THE 4TH REICH

- BOOK THREE -

Patrick Laughy

DEDICATION
This book is dedicated to all Second World War history buffs out there who, from time to time wonder...what if?

ACKNOWLEDGEMENTS
Thanks to Suzy for her long hours of research and editing, David for another great cover and Linette for her continued support.

Nineteen Forty-One

CHAPTER ONE

- January -

- Hitler's Mindset -

- Operation Barbarossa

On December seventeenth nineteen-forty Adolf Hitler signed off on the plan for the Nazi attack against Soviet Russia. He'd done so after altering it to delay the drive on Moscow until the Baltic States had been cleared and Leningrad captured. He had also changed its codename from the original *'Operation Otto'* to *'Operation Barbarossa'*.

The decision to commit Germany to war in the east under the current conditions had been agonizing for the Fuhrer. He'd made it clear in *'Mein Kampf'* that the main enemy of the formation of a new German Reich was a Jewish-Communist conspiracy. That the central aim of National Socialism, was to engineer the eventual destruction of *'Judeo-Bolshevism'*.

He had been convinced for years that the communist movement served Jewish interests and that all Jews were communists. It was something he passionately believed in. So much so, that he'd gone so far as to put his beliefs in writing and published them under his name.

These *'absolute truths'* had since become a major plank in the platform of his governing Nazi party.

In January of nineteen forty-one Hitler had little support from within his military leadership for such a move, the vast majority of whom counselled moderation in triumph and pushed for a cessation in aggression and an extended period of inertia to enjoy the fruits of their recent conquests. The Fuhrer had not intended turning the German war machine to the east before he had either defeated or reached a peace agreement with the British, but to his frustration, neither of these situations, which he had genuinely considered as probabilities, had come to fruition.

And why not stop to savour his successes to date?

Hitler now controlled most of Europe and while he had to admit even to himself that the British were putting up a good front, it was generally agreed that they would have to eventually see the error of their ways and accept capitulation through some form of peace agreement with the Reich.

Hitler was the messiah, the savior and deliverer of the new German Reich: destined to create a new world order. He was at the height of his power and drunk on his successes.

'His successes', which had rarely been openly supported by his Generals and who now counselled him to instead choose inertia and grow fat. More importantly those around him were attempting to prevent him from fulfilling his long held dream of the absolute necessity of the total destruction of *'Judeo-Bolshevism'*.

He was mentally incapable of turning his back on his mission in life and he had no difficulty in justifying that decision to himself.

'I had always maintained that we ought at all costs to avoid waging war on two fronts and you may rest assured that I pondered long and anxiously over Napoleon and his experiences in Russia. Why then, you may ask, this war against Russia? And why at the time I selected? There was no hope of ending the war by invasion of England and hostilities would have gone on interminably with the Americans playing an increasingly active role. The one and only chance of vanquishing the Soviet Union was to take the initiative.

Why attack in nineteen forty-one?

Because time is working in Russia's favour and against the Germans. Only when he held the territories of Russia would time be on Germany's side'.

There was to be no further discussion.

'Barbarossa' was to go ahead and it was to go ahead soon.

In order to succeed against the Russians Hitler knew that he must continue to maintain the facade of the Nazi/Soviet Non-Aggression Pact right up to the point of the invasion. This would ensure he had the element of surprise on his side when he turned his *'Blitzkrieg'* loose against the Soviet Union.

He had been able to maintain this pretence thus far and on the surface, relations between the two unnatural allies prospered.

On the tenth of January, nineteen forty-one, within days of his signing off on plans for the invasion, Hitler authorized the promulgation of two new agreements with the Soviets; an economic treaty specifying reciprocal deliveries of commodities and a secret protocol in which Germany renounced its previous claim to a strip of Lithuanian territory for the price of seven million, five hundred thousand gold dollars.

Below the surface however, dissension was beginning to rise between the two trade delegations. While the movement of raw materials from the Russians was flowing steadily and on schedule, the German deliveries were slow and erratic.

Often machine tools destined for delivery to the Soviet Union would suddenly be declared by inspection personnel as *'necessary for national defence'* and seized for internal use. The Germans had agreed to build a heavy cruiser for the Russians, however Hitler had personally ordered that work on the partially-built craft be stopped in order to use the raw materials necessary to complete the project for an increase in Germany's U-boat production. He had then ordered his trade negotiators to begin to wrangle over the price of the ship to the point that it became so overpriced the Soviets balked at the deal.

Stalin, to all intents and purposes, as much a dictator as Hitler and a man who, as did Hitler, literally held sway over life and death of his citizens, had good reason to ensure that relations with the Germans did not deteriorate.

The Russian leader had ordered tremendous purges of his senior military commanders over the past decade and his armed forces were currently ill-led, ill-supplied and in massive disarray.

He needed to buy time in order to rebuild and bring the army up to fighting strength and rearm the entire Soviet military machine.

Stalin kept a close eye on his delegation, allowing them to offer up reasonable complaints over the slow deliveries by the Germans but instructing that these grievances not be pushed to the point of cessation and/or a breakdown in relations between the two countries.

As a result, the last train hauling grain from the Soviet Union to Germany under the mutual trade agreement between the two countries rolled into German territory at the same time as the first attacks of *'Operation Barbarossa'* were launched.

Although Hitler held to his policy of keeping his plans for expansion in the east and the eradication of the *'Jewish-Soviet'* entity secret, he had sensed a need and an obligation to prepare his people for war and garner their support for the forceful measures that would be needed to create his vision of a *'New Order of Europe'*.

Accomplishing these two aims meant he had to walk a tightrope, keeping the Soviets off guard, while all the while doing his level best to prepare his people for what was to come.

A prime example of this strive to rouse the German populace to his cause occurred during Hitler's annual address given at the *'Berliner Sportpalast'* on January thirtieth of nineteen forty-one.

After a stirring introductory speech by Propaganda Minister, Goebbels, Hitler strode severely to the platform, raised his arm slowly in the Nazi salute and waited patiently for the enthusiastic cheers to eventually recede. He then allowed for a few minutes of silence to reign before he began speaking.

His first words were delivered in a measured, muted, rumble and then with sudden vehemence he began to wave his arms in wide sweeping gestures and both the tone and level of his speech rose as he stated:

'I am convinced that nineteen forty-one will be the crucial year of the great New Order of Europe'.

The enemy he chose to attack during the speech was that of Great Britain, whom he described as the *'leader of the 'pluto-democracies'* and went on to explain, were under the control of an international Jewish clique and supported by dissident émigrés.

Throughout this speech he made no mention of the Soviet Union, but strongly indicated to his audience, that Germany's struggle in Europe were not yet complete and despite what had been accomplished so far, it would be crucial to the good stability of the New Order of Europe to make a final assault against Jewry.

* * * * *

- The Inner Circle -

Goebbels is in awe of Hitler.

He has one aim in life and that is to please the Fuhrer.

Consequently, once he had played his major part in bringing the Nazi party to political power within Germany and despite privately professing his desire for peace, he threw himself firmly and deliberately towards Hitler's wish, which was for the push for military confrontation.

Knowing that Hitler wanted war, he became one of the inner circle's most enthusiastic proponents of aggressively pursuing Germany's territorial claims sooner rather than later.

After nineteen-forty, Hitler, who was now preoccupied with the war, found it physically impossible to maintain the numerous public appearances and many radio broadcasts which had been staged for domestic consumption and it was Goebbels, in his endless strive to please his Fuhrer, who stepped in to fulfill this need.

Goebbels had sensed a growing power vacuum in the area of domestic policy and he moved to fill it.

By nineteen forty-one he had stepped into the void to

become the new face and voice of the Nazi regime within the new Reich. In so doing, despite his inability to effectively partake in his leader's new day to day life of continuous military planning, he'd found a way to maintain his powerful position safely within Hitler's good graces.

In addition to this new positioning, Goebbels could see that Goering's position and influence with Hitler had been in steady decline since the failure of the Luftwaffe to bring the British to their knees.

Goering had a plethora of shortcomings, but he was no fool.

He was in opposition to moving against Russia and opening a second front. He held this position for one reason and one reason only. Not only had the Luftwaffe failed to beat the British into submission or set the stage for an invasion, thereby reducing his importance to Hitler, Goering knew that his air force would not be physically capable of maintaining air superiority in the skies in the event of a drawn-out two front war.

He had counselled Hitler against the move and when it had become apparent to him that the Fuhrer was determined to carry out *'Operation Barbarossa'* he had had privately washed his hands of the whole situation. From that point on, he began to avoid direct one on ones with his boss and became increasing lethargic and demoralized as he slipped yet further from Hitler's favour.

Despite Hitler's displeasure with him, Goering still held the important responsibility for Germany's economic health as head of the Four Year Plan Ministry, and he now clung on to this position with desperate determination.

Goebbels, who had been watching this situation between Hitler and Goering, felt that since civilian morale within the Reich was his responsibility, he could now make inroads into Goering's empire and influence with the Fuhrer.

He did this by beginning to publicly step into areas under Goering's economic control to play a part in solving the current problems which were affecting German morale and therefore productivity, which was Goering's responsibility and had begun to founder under his leadership.

Determined to further undermine Goering while simultaneously impressing Hitler with his own value, Goebbels moved to forge an alliance with Himmler against the *'Reichsmarschall'*.

Himmler found himself in somewhat the same boat as the Minister of Propaganda now found himself, in that he had also been somewhat sidelined by Hitler who was by this point in time, deeply involved with military planning. Skeptical of the offer, Himmler nevertheless decided that it was in his best interest to agree to the concept.

For reasons similar to those facing Goebbels and Himmler, von Ribbentrop and to a somewhat lesser degree, Spear, were also eager to ally Goebbels in pursuing the delightful goal of undermining Goering.

Himmler's answer to the current situation, vis-á-vis keeping himself important to the Fuhrer, was to focus his activities on the solving of the Jewish and other *'special'* problems in the expanded territories of the east. These were things that the Fuhrer held close to his heart and always managed to find some time for, despite the demands now being made upon his time by military planning.

As with the other members of the inner circle, he did not like, nor trust Goebbels as far as he could throw him, but…a chance to do damage to Goering's position was always appealing and he was willing to help wherever he could.

While the majority of Himmler's energy was directed at the preparation for the *'Generalplan Ost'* for Hitler, which was his responsibility in relation to the upcoming invasion, he could always find time to throw a damp blanket on the abilities and responsibilities of the other members of the inner circle with the hope of absorbing their duties and responsibilities into his own growing empire.

* * * * *

- Norway -

Hitler appointed Josef Terboven to the position of *'Reichskommissar '* of Norway on April twenty-fourth, nineteen-forty-two, months before the German invasion of that country had come to a successful conclusion on June seventh of that year.

Terboven was born on May twenty-third, eighteen ninety-eight in Essen, Rhine Province, Germany, the son of minor landed gentry. He studied political science and law at the universities of Freiburg and Munich and it was while at university that he became interested in politics.

Terboven quit university in nineteen twenty-three and joined the Nazi party.

He participated in the abortive, Nazi orchestrated Beer Hall Putsch in Munich which led to Hitler's arrest and incarceration as well as the temporary outlawing of the party.

During the period the party was banned Terboven found employment in a bank but was laid off in nineteen twenty-five. He immediately returned to working for the Nazi party, which had by this point been resurrected.

On June twenty-ninth, nineteen thirty-four Terboven married Nazi Propagandist, Joseph Goebbels's former secretary and mistress. Adolf Hitler was the guest of honour at the wedding.

In nineteen thirty-five Terboven was appointed *'Oberprasident der Rheinprovinz'* (President of the Upper Rhine Province) and quickly developed a reputation as a loyal party bureaucrat as well as that of a petty and ruthless tyrant.

In September of nineteen-forty, in his new position as *'Reichskommissar '* of Norway, Terboven took up residence in the Norwegian crown prince's palace at Skaugum, located in the Asker municipality, which was situated fifteen miles southwest of Oslo.

He set up his operational headquarters in 'Stortinget' (Norwegian parliament buildings).

The Nazi sympathiser, Vidkun Quisling, led the

Norwegian Nazi party known as the *'Nasjonal Samling'* (National Gathering) at the time of the German invasion. This organization was a Nazi styled political movement and only a minor faction on the overall Norwegian political scene at that time.

Prior to the invasion Quisling had attempted to convince Hitler that he could bring the Norwegians over to the Nazis without a major struggle and without the need for German military action. He had done this before the Germans had reached their decision to invade but when given tentative support from Hitler to bring about such an accomplishment he had proven completely ineffective at delivering on his promise. He had subsequently been marginalized by the Germans prior to the actual attack.

Despite his party's small following among the people of Norway, Quisling, on the first day of the German attack, had the audacity to attempt to seize control of the Norwegian government and had gone on radio to nominate himself as the new Prime Minister.

Hitler had already dismissed Quisling as an ineffective and uncommitted politician who was simply an opportunist and a man primarily concerned with improving his own lot in life by supporting the Germans in their expansionist endeavours into the Nordic states.

The Fuhrer's aim at the time of the invasion was to maintain the legitimate Norwegian government in place. He believed that after the invasion was complete he could hold sway over the current parliament and bring it to heel.

The victorious Germans quickly sidelined Quisling publically and went ahead with their plans to attempt to subordinate the current members of the Norwegian government.

Haakon VII, the King of Norway and part of the government, had been able to escape from Norway and had gone into exile in England before Hitler's invading troops could capture them.

As a result the Germans found themselves dealing with

the ragtag Norwegian administrative council led by Ingolf Elster Christensen which had been established on April fifteenth to administer those areas which had so far come under German control.

All attempts by the Germans to subjugate this council prior to Terboven's arrival in the country in September of nineteen-forty had failed miserably and the moment the new *'Reichskommissar'* came onto the scene he quickly moved to abolish it.

With this accomplished, Terboven then formed his own cabinet.

After doing so he began to negotiate with the old government members with a view to forming a puppet Norwegian parliament that would provide his new Nazi cabinet with a façade of legitimacy.

The German occupation force in Norway numbered in excess of three hundred thousand men at arms. Of this number of the permanently garrisoned German troops in Norway, the SS had only a small presence, that of approximately six thousand men.

These members of the SS were under the separate command of *'SS-Obergruppenfuhrer'* (Lieutenant General) Wilhelm Rediess and were split between the Waffen-SS and those assigned under the command of the 'SS- *und Polizefuhrer'* (SS and Police Leader), who included members of the Gestapo and other Police organizations.

* * * * *

- Lebensborn Program: Occupied Countries -

Initially envisioned in nineteen thirty-five by SS-Reichsfuhrer Heinrich Himmler as a domestic German programme intended to prevent abortions and enhance the Aryan birthrate, the *'Lebensborn Program'* was put into place to provide single mothers and their illegitimate children of pure bloodlines, SS-staffed, all inclusive and state funded care and adoption facilities.

Openly at first, Himmler encouraged as part of the program, that his pure-blooded SS officers eagerly apply themselves to the job of producing illegitimate children with willing young women of like stock. There was a backlash of sorts over this suggestion, one that should have been reasonably expected from a Christian country of the era, but despite this, Himmler continued to support the concept if less openly.

Over time the program had limited success domestically.

Like many of the original Nazi policies and programs, the priorities and methods used in the development of the initial *'Lebensborn Program'* began to evolve as Hitler gained new territory for the Reich through diplomatic conquest and military invasion.

What had been policy applied within the borders of Germany in nineteen thirty-five for dealing with a domestic situation involving an alarming abortion rate and a perceived need for an increased birthrate of an eugenically sound generation of pure Aryan children; was also applicable to those Nazi overrun areas that had been previously populated by expatriate Germans, or those of Nordic bloodlines.

It was however, definitely not applicable to the non-Aryan citizens of the majority of the newly conquered territories of the east which had now been incorporated into that of the new Reich.

All conquered peoples were not to be considered as equal in the eyes of the Nazis - far from it.

* * * * *

- GPO -

'Generalplan Ost' (GPO), (Master Plan East) was the Himmler designed Nazi blueprint for the colonization of Central and Eastern Europe.

The planning for GPO was begun in nineteen thirty-nine

in preparation of the fulfilment of Adolf Hitler's *'Lebensraum'* (living space) policy and the Nazi envisioned *'Drang nach Osten'* (Drive towards the East) ideology, the plan for the German expansion to the east and the establishment of the New Order in Europe.

The plan had been drawn up by the *'Reichssicherheitshauptamt'* (Reich Main Security Office) (RSHA), the security organ of the SS which had the responsibility of fighting all enemies of Naziism.

Due to the plan's necessary requirement for genocide and ethnic cleansing to be conducted on a massive scale in the Eastern European territories, it was considered to be top secret and was known only to those belonging to the upper echelon of the Nazi Party.

Initial research for the plan was provided by the *'Ostforschung'* (Research of the East), an organization made up of German Historians and Anthropologists which had been studying the development of the area since the eighteenth century and looking at the concept of cleansing Central and Eastern Europe of local non-German populations and its eventual resettlement with German colonists in order to *'Germanize'* Europe.

The preliminary versions of this research were discussed by the leader of the SS, Heinrich Himmler and a few of his most trusted colleagues before the outbreak of war.

The final version for the *'Germanization'* of conquered territory, within the envisioned New German Reich under *'Generalplan Ost',* was completed in nineteen-forty.

Implementation was anticipated by way of two separate thrusts; the *'Kleine Planung'* (Small Plan) which was to be instituted during the war itself and the *'Grosse Planung'* (Big Plan), which was to come into force after the war had been won and spread over a number of decades.

The plan envisaged the likelihood of a successful *'Germanization'* in any given country based on the historical research that had been undertaken in the forming of the plan, as well as a current evaluation of the indigenous people by the

Nazis which led them to believe that those chosen would demonstrate the formation of a desirable element for the future success of the Third Reich.

This later criterion was of course based upon the Nazis singular point of view with regard to racist policies.

Of necessity, there were to be different approaches taken in relation to each conquered nation and the plan went into great detail as to how to deal with specific ethnic and political groups within these individual nations.

Specific criteria were contained within the document, having been formulated as a guideline to be used prior to accepting any of the subjugated countries' citizens into the *'Germanization'* process.

These criteria could be applied more liberally when dealing with a nation who's *'Rassische Substanz'* (basic racial makeup) and the level of its cultural development suggested that they were more likely to be of value to the Reich than those of a lower standard could ever expect.

A rough prediction of what portion of the citizenry of each nation would have to be removed in order to provide the opportunity of the successful *'Germanization'* of that nation was part of the overall plan.

Between eighty and eighty-five percent of Poles would require removal.

Fifty to sixty percent of Russians would have to be eliminated outright and another fifteen percent would require relocation to Western Siberia.

One hundred percent of the Latgalians had to go, as did eighty-five percent of the Lithuanians, seventy-five percent of the Belarusians, sixty-five percent of the Ukrainians, and fifty percent of the Latvians and Czechs, while almost all of the Estonians could remain in place.

Needless to say, one hundred percent of the Jew must be removed from the New Reich.

Under the plan, deportation numbers would reach approximately forty-five million *'non-Germanizable'* people, of whom thirty-one million had already been pre-classified as *'sub-human'* or *'racially undesirable'*.

Fourteen million of the original occupants of the captured territory were to be allowed to remain within the Reich as slave labour and between eight and ten million Germans were to be settled in the resulting extended *'Lebensraum'*.

The contents of *'Generalplan Ost'* was now, under the watchful eyes of the SS, Nazi state policy and as such was bound to have a definite effect on how the *'Lebensborn'* and other Programs were to be followed in the various eugenic demographics of the expanded eastern territories of the New Reich.

'Generalplan Ost' was a plan for Central and Eastern Europe and did not directly affect the governing of the Nordic territories of Denmark and Norway, which were now under Nazi occupation.

* * * * *

- Oslo -

The Norwegian winter of nineteen forty/forty-one was one of the coldest on record.

Gabriella and Konrad had boarded the train in Berlin directly after their wedding reception and headed for Oslo to take up Dr. Kauffmann's new assignment.

When they arrived at the Norwegian Capital an SS staff car was parked in front of the station awaiting their arrival.

As they stepped out onto the platform they were greeted by the uniformed driver who took them out to the car and drove them directly to their hotel. The driver carried their personal luggage inside and after advising them that he would return in one hour to pick them up and transport them to the offices of Obergruppenfuher Wilhelm Rediess, who was expecting them, the soldier retuned to the car, leaving them to register and settle in.

The General had earlier received detailed orders directly from the *'Reichsfuhrer of the Schutzstaffel'* Heinrich Himmler himself no less, with regard to this new assignment for SS-Major Dr. Konrad Kauffmann and his new bride.

Konrad had been provided with a copy of the document which had been previously sent under Himmler's signature to Rediess. He had been both surprised and pleased with the depth of personal commitment for the *'Lebensborn'* programme Himmler had articulated in the letter.

Added to that strong support for the project itself was the level of confidence expressed by the Reichsfuhrer in Konrad's ability to fulfill the responsibilities to be incurred in expanding the clinics into Norway.

This fact had also been contained within the document and therein relayed to the Obergruppenfuher prior to the couple's arrival in Oslo.

In specific terms, the General had been ordered to provide any and all assistance required to ensure the swift expansion of the Lebensborn programme into Norway under Major Kauffmann's guardianship.

The General had been further advised that this programme was of prime importance to the Reich as Norway was the birthplace and source of pure Aryan Viking stock - stock whose progeny would serve to support the creation of the new German Aryan race. As such, it was necessary that the *'Lebensborn'* programme be rapidly expanded into Norway and was to take priority over all other matters until it had firmly taken root and was functioning at optimum levels as adjudged by the said Major.

Himmler had ended the letter by advising the General that he would be taking a personal interest in the progress of the operation and had asked the Major to not hesitate to contact him directly if he experienced any difficulty in achieving the cooperation he required to reach his goal.

* * * * *

- Gabriella -

Despite the low temperatures and massive accumulations of snow clearly visible as the train had travelled north and eventually rolled into the port city of Oslo, Gabriella was in good spirits.

Still wrapped snugly in the romantic glow of her recent wedding and the comfort of travelling first class, she was generally happy and looking forward to entering into her new role as Konrad's wife and right hand in the expansion of the *'Lebensborn'* programme into the newly conquered country.

Since the wedding, Konrad had become even more attentive to her and it was apparent to all who met the couple that the SS-Major blatantly idolized his new wife. As a result, Gabriella's feelings for him had deepened since the ceremony and she had not found him in any way lacking in the support she desired, finding him definitely stimulating from both a physical and mental point of view.

Her new situation was giving her more satisfaction than she felt she had a right to expect based upon her past party-girl existence. She was surprisingly content and distinctly certain that she had made the right choice in marrying Konrad.

She was very excited by the prospect of fully supporting him in the expansion of the program into the new Reich territory of Norway and was eagerly discussing various ideas with him as she and Konrad unpacked their cases in the hotel suite that was to be their temporary residence until proper quarters had been arranged for them.

They were waiting in the Hotel lobby when the SS-staff car and driver returned to pick them up for their appointment with SS-Obergruppenfuher, Wilhelm Rediess.

The initial meeting between Gabriella, Konrad and Rediess went extremely well.

Gabriella had been a little unsure as to what to be expect as they were ushered into the General's large office but any perceived unease had been immediately dispelled.

Rediess had obviously been made aware of the importance of the young couple's project and he greeted them warmly, smiling broadly as he exchanged salutes with Konrad, then clicked his heels and bent to kiss Gabriella's hand.

The General then waved them to seats in front of his desk.

Once they were comfortably seated he directed his secretary to bring in coffee before moving to his own chair and seating himself across from them.

He congratulated them on their recent marriage and asked them about their trip and a few moments later when the coffee arrived he spoke to his secretary.

"Have *'Untersturmfuhrer'* (Second Lieutenant) Biermann join us please."

CHAPTER TWO

- January -

- Air Operations -

Both the German and British air forces continue their bomb runs.

Principal targets for the Luftwaffe are London, Cardiff, Portsmouth and Bristol.

RAF bombers target Hamburg, Bremen, Brest and Wilhelmshaven.

* * * * *

- Battle of the Atlantic -

The Germans have only twenty-two operational U-boats at sea, however, ramped up production had made for a total of sixty-seven more, either on sea trials or in training.

Those on war patrols sink twenty-one ships for a total tonnage of one hundred and twenty-six thousand. Attacking U-boats find that their greatest chances of success prove to be after convoys have been dispersed, usually beyond twenty degrees west.

German aircraft, while either scouting for the U-boats or on patrol at sea sink fifteen ships on their own.

Experimental new British radar systems that are specifically aimed at reaching a level of sensitivity that will allow for the detection of U-boats are making their way onto convoy escorts; however these are early models with the to-be-expected failings which normally exhibit themselves when new products are given practical applications.

The bugs are being ironed out and the instruments are

slowly being improved.

The Allies lose seventy-six ships for a total of three hundred and twenty thousand, two hundred tons during the month.

* * * * *

- January First -

- Balkans -

On January first, nineteen forty-one Joachim von Ribbentrop, Germany's Foreign Minister, meets in Berlin with the Bulgarian Prime Minister Bogdan Filov.

Earlier Filov had proposed the Bulgarian *'Law for protection of the nation'*, mimicking the Nazi Nuremberg Laws of the Third Reich. This document had been promptly voted into law in December of nineteen-forty.

The purpose of this current meeting, which was initiated by the Germans, was to arrange for the free passage of German troops through Bulgarian territory and to provide an opportunity for the Germans to apply pressure to encourage the Bulgarians to join the Axis Tripartite Pact.

While no firm agreement was reached at this meeting, Filov, who was a known Nazi sympathizer, managed to hang on to the position of neutrality for his country while sympathizing with and warmly expressing his support for Germany's current endeavours.

* * * * *

- Mediterranean -

The German X Fliegerkorps based in Sicily has now reached a total of ninety-six bombers and twenty-five fighters and is still growing.

The British have only fifteen Hurricanes in the

Mediterranean. These are stationed on Malta.

* * * * *

- January Second -

- North Africa -

The Italian held, Libyan port city of Bardia, is hit by British bombers in conjunction with a systematic bombardment from the sea by British naval units.

* * * * *

- January Third -

- North Africa -

The 6th Australian Davison arrives with considerable tank and artillery support and the British attack on Bardia in Libya begins.

RAF bombers attack the Kiel Canal in Bremen Germany. A direct hit on the Canal Bridge is achieved and the bridge collapses.

* * * * *

- January Fourth -

- Albania -

A new offensive is undertaken by the Greeks. They begin to drive westward in a move against Valona. The Greeks find themselves vastly outnumbered by the Italians, but despite this, they begin a steady grind forward.

* * * * *

- January Fifth -

- Libya -

The newly-arrived Australian troops of XIII Corps capture Bardia. They take forty-five thousand Italian prisoners.

* * * * *

- January Sixth -

- Albania -

The Greeks begin their advance toward the Klisura Pass in Southern Albania.

* * * * *

- USA -

Roosevelt makes his State of the Union address in which he speaks of four essential freedoms, those of speech and worship and from fear and want.

He reaffirms that in the current circumstances, the United States will act as the world's *'arsenal of democracy'*.

* * * * *

- North Africa -

Advance units of the Allied forces reach the outer defences of Tobruk after overrunning El Adem airfield to the south of the city. Patrols are immediately sent out to begin an assessment of the Italian defences.

Tobruk is held by a garrison of twenty-five thousand men, two hundred and twenty artillery pieces and seventy tanks and there are additional Italian units still holding positions farther west in Libya.

* * * * *

- January Eighth -

- USA -

President Roosevelt presents his budget to congress. Out of over seventeen billion requested almost eleven billion will go toward defence spending. The United States may not be at war but the President is certainly determined to strengthen the country's defences.

* * * * *

- Albania -

The Greeks push forward against the Italians, beginning their attack on Klisura. They are running into strong enemy resistance on their northern flank around Berat.

* * * * *

- Mediterranean -

The British carry out a bombing raid against the port of Naples targeting units of the Italian fleet moored in the harbour. The Battleship *'Vittorio Vento'* is hit but suffers little damage while the battleship *'Giulio Cesare'* is seriously damaged.

* * * * *

- January Tenth -

- USA -

The *'Lend-Lease Bill'* is introduced into the U.S. Congress to a good deal of opposition from prominent isolationists including Senators Wheeler and Nye, former ambassador Kennedy and Charles Lindbergh.

President Roosevelt announces a plan to build two hundred, seventy-five hundred ton freighters to a standard design. These cargo carriers, based on a British design, are to be called *'Liberty ships'* and will be used for lend-lease deliveries to Britain.

* * * * *

- Berlin/Moscow -

A new joint pact between Germany and Russia is signed. This is a clean-up agreement between the two countries that will serve to clarify the Molotov/Ribbentrop Pact of nineteen thirty-nine.

The *'Border and Commercial Agreement'* settled a dispute that had arisen regarding land in Lithuania that had been split between the two countries under the previous pact and tweaked other commercial agreements between the two countries that had been reached over the previous two years.

Germany agrees to provide the soviets with industrial equipment while the Russians commit to provide Germany with much needed raw materials and food.

Discussions are also held with regard to the Russians joining the Axis Tripartite Pact. The Germans put their offer on the table for such an agreement and the Russians, eager to join, respond with a counter-offer containing minor changes.

No immediate agreement on this concept is finalized.

* * * * *

- Albania -

The four Italian Divisions holding the Klisura Pass retreat and the Greek forces move in to take this strategically important position.

* * * * *

- Mediterranean -

Two Italian torpedo boats and forty bombers from the German X Fliegerkorps attack a British convoy in the Straight of Sicily off the Italian island of Pantelleria.

One of the torpedo boat is sunk and the other does no damage but the bombers manage to get six hits on the aircraft carrier HMS *'Illustrious'* and other ships suffer minor damage.

The British send additional troops and eighteen more fighters to Malta.

* * * * *

- January Eleventh -

- Berlin -

Hitler puts forward his plan for reducing British influence in the Mediterranean with the introduction of Directive 22.

Among other things, this directive orders the creation of the famous *'Afrika Korps'*.

* * * * *

- Mediterranean -

The British cruisers HMS *'Southampton'* and *'Gloucester'* leave Malta and make way for Gibraltar. They come under attack by German Stuka dive bombers and both ships are damaged. *'Southampton'* is sunk.

* * * * *

- Battle of Britain -

One of the bombs dropped by the Germans on London strikes next to the Bank of England. This single piece of ordinance leaves a crater measuring one hundred and twenty feet across, demolishes the underground station below, killing fifty-seven people and injuring a further sixty-nine.

* * * * *

- January Twelfth -

- Libya -

British and Australian troops of XIII Corps execute *'Operation Compass'* in preparation for their assault on the Italian forces holding Tobruk.

* * * * *

- Malta -

Malta-based British aircraft attack Catania airfield on the east coast of Sicily in a preventative action to deter German and Italian planes from striking at Malta while the rushed temporary repairs are being carried out on the damaged aircrafts carrier HMS *'Illustrious'*.

* * * * *

- January Fourteenth -

- Greece -

British General Wavell, accompanied by Air Marshall Longmore, arrives in Athens for talks with Prime Minister Metaxas and the Greek Commander in Chief, General Papagos.

The Greeks, with only thirteen divisions are up against much stronger Italian forces in Albania and they have only four divisions facing the Bulgarians. The Germans currently have twelve divisions in Rumania and reserves in Bulgaria.

Holding their own to date, the Greeks ask the British for substantial air support and nine divisions to assist them in their struggle on both fronts.

The British have little to offer, but promise to do what they can.

* * * * *

- January Sixteenth -

- East Africa -

The British begin their East Africa counter-offensive by attacking Italian-held Eritrea in Ethiopia from bases in Kenya.

* * * * *

- Malta -

The Germans and Italians begin attacks on Malta with specific attention being paid to the damaged aircraft carrier HMS *'Illustrious'*.

The opening attack consists of eighty Stuka dive-bombers and while they lose ten planes the Germans succeed in hitting the carrier yet again and also damage the cruiser HMS *'Perth'* as well as doing a great deal of damage to the harbour facilities.

These attacks continue through to the nineteenth when additional damage is done to the *'Illustrious'*.

The emergency repairs to the ship are finally completed

on January twenty-third and she sails for Alexandria and thence to the U.S. where she will undergo full repair.

* * * * *

- January Seventeenth -

- Moscow -

Molotov, the Russian Foreign Minister, meets with the German Ambassador to the Soviet Union, Schulenburg and expresses surprise that the Germans have, as yet, not responded to the Russian offer to join the Axis Tripartite Pact.

The ambassador puts him off, with the explanation that the situation must first be discussed with the Italians and Japanese.

* * * * *

- January Nineteenth -

- East Africa -

British forces under General Platt, including the 4th and 5th Indian Divisions and units of the Sudan Defence Force, go on the offensive. The Italians have a force of approximately seventeen thousand troops spread in a defensive line along the border and an additional force of four divisions stationed inland and available for support if and when needed.

In their initial thrust British forces take the city of Kassala in Easter Sudan.

* * * * *

- Berghof -

Hitler, Mussolini and their respective generals meet at the

Fuhrer's home in Berchtesgaden for two days of meetings.

While appearances of equal partnership are maintained between the two leaders and their staffs during the discussions, everyone present is well aware of the fact that the Germans, after several diplomatic and military successes, are riding high and the Italians, whose troops are retreating on all fronts, are placed in the position of having to put on a good face.

Hitler has called the conference because he sees a need to militarily bolster the faltering Italians, who are his oldest and strongest allies and whose performance in the field are frankly becoming an embarrassment.

He interacts warmly with Mussolini, demonstrating none of the disappointment he harbours over what he sees as Italian ill-planned and over-ambitious campaigns.

He eagerly offers Mussolini military support for both North Africa and Albania.

The Italian dictator, striving to save what he can of his pride, waves off the proffered support for Albania, indicating that his forces there are regrouping and will soon be on the offensive again but accepts the offer of German assistance in North Africa, having already privately acknowledged that it is a theatre where he has little chance of succeeding on his own.

They discuss the situation in Greece and Hitler advises Mussolini that he will attack the Greeks if a British presence there should grow to a point where it threatens the oil refining operations at Ploiesti in Romania.

* * * * *

- January Twentieth -

- Romania -

The fascist Iron Guard party revolts in Romania.

General Antonescu uses the Romanian army and the German troops billeted in the country to put the insurgency down and it is forcefully quelled within a few days.

* * * * *

- January Twenty-first -

- North Africa -

The 6th Australian Davison moves against Tobruk which has already been isolated by the advance of the British 7th Armoured Brigade which is moving toward Martuba and Mechili.

A weak point in the Italian defences at the southeast corner of the city is put under heavy bombardment and then assaulted by the Aussies who smash through the Italian defences.

Fort Palastrino is taken and Italian General, Mannella is captured.

* * * * *

- Romania -

The Iron Guards are on the second day of their revolt and there are reports that they are executing Jews in Bucharest.

* * * * *

- January Twenty-Second -

- North Africa -

After destroying harbour facilities the last of the Tobruk garrison surrenders to the British who suffer only five hundred casualties while taking twenty-seven thousand prisoners.

A large stash of Italian military equipment is also captured.

Work immediately begins on getting the port back into

service for use by the Allies.

* * * * *

- East Africa -

General Platt's troops are pushing the Italians back toward the city of Agordat in the western lowlands of Eritrea and minor border skirmishes are taking place on the border between Kenya and Italian Somaliland.

* * * * *

- January Twenty-Third -

Still heavily damaged but having completed emergency repairs, HMS *'Illustrious'* slips out of Malta and heads for the relative safety of Alexandria where she will undergo further work in preparation for her trip to a U.S. dockyard.

* * * * *

- Balkans -

The Prime Minister of Bulgaria agrees to bring his country into the Tripartite Pack as soon as ongoing military arrangements with the Germans are completed.

- USA -

Well known for his isolationism, Charles Lindbergh appears before the U.S. Congress and strongly recommends that the USA commence negotiations with Adolf Hitler for a neutrality pact.

* * * * *

Patrick Laughy

- January Twenty-Fourth -

- North Africa -

The British 4th Armoured Brigade tangles with the Italians near Mechili. The losses sustained are about equal on both sides and the Italians retreat.

Italian forces in Libya are now split in two.

Those at Mechili are currently facing the British 4th armoured and the 7th Armoured Brigade is moving in to support and encircle the Italians.

Those on the coast at the port city of Derna are about to be attacked by the 19th Australian Brigade.

* * * * *

- East Africa -

British forces in Kenya continue the East African counter-offensive, pushing into Italian Somaliland.

* * * * *

- January Twenty-Sixth -

- Albania -

The Italians counter-attack near Klisura with some, but insignificant, success.

* * * * *

- North Africa -

The Italians abandon Mechili.

Unprepared for the move and badly commanded, the British 4th Armoured Brigade sits idle while the Italians pull out unchallenged.

* * * * *

- January Twenty-Seventh -

- East Africa -

Advancing into Eritrea, the British reach Agordat and the opposing sides begin to interact.

* * * * *

- Albania -

Mussolini's son-in-law, the Italian Foreign Minister, Galeazzo Ciano, accompanied by other senior members of the Italian government arrives in Albania to take up active army commands.

Mussolini, completely frustrated by, and depressed with the continued defeats being suffered by his troops has ordered this measure in a bizarre attempt to reverse the the Italians dismal military performance to date.

* * * * *

- January Twenty-Ninth -

- Greece -

The Prime minister of Greece, Ioannis Metaxas dies.

He is succeeded by Alexander Korizis, a man less decisive than his predecessor and one who does not have as good a relationship with his Commander in Chief, General Papagos.

This briefly throws a small monkey-wrench into the ongoing negotiations with the British but results in only a minor ripple, as there is no question that the Greeks need British help in their struggle.

* * * * *

- East Africa -

Under the command of General Cunningham the 11th and 12th East Africa Divisions and 1st South Africa Division begin to push across the border from Kenya into Italian Somaliland.

* * * * *

- North Africa -

The Italian forces withdraw from the city of Derna and begin a hasty retreat westward along the coast road.

* * * * *

- USA -

Secret talks between the British and the *'neutral'* USA begin in Washington.

These joint military talks will continue until late March and will result in agreement under the code name *'ABC1'* that allied policy in the event of war with Germany and Japan should be to put the defeat of Germany as its first priority.

In March an American military contingent will visit Britain to begin the selection of proposed sites for naval and air bases for use in case the Americans go to war with Germany. It is intended that initial work to equip these bases will be undertaken later in the year.

* * * * *

- January Thirtieth -

- North Africa -

The 19th Australian Brigade moves in to occupy the abandoned city of Derna which lies one hundred miles west of Tobruk.

* * * * *

- January Thirty-First -

- East Africa -

The Indian 4th Division takes the city of Agordat in Eritea capturing one thousand Italian troops and forty-three field guns.

* * * * *

- Berlin -

On this day the German Army High Command completes its preparations of the operational and deployment plans for the German invasion of Russia.

CHAPTER THREE

- February -

- Hitler's Megalomania -

Having signed off on *'Operation Barbarossa'* in January, Hitler clearly believes that the conquest of Russia is all but a fait accompli.

A few days after making his speech in the *'Sportpalast'*, he is advised by General Halder that Germany's troop strength will soon be equal to that of Russia and far superior in quality. Hitler responds with: *'When Barbarossa commences the world will hold its breath and make no comment'*.

By this point in time the Fuhrer's concept of German conquest had moved well beyond Europe. This is demonstrated by his order, on February seventeenth, nineteen forty-one, to prepare plans for a drive into India, the heart of the British Empire.

He further advised that this attack was to be accompanied by the seizure of the Near East which would be accomplished by a pincer movement, on the left, from Russia across Iran and on the right, from North Africa toward the Suez Canal.

That would soon bring the bloody British to the table to assume their proper role as an ally with the Axis powers in the worldwide battle against the *'pluto-democracies'*.

Then he would deal with America and Roosevelt and quickly bring them to heel.

* * * * *

- Access to the Atlantic -

With the fall of France came the opportunity for the

Nazis to garner open access to the Atlantic without having to move their ships through the North Sea.

The Germans quickly moved to create U-boat bases on the French Atlantic coast.

Lorient, Brest, St. Nazaire, La Pallice and Bordeaux were selected as suitable for new home bases for the German submarine fleets, substantially increasing their effective war patrol range.

A U-boat communication center was then established inland at *'Saint-Barthelemy-d'Anjou'* in western France.

By this time Hitler had effectively lifted his earlier restrictions upon U-boat activity.

In nineteen forty-one the delivery of the new German *'Type VII'* U-boats and new and improved torpedo designs had been enhanced to the point where the German submarine war patrols were having a serious effect on the British wartime economy.

The British losses were such that, if the status quo were maintained, the English would not be able to sustain their island economy.

The Nazis were winning the battle of the Atlantic.

* * * * *

- U-boat Pens -

Harbour protection for submarines was not a new concept for the Germans.

The concept of building protective enclosures for moored U-boats began in the Great War, at a time when bombs were dropped by hand from bi-planes, and protection had amounted to wooden structures.

By the mid nineteen-thirties both the size and delivery of bombs caused the Naval Construction Office in Berlin to re-evaluate the need for protection in view of their plans for a much expanded U-boat arm should Germany ever go to war again.

The RAF raid on Berlin in nineteen-forty and the inability to bring the British to heel either militarily or by way of an agreement provided stimulus to this re-evaluation of the need to protect the U-boat fleet and was enough to trigger a massive building programme of sub-pens and air raid shelters.

Four types of bunkers were designed to be built for U-boats.

Covered locks were bunkers constructed over existing locks to give a U-boat protection when it was most vulnerable during the period of the filling and emptying of the large water containment areas.

Construction bunkers were used to cover U-boat manufacturing plants.

Fitting-out bunkers were used to enclose U-boats that had completed the building phase and were in the final process of being fitted out.

Repair bunkers were built to cover docked U-boats and those requiring repairs.

The majority of bunkers built for the U-boats were for the repair and storage of docked submarines and these had to be constructed over water while the others were built on dry land where the craft were moved about on ramps.

By the autumn of nineteen-forty construction of pens had been started. The first two were built on the *'Elbe II'* on the southern bank of the Elbe River at the Vulkanhafen in Hamburg and the *'Nordsee III'* on the island of Helgoland in the North Sea.

This type of construction would obviously also be required for the U-boat's new French ports.

The Kriegsmarine was unable to take on such an extensive project and it fell to the *'Organisation Todt'* (Todt Organization) or *'OT'* to take on that task.

* * * * *

- OT -

Organisation Todt, (OT) was a Third Reich civil and military engineering group named after its founder, Fritz Todt, who was an engineer and early Nazi member.

It was a massive organization which was responsible for a huge range of engineering projects both in pre-war Germany and in the occupied territories from France to the Soviet Union during the war years.

In the pre-war era, from nineteen thirty-three to nineteen thirty-eight, Todt held the position of *'Generalinspektor fur das deuscher Strassenwesen'* (General Inspector of German Roadways). At that time his primary responsibility was for the construction of the huge German Autobahn network.

In his position, Todt was given the authority to conscript labourers from within Germany through the *'Reichsarbeitsdienst'* (Reich Labour Service) or RAD.

OT proper was founded at the beginning of the war when Todt was named *'Reichminister fur Bewaffnung und Munition'* (Minister for Armaments and Munitions) and nearly all OT projects from that point on were exclusively military.

The extraordinary increase in the demand for labour created by the many military projects was met by a series of adjustments in the laws on compulsory service, with the end result being a situation called *'Zwangsarbeit'* in which all Germans were obligated to an arbitrary determination of compulsory labour for the state.

Between nineteen thirty-eight and nineteen forty almost two million Germans were conscripted into the labour service.

Beginning in nineteen-forty labourers for the various projects were also drawn from sources known as *'Gastarbeitnehmer'* (Guest Workers), *'Militarinterniete'* (Military Internees), *'Zivilarbeiter'* (Civilian Workers), 'Ostarbeiter' (Eastern Workers) and *'Hilfswillige'* (Volunteer Prisoner of War workers).

* * * * *

- Ghettos -

The term *'Ghetto'* originated in Italy from the name of the Jewish quarter in Venice, which was established in the sixteenth century. It described an area or street where Jews were required to live.

The Nazis adopted the concept of placing the Jews into *'Ghettos'* as a method of dealing with the growing *'Jewish Problem'* that had burgeoned exponentially after they began to take territory.

These walled enclosures were seen as a short term answer to the problem of quickly *'cleansing'* these new territories by enclosing the Jews into restricted areas isolating them and separating Jewish community's both from the population as a whole and from neighbouring Jewish communities.

Eastern Poland was not occupied by the Germans until June of nineteen forty-one at which time the Nazis set up their own *'Generalgouvernement'* where most of the early 'Ghettos' were established. The first of these was created in the town of Piotrkow Tryybunalski, with the first large one being set up in the city of Lodz in February of nineteen forty.

These 'Ghettos' constructed by the Nazis were soon overcrowded and dirty. Starvation, chronic shortages and the curtailing of most urban services led to repeated epidemics and a high death rate within these contained holding areas.

The largest of these facilities had been set up in Warsaw in October of nineteen-forty. It grew to hold more than three hundred and fifty thousand Jews which was about thirty percent of the city's population, all of whom were eventually being confined in under three percent of the total area of the city of Warsaw.

* * * * *

- Bordeaux -

Alert and intent upon his purpose, Eric stood high on the conning tower of his massive U-boat as he snapped off a string of orders and the huge craft began to inch its way into the protection offered by its new home port.

The last weak rays of February sunshine were abruptly replaced by the cold artificial light as the sub slipped deeper into the pen, which was still under construction and his nostrils filled with the smell of newly formed and still curing steel-reinforced concrete.

Moments later it was with some satisfaction that Eric gave the orders to tie up the Massive U-boat and turned his attention to the small group of people waiting on the covered cement jetty to his right.

He recognized his father standing among them.

After completing his sea trials and workups Eric had received a promotion to the rank of *'Oberleutnant Zur see'* (Senior Lieutenant), placed in command of the vessel and taken the newly commissioned U-boat and its mixed human and equipment cargo on its maiden trip to Brazil.

The voyage had gone well, the massive submarine performing beyond all his expectations.

Upon arriving in Brazil and after he'd given instructions for the offloading, he'd left the U-boat anchored off the deserted coast and accompanied by a distant cousin, whom he'd never met before, spent an enjoyable week surveying the ongoing work for the new mine. The project was to be a massive commercial operation in itself, while its business would serve as a form of camouflage for the secret *'Operation Fatherland'* compound it would conceal.

Eric had a general idea of what was intended but that in no way prepared him for the scale and the complexity of the huge undertaking.

He had been absolutely astounded by what he saw on this first short visit and had initially been mentally unable to take it all in.

Greeted with warmth by his much-removed cousin, Hans Schultz, who was a big strapping lad in his early twenties and whom he immediately took a liking to, Eric was led to an open four-wheel-drive vehicle where he was introduced to another distant cousin, this time a tall, deeply tanned blonde female beauty in her late teens, named Heidi, who turned out to be Han's younger sister.

Heidi, dressed simply and for the Brazilian summer, wore a full skirt and a deeply cut peasant blouse. She radiated the outdoor healthiness and unblemished beauty that could only be gleaned through a lifetime of country living.

Heidi greeted him with a big smile which consisted of full lips framing twin rows of remarkably straight white teeth below which, upon closer inspection, proved to be a deliciously curved body and just above by deep blue eyes that sparkled mischievously with obvious interest and appreciation.

He had then spent several hours each day driving for hundreds of miles while being whisked from place to place from construction to construction and receiving a running commentary by the brother and sister combination, all of which had been delivered in perfect German.

From their first meeting both Hans and Heidi had used the plural possessive when referring to the newly constructed mine buildings and the small city that seemed to be sprouting up around it.

It was always *our* mine and *our* bakery and *our* family, and this inclusiveness continued each evening as he was transported in a small convoy of vehicles to several more newly built homes where he met more and more distant family members at different residences for dinner on succeeding evenings.

After the first family dinner he was taken directly to the domicile of the patriarch of the extended and obviously vast von Stauffer clan who also turned out to be the Grandfather of Hans and Heidi.

Klaus von Stauffer proved to be a structural engineer who while in his early seventies was still unretired was both spry and quick of mind and one who left no doubt that he was the one guiding the entire project and acting directly on behalf of Eric's father.

It was made clear to Eric that during his stay and while he

awaited the unloading of his U-boat, that while with them he would be based within the household of the senior von Stauffer who accepted him readily and treated him very much like a long lost son.

Eric's accommodation within the large structure proved to be more than comfortable.

It consisted of a self-contained suite of rooms on the second floor of the obviously new and distinctly impressive mansion which had been built upon a small rise and was surrounded by several heavily forested acres on the edge of the rapidly growing town. It showed signs of having been recently entirely fenced.

Eric breakfasted each morning with Klaus, who was a widower, and then he would be taken by the elder von Stauffer, away from the native domestic staff that cared for the old man, into the privacy of his large study where he would be shown the detailed plans and designs of the humongous operation currently well underway.

Eric paid special attention to the plans for the subterranean facilities that were to be cut out of solid rock for use by those involved in *'Operation Fatherland'* and was particularly interested in the submarine pens that would be hewn out of the solid granite of the sheer mountain where it dropped to the sea.

These pens would be accessible only from the ocean and the entrance to them would be well beneath the surface of the water.

Surprisingly, Klaus informed Eric that tunnelling was well under way for both projects and at the current rate would be completed by the end of the year.

At nine each morning, after these private sessions between the two men, Hans and Heidi would arrive in the four-wheel-drive all-terrain vehicle and they would eagerly gather him up, along with a packed lunch and then be off for more sightseeing.

Everywhere they drove the pace of construction was vast and hectic.

Eric had found little time and less opportunity for sexual dalliance once the sea trials for the big U-boat had been completed and both he and the sub had been reposted to the port of Bordeaux. There, he had immediately re-provisioned, loaded men and material and immediately taken up the responsibility of transporting his cargo in his first cross-Atlantic cruise using the massive craft.

Needless to say, he had by this time found himself sorely missing his twin blond playmates. He was now finding himself becoming strongly attracted to his much removed distant cousin Heidi who had done little to hide her returned interest in him and had taken every opportunity to brush up against him and make her desires obvious.

Not for lack of trying on either of their parts, this had unfortunately come to little in that her big brother Hans had diligently and dutifully fulfilled his obvious assigned task, which, in addition to being that of co-guide, was also to fulfill the duties of chaperone for his nubile younger sister.

The mutual frustration between the two of them was palatable and did not go unnoticed nor discouraged by the rest of the family who seem to find it both understandable and something they could take in stride, providing of course, that it did not reach fruition prior to the U-boat's return trip to Germany.

In the afternoon of the last day the brother and sister took him to the bottom of the huge mountain which rose majestically to separate the construction going on in the valley from the ocean beyond. Here they found the opening of the mines main tunnel complex.

Once inside and under the watchful eyes of several fully-uniformed and armed SS guards they'd boarded a small upholstered car that was sitting just inside the entrance on obviously recently placed steel rails running through the centre of the large opening.

Artificial light which filled the tunnel was being generated from large panels hanging from the high ceiling. The twin metal surfaces of the steel rails reflected the brightness from above as they disappeared into the distance on a gentle downward curve.

They were obviously expected and once they had climbed into the small car with its uniformed SS driver it began to move into the depths of the mountain. It took them some time to reach the end of the shaft where they exited the car.

Eric was astounded by the amount of work that had been completed once they passed through an SS guarded rock face that, at the push of a concealed button, slowly and silently slipped open on well-greased runners and under hydraulic power to provide entry into the initial construction phase of the *'Operation Fatherland'* Brazilian Headquarters and promptly closed after they passed through.

Eric noted that all personnel in the shaft on this side of the doors were clearly of Aryan German descent.

There was not a single native Brazilian face to be seen.

CHAPTER FOUR

- February -

- Air Operations -

The German air force's *'Blitz'* of England continues with the range of targets including the first heavy attacks on Swansea. Damage is extensive and two thousand civilians are injured or killed.

The British RAF drops fourteen hundred tons of bombs on the Germans, striking Dusseldorf, Brest, Wilhelmshaven and Cologne.

* * * * *

- Battle of the Atlantic -

German U-boats manage to sink thirty-nine ships for a total tonnage of one hundred and ninety six thousand, eight hundred, despite the fact that their operational strength of twenty-two is the lowest since the start of the war.

Over half the U-boat successes are composed of stragglers or independents which reflects the growing strength and deterrent effect of the convoy escorts that are now being provided.

There are command and organizational changes undertaken by both the British and the Germans.

German aircraft add another four hundred and three thousand, four hundred tons to those sinkings to bring the total carnage for the month to over six hundred thousand tons.

* * * * *

- February First -

- USA -

The US navy goes through a massive reorganization. It will now be formed on three major fleets, Pacific, Atlantic and Asiatic. The Atlantic fleet is to be strengthened considerably and is put under the command of Admiral King. Admiral Husband Kimmel is appointed Commander of the Pacific fleet.

* * * * *

- Brest -

The German heavy cruiser '*Admiral Hipper*' sails from its home port and heads out on a war patrol in the North Atlantic to begin a search-and-destroy mission aimed at merchant shipping.

* * * * *

- Japan -

The government of Japan announces the rationing of rice.

* * * * *

- East Africa -

In Eritrea, after a difficult three days of fighting, Agordat falls to forces under the command of Platt. The troops under the Italian command of General Frusci retreat to take up mountain positions near Keren. In the south Barentu is taken by Indian troops.

* * * * *

Patrick Laughy

- February Second -

- East Africa -

The British aircraft carrier HMS *'Formidable'* while on route to replace the damaged HMS *'Illustrious'* in the Mediterranean uses its aircraft for an attack on the harbour facilities of Mogadishu in Somalia.

* * * * *

- North Africa -

Australian forces moving west along the coast from Derna realize that the Italians are retreating rapidly. As a result the British commanders send the 7th Armoured Division scurrying across the center of Cyrenaica in the eastern coastal region of Libya in the hopes of cutting them off.

Due to the urgency of this thrust the 7th travels at haste and without full supplies.

* * * * *

- February Third -

- Berlin -

Hitler appoints Lieutenant-General Erwin Rommel to the position of Command for all German Army troops in Africa.

* * * * *

- Vichy France -

The Nazis apply pressure and have pro-German, Pierre Laval, appointed to the position of Vichy Minister of Foreign Affairs.

* * * * *

- North Atlantic -

Under the command of Admiral Lutjens the German battle cruisers *'Scharnhorst'* and *'Gneisenau',* sailing in tandem, slip through the Denmark Strait into the Atlantic to search for merchant targets.

* * * * *

- February Fourth -

- East Africa -

British forces launch their first attack against the Italian defensive positions around Keren in Eritrea.

* * * * *

- North Africa -

The British 7th Armoured advance across Cyrenaica, take Msus and immediately move ahead toward Antelat.

* * * * *

- February Fifth -

- North Africa -

The first units of the swift moving British 7th reach the coast road near Beda Fomm. These consist of armoured cars and light tanks which have swept ahead of the heavy tanks. They immediately engage the retreating Italians and capture nearly five thousand troops.

To the north the Australian troops take the ancient city of Barce on the coast of Libya.

* * * * *

- February Sixth -

- North Africa -

The Australian troops following the fleeing Italians take Benghazi.

The Italians, who are in full retreat, are streaming along the coast road and are forced to make desperate attacks against the British 7th armoured units who have them bottlenecked at Beda Fomm. The small British force holding them takes heavy losses and is forced to give some ground but manages to hold its position.

* * * * *

- February Seventh -

- North Africa -

After failing to break through the British position at Beda Fomm despite numerous frantic attempts to continue their retreat, the Italians begin a large-scale surrender. Twenty-five thousand are taken prisoner and two hundred guns and one hundred and twenty tanks are captured by the British.

* * * * *

- February Eighth -

- USA -

The US House of Representatives passes the Lend-Lease

bill.

* * * * *

- Berlin -

Negotiations are completed and the Bulgarian's agree to allow Nazi troops free passage through their country.

* * * * *

- North Atlantic -

The German battle-cruisers *'Scharnhorst'* and *'Gneisenau'* spot the Convoy HX-106 but do not engage due to the presence of the British battleship HMS *'Ramillies'* as part of the escort.

They take this action because Hitler has specifically ordered that no risk of damage to the German ships is to be undertaken if it can be avoided.

* * * * *

- February Ninth -

- Berlin -

Hitler informs Mussolini that the previously promised German military assistance for the Italians in North Africa is on its way.

- North Africa -

The rolling British advance comes to a halt at the coastal city El Agheila which is located at the bottom of the Gulf of Sidra in far western Cyrenaica, Libya. The offensive cessation is not brought about by any Italian resistance, but is due to the fact that a good portion of the British troops on this front are being siphoned off and sent to the defence of Greece.

* * * * *

- Mediterranean -

British aircraft attack the Italian port city of Livorno on the west coast of Tuscany.

The British battleship HMS '*Malaya*', in company with the battle-cruiser HMS '*Renown*' conducts a daring bombardment of the harbour at Genoa, Italy. A total of five ships are sunk in the port and eighteen are damaged.

The carrier HMS '*Ark Royal*' who accompanies the '*Malaya*' and '*Renown*' sends her aircraft in an attack against Leghorn and La Spezia.

* * * * *

- February Tenth -

- London -

Churchill instructs General Archibald Wavell of the Middle East Command to treat Greek requests for assistance as a top priority. He stresses to the General that world opinion, especially that held by the United States must be considered when it comes to the British determination to fulfill its commitments with regard to the current agreements it has in place with smaller countries.

Such commitment will, in Churchill's opinion, also play a part in strengthening British relations with Turkey and could possibly make it easier for them to make an attempt to establish a Balkan coalition against the Nazis.

* * * * *

- Malta -

Heavy daily air attacks upon Malta begin.

* * * * *

- East Africa -

The British 4th Indian Davison goes on the offensive against the Italian units holding Keren. The Italians are solidly ensconced and routinely counter attack which leads to a standoff situation. The British recognize that more troops will be required to take the city and arrange for these to be brought up to the front.

* * * * *

- February Eleventh -

- North Africa -

The first German elements of what will soon become known as the *'Afrika Korps'*, begin to arrive at Tripoli and Tripolitania.

* * * * *

- East Africa -

The British forces advancing from Kenya into Italian Somaliland take Afmadu.

* * * * *

- Vichy France -

Admiral Darlan is nominated as the successor to Petain

and is to become his deputy. In addition he is to hold office as Foreign Minister, Minister of the Interior and Minister of Information.

He retains his rank as Commander in Chief of the Navy.

* * * * *

- February Twelfth -

- Atlantic -

The *'Admiral Hipper'* finds convoy SLS-64. This convoy contains nineteen ships and has no major allied warship in protection.

The Hipper attacks immediately and with her massive guns sinks seven of the ships before they can effectively scatter.

Hipper also comes across and sinks a single, independent merchantman before she turns back for her home port in Brest.

* * * * *

- Russia -

Stalin appoints General Zhukov to the position of Chief of the General Staff and Deputy Commissar for Defence. Soviet General Meretskov is appointed to lead the Red Army's training directorate.

* * * * *

- North Africa -

Rommel, the Commander of the newly formed German *'Africa Korps'* arrives in Tripoli.

Field Marshal Albert Kesselring is in Rome as the Nazi's military representative.

Mussolini appoints General Garibaldi as the new Italian Commander in Chief for Libya.

* * * * *

- February Thirteen -

- East Africa -

The British aircraft carrier HMS *'Formidable'*, unable to clear the Suez Canal on her way to join the Mediterranean Fleet due to mines which the German air force has dropped, unleashes an attack on the ancient port city of Massawa in Eritea.

* * * * *

- February Fourteenth -

- North Africa -

Units of the *'Africa Korps'* begin to move eastward toward the advance positions for the British forces at El Agheila.

* * * * *

- East Africa -

With supporting fire from the cruiser HMS *'Shropshire'* and a fleet of smaller support ships the British 22nd East African Brigade takes the port city of Kismayu.

* * * * *

- Berchtesgaden -

Hitler meets with Yugoslav Premier Cvetkovic and his Foreign Minster to urge them to join the Tripartite Pact.

Cvetkovic is hoping that the Nazis will soon find themselves embroiled in and pre-occupied with their relations with the Soviet Union and that in this eventuality Yugoslavia many turn to the Allies side with the expectation of getting aid from both Britain and the USA.

Riding a diplomatic razorblade the Yugoslavians talk the talk with Hitler but refuse to agree to immediately commit their country to the Axis cause.

* * * * *

- February Fifteenth -

- Berlin -

The order goes out to begin the deportation of the unwanted Austrian Jews eastward to waiting ghettos in Poland.

* * * * *

- February Seventeenth -

- Balkans -

Crumbling under pressure from the Nazis, Turkey and Bulgaria sign a friendship agreement in which Turkey allows that the movement of German troops through Bulgaria is not an act of war.

With this agreement goes any reasonable chance that Turkey might be persuaded to join the Allies.

* * * * *

- February Eighteenth -

The 4th Reich

- East Africa -

South African forces advancing from Kenya into Abyssinia attack the town of Mega, capture it and take one thousand prisoners.

* * * * *

- February Nineteenth -

- Blitz -

The Nazis begin three nights of heavy bombing over Swansea, South Wales.

* * * * *

- East Africa -

Emperor Haile Selassie arrives at Dangilla in Abyssinia in support of the British troops commanded by Major Orde Wingate who had named his small force of one Battalion of the irregular Sudan Defence Force accompanied by one battalion of Ethiopian solders of the 2nd Ethiopian Battalion, the *'Gideon Force'*.

They immediately go into action against Italian troops around Bahrdar Giorgis and Burye with considerable success, despite the fact that the British led force consists of only seventeen hundred men, while the Italians have four full brigades in the area.

* * * * *

- Cairo -

Anthony Eden, the British Secretary of State for War, accompanied by the Chief of the Imperial General Staff,

General John Dill attend a conference with the local area commanders, Generals Wavell and Cunningham.

Their mission is to fulfill Churchill's orders to free up as many troops as possible from their current forces within Africa for immediate transport to the aid of Greece.

* * * * *

- February Twentieth -

- Western Libya -

British and German troops come face to face in North Africa for the first time at El Agheila.

* * * * *

- February Twenty-First -

- Bulgaria -

German forces enter Bulgaria and begin their move toward the Greek front.

* * * * *

- Russia -

Stalin shakes up the Communist Party Central Committee. Among others, the Foreign Minister and the former Ambassador to the USA are dismissed.

* * * * *

- February Twenty-Second -

- Athens -

The British delegation travels from Cairo to Athens where they meet King George and Premier Korizis and conduct further meetings regarding British military aid.

* * * * *

- February Twenty-Third -

- East Africa -

Italian forces in defensive positions at the Juba River in Somaliland are routed by the British. The Allied troops are now advancing at speed towards Mogadishu.

A small Free French force lands in Eritrea.

* * * * *

- Athens -

After discussions, the British offer the Greeks a force to consist of one hundred thousand troops supported by appropriate numbers of artillery pieces and tank support.

The Greeks feel that a lesser force would only serve to put them in the position of being unable to defend successfully against the Nazis and simply encourage the Germans to launch an immediate attack.

No agreement acceptable to both sides can be reached however, with regard to the specific displacement of these additional troops.

* * * * *

- February Twenty-Fourth -

- Vichy France -

Admiral Darlan is appointed to head the Vichy government.

* * * * *

- February Twenty-Fifth -

- East Africa -

After traversing two hundred and thirty miles in three days, the British forces take Mogadishu.   Massive fuel reserves, supplies and equipment are captured.
* * * * *

- Mediterranean -

While on convoy duty for a Naples to Tripoli run the Italian light cruiser *'Diaz'* is sunk by the British submarine *'Upright'*.

* * * * *

- February Twenty-Sixth -

- Balkans -

Eden and Dill visit Ankara with a view to pressing for an alliance with Turkey but the talks bring about no resolution of the Turkish position.

- February Twenty-Seventh -

-Indian Ocean -

The New Zealand cruiser *'Leander'* sinks the Italian Merchant cruiser *'Ramb I'* Off the Maldive Islands.

* * * * *

- February Twenty-Eighth -

- East Africa -

The RAF has now established aerial superiority in the area and Asmara in Eritrea is bombed.

CHAPTER FIVE

- March -

- Alfred Rosenberg -

Rosenberg was born into a family of Baltic Germans, in Reval, which at that time in history was part of the Russian Empire, on January twelfth, eighteen ninety-three. He studied architecture at the *'Riga Polytechnical Institute'* and then engineering at Moscow's *'Highest Technical School'*, completing his PhD in nineteen seventeen.

While a student at Riga he became a member of the Baltic German student fraternity *'Rubonia'*, and during the Russian revolution in nineteen seventeen Rosenberg supported the counter-revolutionaries. Following the successful revolution his family fled Russia, immigrating to Germany in nineteen eighteen and upon his arrival in Munich he began to contribute to the publication *'Volkischer Beobachter'*, which was to become the official newspaper of the Nazi party in nineteen-twenty.

At this point in his life Rosenberg was firmly, both anti-Semitic and anti-Bolshevik. As such, he found himself strongly attracted to the, then-named, *'German Workers' Party'*. He joined this party a year after his arrival in Germany, nine months before Adolf Hitler became a member. He was one of its earliest members. This party later changed its name to *the 'Nation Socialist German Workers Party'* or what quickly became known as the Nazi party.

In nineteen twenty-three Rosenberg became the editor of the official Nazi paper. In the year after the failed *'Beer Hall Putsch'*, and Hitler's resulting imprisonment, *'The Fuhrer'* appointed Rosenberg as the interim leader of the Nazi party during the period of his imprisonment. Hitler was released from prison on December twentieth, nineteen twenty-four, at which time he reassumed the leadership of the party.

In nineteen twenty-nine Rosenberg founded the *'Kampfbund fur deutsche Kultur'* (Militant League for German Culture), a nationalistic anti-Semitic political society that flourished during the Weimar Republic. The name of this organization changed to *'Nationalsozialistische Kulturgemeinde'* (National Socialist Culture Community) in nineteen thirty-four after the Nazis had come to power. He also formed the *'Institut zur Erforschung der Judenfrage'* (Institute for the Study of the Jewish Question) which was dedicated to searching for and then attacking Jewish influence in German culture and to the recording of the history of Judaism from an anti-Semitic perspective.

In nineteen thirty-four Hitler gave Rosenberg responsibility for the shepherding of the spiritual and philosophical education of the Party and all its related organizations.

* * * * *

- ERR –

The *'Einsatzstab Reichsleiter Rosenberg'* (Reichsleiter Rosenberg Taskforce) or ERR was formed in nineteen forty. Headed by the now chief ideologue of the Nazi party, Alfred Ernst Rosenberg, it was overseen from within the office of the *'Aussenpolitischen Amt der NSDAP'* (Foreign Affairs).

The ERR was initially a project of the *'Hohe Schule der NSDAP'* , a Nazi created elite university which was subordinate to Rosenberg who envisioned it as a research institute filled with seized cultural material from all those associations who opposed Nazi ideology. These were to include Jewish, Masonic, Communist and Democratic organizations within Germany and from all new German occupied territories.

After the occupation of France the staff of the ERR

established itself in *'Office West'* in Paris and immediately joined the SS in the search for all books, archival material and artifacts found to be in the possession of Jews. In the Fuhrer Directive issued on July fifth nineteen-forty Hitler had officially authorized the ERR to confiscate from occupied territories: precious manuscripts and books from national libraries and archives, important artifacts of ecclesiastical authorities and Masonic lodges and all valuable cultural property belonging to Jews.

On the first of March nineteen forty-one the ERR central administration was transferred to Berlin.

* * * * *

- Einsatzgruppen -

The *'Einsatzgruppen der Sicherheitspolizei un des SD'* (SS paramilitary death squads) were mobile killing units initially brought into being with the invasion of Poland.

These Special Forces were under the direction of SS-Reichsfuhrer, Heinrich Himmler and the direct supervision of SS-Obergruppenfuhrer Reinhard Heydrich.

The group's origins were loosely formed after the Nazis came to power in Germany. The *'Einsatzgruppen's'* predecessor was the ad hoc *'Eisatzkommando'* which was initially formed by Heydrich to secure government buildings and documents following the Anschluss in Austria in March of nineteen thirty-eight. It had originally been an arm of the *'Sicherheitspolizei'* (Security Police).

The job assigned to this force was the responsibility for the confiscation of government papers and police files in any area newly occupied by German forces and subsequently absorbed into the Greater German Reich.

As part of their duties, once the German military forces had taken control of new territory, they followed the troops to immediately secure government buildings, questioned senior civil servants and arrest anyone they considered as potentially dangerous to the ideals and aims of the occupying Nazi forces.

Shortly before Poland was invaded Heydrich re-formed this ad-hoc political policing agency and renamed it *'Einsatzgruppen'*. As such it played a role in the *'Action T4'* programme of the euthanization of the physically and mentally handicapped.

When the invasion took place Heydrich placed *'Obergruppenführer'* Werner Best in command and gave the organization the overall responsibility of removing all undesirable elements from the expanding German controlled territories and ordered them to travel in the wake of the German armies.

Membership in the expanding force whose total strength was approximately twenty-seven hundred at this point, was drawn from the SS, *'Sicherheitsdienst'* (Security Police) and the police. Leaders for the various subgroups within the organization, which were called *'Einsatzkommandos'*, were selected with a view to garnering those who held higher education and possessed some form of military experience.

The mission of this newly expanded force was now narrowed somewhat, its mission being that of the forceful de-politicisation of the Polish people and the elimination of groups most clearly identified with the Polish national identity. The intelligentsia, members of the clergy, teachers and members of the nobility. Hitler had stated his wishes clearly to Himmler. He wanted no Polish leaders left within the occupied territories.

They were to be completely eradicated.

Himmler was completely under the Fuhrer's thrall and determined to stand out within Hitler's inner circle as the man who did not have to be asked twice to fulfill his Fuhrer's needs.

With typical German thoroughness and organization he ordered the creation of the *'Sonderfahndungsbuch Polen'* (List of persons to be eliminated in Poland) to be drawn up prior to May of nineteen thirty-nine and directed that these *'Einsatzgruppen'* actions were to be supported by the *'Volksdeutscher Selbstschutz'* (an ethnic paramilitary group consisting of Germans living in Poland). He also instructed that members of the SS, Wehrmacht and the *'Ordnungspolizei'* (Order Police) were to actively support the individual members of the *'Einsatzkommandos'* in carrying out their work.

Seven *'Einsatzgruppen'*, each at battalion strength, operated in Poland and each was subdivided into four *'Einsatzkommandos'* of company strength and functioned separately from the army and under the direct orders of Heydrich.

Many senior army officers choose to ignore these genocidal actions, as the killings violated the rules of warfare as set down in the Geneva Conventions, however Hitler had told them up front that they would have to tolerate and offer logistical support to the *'Einsatzgruppen'* whenever it was tactically possible to do so.

Some old school officers abhorred the unauthorized shooting, looting and rapes committed by the members of the individual *'Einsatzgruppen'* to little or no effect. As an example, in May of nineteen forty, Gerneraloberst Johannes Blaskowitz sent a memorandum of complaint directly to Hitler which the Fuhrer dismissed as 'childish' and promptly relieved Blaskowitz of his command.

Those given *'special handling'* included Jews, prostitutes, Gypsies, and the mentally and physically disabled. Approximately sixty-five thousand Polish civilians had been executed by these units by the end of nineteen thirty-nine.

The final task of the *'Einsatzgruppen'* in Poland was to round up the remaining Jews and place them in Ghettos.

On the thirteenth of March nineteen forty-one in the lead-up to *'Operation Barbarossa'* (the invasion of Russia), Hitler dictated his *'Guidelines in Special Spheres re: Directive no. 21'*.

Sub Paragraph 'B' of this document specified that the *'Reichsfuhrer-SS Heinrich Himmler would be given 'special tasks' on direct orders from the Fuhrer. Which he would carry out independently'*.

This was aimed at ensuring that there would be no conflict between the army and the SS when it came to the necessary *'special handling'* the Fuhrer envisioned as an essential part of dealing with the Polish sub-human race.

Taking that concern a step further, Hitler specifically proclaimed within the directive that any criminal acts committed against Russian civilians by members of the Wehrmacht during the upcoming campaign would not be considered for prosecution in the military courts.

Absolution from the top: no later punishment for crimes committed by the troops going into Russia, issued before the attack began.

Carte blanche delivered on a platter by the Supreme Commander to his invading troops.

Hitler's position on the war against Russia was no secret to his military commanders.

In a speech delivered to his top generals on the thirtieth of March of forty-one he spoke at length about the upcoming engagement, dwelling on the ongoing struggle between two opposed ideologies, providing a contemptuous evaluation of the Bolshevised system of corrupt government, berating the encouragement in the Soviet Union of antisocial criminality, classing the Communist system as an immense future danger to Germany.

He classed the invasion as a fight to the finish, explaining that the struggle against Russia would have to be similar to the removal of a cancerous growth from the human body. The invaders would have only one chance to deal with the problem. If it was not immediately and completely eradicated, it would simply regress, then build and expand to again confront the pure German race in years to come.

In ending this tirade he told them that the fight in the east could not be fought in the same manner as that in the west. That the war against the Russians had to deliver the extermination of Bolshevik Commissars and of the Communist intelligentsia and GPU personal. That these individuals were criminals and had to be treated as such; that in the east harshness now will mean mildness for the future of the new world order.

Although Hitler did not refer to the *'Jewish problem'* inherent in Russia during this speech, he had often spoken publicly and succinctly about the necessity of Germany conducting a war of annihilation against *'Judeo-Bolshevism'*. It can be reasonably argued then that, at this time of the pinnacle of the Fuhrer's power, his audience would have clearly understood that Hitler's call for the destruction of the Soviet Union was also a call for the destruction of its entire Jewish population. And no matter the fact that this *'Jewish Problem'* was couched in euphemisms like *'special tasks'*, *'executive measures' and 'shot while attempting escape'*, the Fuhrer's wish was for the total and utter genocide of the Jewish race.

* * * * *

- Castle von Stauffer –

Three days after the double wedding of her daughters, the Countess Erika had left Berlin in the family's chauffer driven nineteen thirty-eight Mercedes-Benz 150 series Pullman limousine for the trip to the von Stauffer castle nestled above Lake Constance and the city of Friedrichshafen.

This would not have been Erika's first choice for travel of this length; she would have preferred to travel by rail.

However, as Ursula and Friedrich had, with her blessing - after all it was their honeymoon chosen to make use of the family's private rail cars for their brief weeklong sojourn to Friedrich's ancestral home in Frankfurt and then their own onward journey to the castle; she had not been afforded the opportunity to make use of the private von Stauffer railcars.

Which meant that, should she have chosen to journey by train, she would have been restricted to travelling first class, which was simply not the same as having the use of one's private units and quite unworthy of consideration.

Added to that was the fact that the car would likely be a convenience to have during the stay at Lake Constance, especially if it should turn out that the visit would be of an extended nature since Karl had his own driver and staff car the chauffeur would be of little use at the Berlin mansion, therefore it seemed only sensibly that she should travel to the castle by personal car.

More than pleased to have her daughters finally safely married to suitable young men, she had been determined to enjoy the solitude of the motor trip and had spontaneously chosen to break it up with an overnight stop at a favorite hostelry.

She had indeed found it pleasant and upon her arrival at the castle had been well rested and eager to get things organized for the arrival of Ursula and her new husband, having already decided that they would be given the upper floor on one of the newer wings, therein providing them with a large degree of privacy, well away from the main rooms of the castle proper.

Although she seemed to remember Karl mentioning something about some new construction that would be underway, something about a storage area for state artworks or some other, somewhere in the depths of the lower areas of the castle, she had been somewhat taken aback at the extent of the goings on when she'd arrived.

Luckily the main thrust of the work was being done far from the occupied areas of the castle and she soon took the construction, which was being supervised by a seemingly very efficient SS Captain on temporary assignment from SS-General Dieter Bichler's personal staff, in stride.

The officer had advised her that the work would be finished within a few days and that upon completion he would be leaving for Berlin after turning the responsibility for security of the area over to Major von Krueger and his Luftwaffe security contingent.

Remembering that Karl had earlier assured her that she would have no need to concern herself with whatever it was all about, she had dismissed the whole thing from her mind until her arrival. When she'd arrived, the SS Captain had given her the same assurance, and from that point on she'd not given it another thought.

She'd set to work, generally whipping things into shape, hiring additional staff and overseeing a good cleaning of the upper floor of the wing she'd previously decided would meet Ursula's needs.

The newlyweds where set to arrive in two days' time.

* * * * *

Harbouring a sense of trepidation, Ursula had been pleased to find after their arrival at her new husband's ancestral home that Friedrich's mother and father had graciously arranged to allow the newlyweds as much private time as they needed.

The young couple spent most of the week, when not buried in the depths of their huge antique, curtained bed, skiing snowshoeing and hiking on or near the estate. They were only expected to spend part of their early evenings with the family members primarily at the evening meal.

Friedrich had a warm and easy relationship with his parents who appeared to be obviously and very sincerely pleased with the match. Ursula was received with an extension of that warmth and immediately found them good company.

Her new spouse had proved to be stimulating company himself and a confident lover and Ursula found herself enjoying her new relationship immensely.

As a result, time seemed to have passed quickly and despite the fact both she and Friedrich were eager to get to the castle and take up their new responsibilities, it was with some regret they boarded her family's private railcars and began the final leg of the journey to Friedrichshafen and Castle von Stauffer.

Major von Krueger had been provided with an aide and had booked the young officer a spot in first class and relieved him from his duties for the length of the remaining trip to Friedrichshafen, allowing the young couple to enjoy the uninterrupted privacy of the family's two private railcars.

They put this seclusion to good use and the aide saw them but twice, both times when he was seated some distance away from them in the dining car.

Upon arrival at the rail yards at Friedrichshafen their private cars were uncoupled from the rest of the train and briefly shunted onto a short siding. A few minutes later a small yard engine puffed its way backward into the siding and attached itself and they were soon moving again, back onto the main line for the short trip to the spur that led to the castle.

There was a short pause when they reached the spur while the switch was thrown to allow entry off the main line and Ursula took advantage of the cessation of motion to lead Friedrich to the back of the train and out onto the observation platform.

They established themselves into two of the comfortably padded chairs and with freshly made drinks provided by the aide, settled down to enjoy the scenery as the little engine began to reverse onto the spur, pushing the cars in front of it.

After the engineer had paused to drop down out of the engine to return the switch to its original position, he had climbed back into the cab and the little engine began to chuff its way along the gently rising incline of rails that led upward toward the base of the castle.

Ursula maintained an historic commentary about the origins of the castle punctuated by comments on various objects and vegetation as they passed them and Friedrich listen avidly as they made their way up the mountainside.

As they reached the face of the massive wall surrounding the estate and then chuffed their way through the railway portal onto the grounds, the distant castle came into view above and Ursula paused in her remarks before turning to him.

"Well that's new."

She raised her hand to point at a second spur line and the switch that attached it to the rails they were currently moving on. This new line ran parallel to the one they were travelling on and ended at a newly constructed rail barn which was adjacent to, but looked much larger than the original one that had been built to house the family's two private railcars when they were not in use.

Friedrich followed her gaze, taking in the sparkling new rail lines and arched his brows.

"Must be for the incoming train cars loaded with the objects coming in from the occupied territories."

Ursula nodded.

"Yes, I had expected some changes but nothing quite this elaborate. Obviously a good deal of construction and preparation have been accomplished already. I suppose additional renovations must have been done within the castle proper as well.

Knowing mother's need for quiet organization, I would imagine she must be at her wits end."

CHAPTER SIX

- March -

- Hitler's View -

Having already dealt with the minor irritants in his own mind, Hitler now turned his attention to an immediate annoyance, his belief that the defeat of the Italian troops in Albania and Greece had indirectly *'struck a blow at the belief of our invincibility, that was held by friend and foe alike'*.

He had decided that this situation had to be eradicated and Greece would therefore have to be occupied and order re-established throughout the area before Barbarossa could be safely launched. Irritated by the Italian's dismal performance in the Balkans he preferred to look upon that debacle as a golden opportunity for Germany to gain more territory and economic assets for herself.

There were several obstacles to be overcome before Greece could be taken, primarily those of geography. Four countries: Hungary, Romania, Bulgaria and Yugoslavia separated Germany from Greece.

Hungary and Romania were by this time under his thumb and he already had troops in each. Bulgaria seemed to be in his pocket now that they had been successfully pressured to join the *'Tripartite Pact'*.

The presence of Yugoslavia however, remained both a military and political concern to the Fuhrer. Despite the political arm-twisting that had been applied to the Yugoslavs, they had made it clear that they wanted neither German nor Russian intervention in the Balkans.

Veiled diplomatic threats and dangled promises had so far been unsuccessful in encouraging them to join the Axis pact and Hitler now decided to intervene personally. He invited

Prince Paul, the Yugoslavian Regent, to a secret meeting at the Berghof for two days on March the fourth and fifth.

Prince Paul was sorely tempted by Hitler's personal promise to guarantee Yugoslavia's territorial integrity but explained that he found himself in a most difficult situation for personal reasons.

His wife's Greek ancestry and her personal sympathies for England as well as his own displeasure with Mussolini made joining the Axis problematic. He left Hitler with a strong impression that despite his concerns, he would in fact agree and returned to Yugoslavia without a full commitment.

Three days later he responded to Hitler in writing. He indicated that he was willing to sign on the Tripartite Pact with the proviso that Yugoslavia would not be required to lend any military assistance nor allow the passage of German troops through its territory.

Hitler was not pleased, but after giving the matter some thought he decided to respond with his acceptance of these additional conditions only to have the Regent send another missive informing the Fuhrer that Yugoslavia could do also do nothing that might involve them in a possible war `with America or Russia`, which would require a further promise to that effect from Hitler.

By the middle of the month Hitler had come to the conclusion that the Yugoslavs were not about to submit to his initial requirements. He was furious, but decided to concede in the hopes of a rapid agreement.

On the sixteenth of March Hitler spoke at the Memorial Day ceremony held at the Berlin War Museum.

The strain of the unsatisfactory negotiations with Yugoslavia had taken an obvious toll on the Nazi leader. Hitler appeared drawn and haggard. He displayed none of the usual fire and oratory normally present in his speeches being broadcast to the German people and instead offered up the usual platitudes required of the occasion without enthusiasm.

The next day The Yugoslavian Crown Council agreed to sign the `Tripartite Pact`.

Hitler, when informed of the decision was satisfied that the Yugoslav problem had been satisfied sufficiently to meet his needs. He had personally achieved the joining of the Yugoslavs in the pact where others had failed, albeit being saddled with unsatisfactory caveats, but he could and fully intended to deal with that later.

Upon the decision by the council there was an instant public outcry in Yugoslavia which brought about the resignation of three ministers who joined the protest and a revolt led by high-ranking air force officers.

By the morning of March twenty-seventh the rebels had overthrown the government and made the youthful heir to the throne, Peter, King.

A telegram from Belgrade arrived for Hitler advising that the former members of the Yugoslav government were under arrest and there would be no signing of the agreement with Nazi Germany.

Hitler took the decision as a personal affront.

He immediately ordered his military commanders to report at once to the chancellery and sent out an emergency call for von Ribbentrop before bursting into the conference room where General Jodl, head of the armed forces operations staff and `Generalfeldmarschall` (Field Marshall), Keitel were waiting for the daily war briefing.

Waving the offending telegram in his hand he announced that `He was now going to smash Yugoslavia once and for all`.

* * * * *

- Air Operations -

The newly designed Halifax bomber joins the British RAF. The German cities of Kiel, Bremen, Hamburg and Brest are the main targets.

Good weather brings an increase in German air attacks in the *'Battle of Britain'*. London, Merseyside. Glasgow, Plymouth and Bristol are the main targets.

* * * * *

- Battle of the Atlantic -

Eighty-two British merchantmen are sunk for a total loss of five hundred and twenty-nine thousand, seven hundred tons. Allied escort forces sink six U-boats, which at the time, is one fifth of the Germans' Atlantic operational fleet.

* * * * *

- March First -

- USA -

Three destroyer squadrons consisting of twenty-seven ships are formed by the U.S. navy as a support force for the Atlantic Fleet.

* * * * *

- Auschwitz -

The new Auschwitz concentration camp, located within the Reich's recently annexed Polish territories, has reached a population of ten thousand nine hundred prisoners and in anticipation of the need for enlarged facilities to allow for the confinement of a hoard of new prisoners, Himmler issues orders to the Commandant, Rudolf Hoess, to begin an immediate expansion of the facility.

* * * * *

- North Africa -

A Free French force from Chad, under the command of Colonel Leclerc, assisted by some units from the British Long

Range Desert Group, takes the city of Kuffra in southeast Libya.

* * * * *

- Balkans -

Prime Minister Filov joins Bulgaria to the terms of the Axis Tripartite Pact.

* * * * *

- March Second -

- Balkans -

A day after Bulgaria has signed on to the Pact, German troops intended to be used for the invasion of Greece begin to move into the country in force.

* * * * *

- March Fourth -

- Norway -

A British commando raid is carried out on the Lofoten Islands and on oil facilities at Narvik. The five hundred strong force lands from naval units including two light cruisers and five destroyers. Ten ships are sunk and two hundred and fifteen German prisoners are taken. In addition, three hundred Norwegian volunteers are picked up for transfer to England.

The enraged Germans respond with fierce reprisals after the attacking force retires.

* * * * *

Patrick Laughy

- North Africa -

British forces in Libya are reduced as the English hastily transfer troops to shore up Greek defences in response to the recent German troop movements into and across Bulgaria.

* * * * *

- Balkans -

Prince Regent Paul of Yugoslavia travels to Berchtesgaden for a meeting with Hitler where he is again pressured to join the Axis Tripartite Pact.

The Prince returns to Yugoslavia of the opinion that a decision as to which side he will ally his country must be made immediately. He sees little hope of the British coming to Yugoslavia's aid and although he still holds back from actually signing on the dotted line, he privately reaches the decision to throw his support behind the Axis powers by joining the Pact.

* * * * *

- March Sixth -

- Holland -

Following communist backed strikes in February over the arrest of Jews, and German steps toward organizing workers for transfer to worksites in Germany, the German occupying forces counter by condemning to death eighteen Dutch resistance members.

* * * * *

- March Seventh -

The first British troops arrive in Greece at Piraeus.

* * * * *

- March Eleventh -

- USA -

Roosevelt signs the *'Lend Lease Act'* into law.

* * * * *

- March Twelfth -

- North Africa -

Twelve German Panzer tanks arrive to provide heavy armour in preparation for the first Major German Offensive.

* * * * *

- March Thirteenth -

- Albania -

The Italian Spring Offensive begun on the ninth using twelve divisions and supervised on the spot by Mussolini, has managed a few local successes but by this date the Greek forces at Klisura are having no difficulty checking any further advancement.

* * * * *

- Berlin -

Hitler issues the directive for the invasion of the Soviet Union in which he gives the administrative control of all captured territory exclusively to the SS, who under Himmler's leadership, is rapidly growing in power within the Nazi Reich.

* * * * *

- March Fourteenth -

- East Africa -

Allied forces set up a new command headquarters at Burye. The nearest Italian forces are now at Debra Markos in Ethiopia where they are negotiating with a local chief in preparation for a joint attack on the British.

* * * * *

- March Fifteenth -

- USA -

In a speech Roosevelt states unequivocally that the U.S. will supply Britain and her Allies *'aid until victory'* and that there will be an *'end of compromise with tyranny.'*

* * * * *

- March Sixteenth -

- East Africa -

The British land a small force at the port of Berbera, Somalia. The troops have been sent from Aden aboard two light cruisers and two destroyers accompanied by seven auxiliary vessels. The force takes the port and begins to advance inland.

British forces also advance toward Keren in Eritrea and the Indian 5th Division takes and holds the Dologorodoc position just south of the Keren road.

* * * * *

- March Seventeenth -

- Atlantic -

The allies suffer huge convoy losses in mid-Atlantic during this week.

This catastrophe is somewhat offset by the sinking of U-99, captained by Otto Kretschmer and U-100, captained by Joachim Schepke in a convoy battle with Allied escort ships.

This loss of German U-boat aces, coupled with the loss of U-47 commanded by Gunther Prien, another U-boat star commander ten days earlier, is a severe shock to German morale.

* * * * *

- East Africa -

General Cunningham's forces march northward into Jijiga Ethiopia, which has already been abandoned by the Italians.

* * * * *

- March Nineteenth -

- Atlantic -

The British battleship HMS *'Malaya'* while on convoy duty in the Atlantic is torpedoed by U-106 and seriously damaged. She immediately steams for New York where she will undergo repairs, becoming the first British warship to take advantage of the now-official American willingness to openly assist the Allied military forces.

* * * * *

- Balkans -

Losing patience with the Yugoslavians, Hitler gives the country five days to reach their decision or else he will make it for them.

* * * * *

- March Twentieth -

- East Africa -

Advancing from Berbera, the British take Hargeisa in Somalia.

* * * * *

- Albania -

The new Italian offensive is abruptly called off.

The Italians have taken twelve thousand casualties and achieved virtually nothing. However in holding off the attacking Italians, the Greeks have been forced to maintain their numbers on this front and are therefore unable to make their intended transfer of troops away from this battle in order to bolster their defensive forces which will shortly be facing the German threat, moving rapidly across Bulgaria toward them to open a new front.

* * * * *

- Balkans -

The 4th Reich

At a meeting of the Royal Council in Belgrade, Regent Paul states that in his view Yugoslavia has no choice but to Join the Tripartite Pact and allow the Germans free passage for their troops. His decision holds, although several ministers resign in protest and street demonstrations occur expressing the deep dislike within the county for the Germans under Nazi leadership.

* * * * *

- March Twenty-First -

- East Africa -

The British 11th African Division attacks Italian positions in the Marda Pass west of Jijiga in Ethiopia and despite the strength of the Italian defences they quickly begin to give ground.

* * * * *

- March Twenty-Second -

- East Africa -

Advancing strongly form Jijiga the 11th African Division overruns another Italian defensive position at the Babile Pass.

* * * * *

- March Twenty-Fourth -

- North Africa-

In his first offensive operation General Erwin Rommel now commanding the German forces in North Africa attacks and reoccupies El Agheila in Libya.

Rommel forces the British, who have recently withdrawn their experienced Desert troops under the command of General O'Connor from this front, to retreat in disarray.

Ironically Rommel, an exceptional commander, has been specifically forbidden to attack by the German High Command and told that he would receive no additional forces.

The German General, soon to be christened *'The Desert Fox'* has chosen to ignore these instructions and therein, his limited forces have easily won a decisive battle.

* * * * *

- March Twenty-Fifth -

- Crete -

An Italian Commando Frogman Unit sinks the heavy cruiser HMS *'York'*, two tankers and a cargo ship in Suda Bay.

* * * * *

-March Twenty-Sixth -

- Mediterranean-

On this date, encouraged by German claims to have sunk two of the British Mediterranean Fleet's battleships and with the promise of German air support and reconnaissance, Admiral Iachino takes the Italian Fleet out on a sortie into the Aegean Sea with the aim of attacking British convoys headed to Greece.

The Italian Fleet that sails consists of one battleship, six heavy cruisers, two light cruisers and thirteen destroyers.

* * * * *

- East Africa -

The Italian forces and their local allies begin their attack against the British near Burye. The British defensive line holds firm against them.

* * * * *

- Balkans -

Prince Paul and his Council of the Regency succumb to a coup led by the air force chief of staff General Simovic and are replaced by seventeen year old Prince Peter as Peter II of Yugoslavia and nominal head of government. Agents of Great Britain have played a part in this coup.

Hitler is outraged and immediately issues Directive 25 which orders planning for the invasion of Yugoslavia to begin. He instructs his staff to mount the attack in conjunction with the German military thrust into Greece and indicates that he will accept a postponement of *'Barbarossa'*, the invasion of Russia, if it is necessary to accomplish this new task.

* * * * *

- Mediterranean -

An English naval force under Admiral Cunningham sails from Alexandria. His strength consists of one carrier, three battleships and nine destroyers.

A second British fleet under the command of Admiral Pridham-Whippell consisting of four light cruisers and four destroyers sails from Piraeus.

The British fleets sight the Italian fleet off southern Greece and the battle of Cape Matapan begins.

* * * * *

- Honolulu -

Takeo Yoshikawa, a Japanese spy, arrives in Hawaii and begins his evaluation of the U.S. fleet at Pearl Harbor.

* * * * *

- East Africa -

In a bloody confrontation the advancing allies clear the Italian positions blocking the roads neat Keren in Eritrea, forcing the enemy to retreat toward Asmara.

* * * * *

- March Twenty-Eighth -

- Balkans -

General Dill arrives in Yugoslavia for talks. He has little to offer and no agreements are reached.

* * * * *

- March Twenty-Ninth-

- East Africa -

South African troops take Diredawa in Abyssinia and advance westward toward Addis Ababa.

* * * * *

- March Thirtieth -

- Berlin -

Hitler approves the invasion plans for Yugoslavia. The

attack is scheduled for April sixth.

Hitler speaks with two hundred and fifty of his top commanders with regard to the upcoming *'Operation Barbarossa'*. He tells them that the war in the east is to be conducted differently than those that have already been fought. There is to be no *'Knightly'* behavior on the part of German troops, and all Russian commissars and card-holding communists are to be treated with the utmost severity.

* * * * *

- USA -

The Government orders that all German, Italian and Danish ships in U.S. ports are to be placed into *'protective custody'*, effectively confiscating them.

* * * * *

-North Africa -

Sensing that the British defensive positions are weak, German General Erwin Rommel moves his forces from El Agheila with the intention of taking Mersa Brega.

* * * * *

- March Thirty-First-

- Mediterranean –

The British aircraft carrier the HMS *'Bonaventure'* is sunk in the Eastern Mediterranean by a torpedo-boat attack.

* * * * *

- North Africa -

Patrick Laughy

Rommel's forces attack infantry units from the British 2nd Armoured Division at Mersa Brega, north of EL Agheila. Mersa Brega is taken by the Germans but the British, who have taken a beating, manage to hold the German advance there.

CHAPTER SEVEN

- April -

- Einsatzgruppen -

On April twenty-eighth of nineteen forty-one Reinhard Heydrich successfully completes negotiations for the co-operation between *the 'Einsatzgruppen'* and the Wehrmacht wherein the German Army is to allow and support the implementation of the *'special tasks'* during the Russian campaign.

As a result of this agreement, Field Marshall Walther von Brauchitsch orders that when *'Operation Barbarossa'* begins, all German Army Commanders are to immediately identify and register all Jews in occupied areas within the Soviet Union and, to fully co-operate with the activities conducted by the *'Einsatzgruppen'* forces.

* * * * *

- Action 14f13 -

Action *`14f13`* named *'Sonderbehandlung'* (Special Handling), was a program initiated by Himmler and the SS with the aim of reducing the burgeoning number of concentration camp prisoners the Reich had to accommodate. `

The designation was derived from the SS record-keeping system, the number *'14'* for the Concentration Camps Inspector, the letter *'f'* for the German word *'deaths'* (todesfalle) and the number *'13'* for the means of killing, in this instance, gassing at the T4 killing centers.

In the spring of nineteen forty-one, the Reichsfuhrer met with `Reichsleiter` Phillipp Buhler, the head of Hitler's Reich

Chancellery to discuss the need to relieve concentration camps' responsibility for the housing of 'excess *ballast'*, (those prisoners who were sick, elderly or no longer able to work).

Buhler had been one of Hitler's approved agents for the earlier implementation of the Action T4 euthanasia program for the mentally ill and disabled inmates of the German hospitals and nursing homes who were unfit for work and therefore were deemed to have no useful place in the new German Reich.

Action T4 was still active at this point in the war, but to date, had been implemented with the usual German efficiency, meaning that raw material for the program within Germany was shrinking rapidly.

Buhler eagerly suggested to Himmler that he could take the euthanasia program which had instituted the use of gas chambers and crematoria to deal with the unworthy, that had worked so well in Germany, and introduce it to the concentration camps.

The proposed operation began in April of nineteen-forty-one. A panel of doctors began visiting concentration camps to make selections of inmates who they deemed sick and incapacitated and made lists of those chosen for elimination.

These panels included many of those who had been working on the T4 operation, Professors Wemer Heyde, Herman Paul Nitsche and doctors Friedrich Mennecke, Curt Schmalenbach, Horst Schumann, Otto Hebold, Rudolf Lonauer, Robert Muller, Theodor Steinmeyer, Gerhard Wischer, Viktor Ratka and Hans Bodo Gorgass.

As had been done under T4, the Commandants of the camps, like the administrators of the hospitals before them, were ordered to make up preliminary selection lists.

Those prisoners being considered for the preliminary selection were often encouraged by the camp administration to come forward if they felt stick or unable to work. They were led to believe that they would go to a *'recovery camp'* if they did and that, once transferred, they would only have light work to do.

Many prisoners readily volunteered.

Officially prisoners for this program were selected based on their medical condition. However, unofficially, racial and eugenic criteria were often used. Jews, the handicapped and those with criminal or antisocial records were subsequently readily selected.

Inmates who had been listed by the Commandants were ordered to report to the medical panel. There was no real medical examination done; questions were put with regard to their participation in the Great War and based on personnel and medical records, the doctors decided under which category to classify each of these prisoners.

They then completed a form indicating the prisoners should face *'withdrawal of service'*, and these reports were then sent to the T4 central office in Berlin.

The first such panel took place in April at *'Sachsenhausen'*.

* * * * *

- Oslo -

Prior to the war, in the late eighteen hundreds and early nineteen hundreds, the prejudice against Jews that was commonly found in Europe and other parts of the world, was also evident in Norway.

In the nineteen thirties the Norwegian *'Nasjonal Samling'* (NS) (Fascist Party) had, as did other fascist parties throughout the world, made anti-Semitism part of their political platform.

Halldis Neegaard, born on may twenty-third eighteen ninety-six, was a Norwegian anti-Semite and prominent member of the NS who became the de facto spokeswoman for its increasingly virulent anti-Jewish propaganda. This was summarized in her book *'Jodeproblemet og dests losning'* (The Jewish Problem and its Solution).

As a result, the NS had begun to gather information about Jewish Norwegians well before the start of the war.

Following the German occupation of Norway,

Reichskommissar Josef Terboven placed all Norwegian civilian authorities under his control.

The arrival of the SS and Gestapo saw the various Norwegian police agencies fall under their control. This included the Norwegian *'Lensmannsetaten'* (District Sheriffs), criminal police and order police.

Terboven had been instructed, wherever possible, to use Norwegian rather than German officials in the subjugation of the newly occupied population and that's what he did.

The SS used the same strategy. They created a new organization which they called The Norwegian Department of Police. This organization was headed, in name only, by senior Norwegian police officials who appeared to issue all instructions to the Norwegian police forces.

The SS held a tight rein on these carefully selected senior Norwegian police officers, who knew exactly what was expected of them.

The roundup and removal of the Norwegian Jews fell to the expanded SS and they moved quickly to get it organized and underway.

Commencing with known lists, several had already been arrested and deported in the early months of the occupation and plans were in the works to facilitate the compilation of additional lists now that the SS had sufficient boots on the ground and were in a position to act.

* * * * *

At their initial meeting with Obergruppenfuher Wilhelm Rediess, he had provided a member of his personal staff, SS-Untersturmfuhrer Hans Biermann, to act as his full-time liaison officer with Major von Kauffmann. Biermann`s assigned duties were to assist Konrad and his wife with the initial setup of Himmler's pet project in the newly occupied country.

The four of them had then met briefly to outline the immediate needs for the expansion of the *'Lebensborn'* project into Norway. Two priorities were identified, the location of a suitable building large enough to house the first clinic for the project, including the German senior nursing staff who would be arriving shortly, and a fitting residence for The Major and his new wife.

This accomplished, Gabriella and Konrad had left in the company of the eager young SS-Untersturmfuhrer who took them directly to the motor pool were he saw to it that a car and driver were assigned to the Major.

He then arranged to meet with them at their hotel at nine the next morning to begin their search for permanent accommodations. Before leaving them, Biermann suggested that the endeavour should not take long. He explained that since the SS had arrived in Norway, they had deported many Jews as political prisoners and had, as a result, seized numerous building and dwellings.

He admitted that this rounding up of Jews had gotten off to a rather slow start, as their quarry had to be first properly identified and lists compiled before they could be removed and transported but he went on to assure them that administrative steps had been taken to speed up this process and the lists of Jews was growing daily.

In his view they would therefore have many properties to choose from.

* * * * *

- Gabriella -

Within days of their arrival Gabriella and Konrad had selected an excellent building to house Norway's first *'Lebensborn'* facility.

The large building, which had been owned by a Jewish doctor who had used it for a clinic, was located in the centre of the city and contained a good deal of equipment that they could utilize.

Biermann advised them that the doctor had abandoned the structure in haste within hours of the German's invasion and taken a ship for London with his family.

The building contained large living quarters that the Doctor had occupied and Hans had suggested that Konrad and Gabriella might also want to use it for their living quarters. Gabriella declined this suggestion before Konrad could reply, indicating that she planned on doing a good deal of entertaining and would certainly want something rather larger and separate from the facility as their home.

She suggested that the area in question could be divided up to provide living quarters for the German staff who were already arriving in small groups and the matter was settled.

Konrad had been very excited at the find and had immediately eagerly immersed himself in getting the operation up and running, leaving Gabriella free to accompany SS-Untersturmfuhrer Biermann on the remaining adventure of locating their new home.

Gabriella was in no rush to make her choice. She had every intention of ensuring the she and Konrad would find a high social position among the Occupying forces and wanted an address that would assist in achieving that aim.

The weather had warmed somewhat now that April had arrived and Gabriella was pleased to note that the snow had begun to melt as she stepped into the staff car and settled into the back seat.

Biermann, who had been holding the door for her, closed it and moved around and got into the passenger seat beside the driver.

"Were you able to get the list Hans?'

The young SS-Untersturmfuhrer flushed slightly as he fished a single sheet of paper out of his tunic and swiveled in his seat so he could face her.

"Yes...I had to hand copy it from the original I'm afraid – it had just come in.

I've done as you asked and selected ten of the best addresses. Based on their locations, I would guess that they must all be large and well-appointed properties. You understand that under the circumstances, these people have no idea that they have been listed…they will likely wonder at what we are about."

Gabriella laughed.

"Well, we'll just tell them what we agreed on yesterday.

We understand that they might want to rent in the near future and we would appreciate a chance to have a look around. I really don't think they will be in any position to refuse us, do you?"

The liaison officer took a deep breath and shook his head.

"No, one has to assume that the Jews on this list are all fools, but must be aware at this point that their days here are numbered. The smart ones have already gone. I'm sure that those still left here in Norway know by now that they are not wanted and are thoroughly regretting having passed up the chance to leave earlier.

It is hard to believe that any of them would want to appear uncooperative."

Excited at the prospect of viewing the properties, Gabrielle smiled.

"Yes, I'm sure they must all want to leave the country as soon as they are able…I certainly wouldn't like to live in a country where I wasn't wanted."

Biermann glanced at the list as he turned back around to face the front.

"These are all in the same area, we should be at the first one in about ten minutes."

He gave the driver the address.

Gabriella turned her attention to watching the passing vehicular and pedestrian traffic.

She had not spent much time away from the hotel since their arrival other than to travel from building to building in the staff car and had really paid little attention to the few native Norwegians she had encountered.

She noted that the people on the sidewalks did not look or dress all that differently from the people of Berlin; that the majority of vehicular traffic consisted of German military vehicles or German staff cars and that civilian traffic was light.

The pedestrians seemed content enough, going about their business, if keeping their heads down and avoiding looking directly at the staff car as it passed.

That could be due to the weather, she supposed, but then again it was reasonable to assume that they were simply reflecting a sensible amount of respect for a car flying SS fender runes.

They were, after all, under German occupation, were being well treated and could look forward to a wonderfully bright future now that they were part of the greater German Reich.

As they turned a corner Biermann raised his hand and pointed ahead to the right before he spoke to the driver.

"That's it; just pull into the curb here."

Gabriella looked out in the direction Hans was pointing and beamed as she took in the massive four story mansion situated well back on a large, mature and well-landscaped and fenced piece of property.

"Well now, this does look interesting. If the inside is anything like the exterior, I would say it would fit the bill perfectly. How soon would we be able to take possession should I decide we want it?"

The young SS-Untersturmfuhrer shrugged his shoulders and turned his head to face her as the big car slipped into the curb and stopped.

"The paperwork is usually completed before we make an arrest. If you like the house we can take immediate steps to complete the required process. I will call the office and they will get to work on the paperwork straight away. Once it's ready they'll send it out with a squad to make the arrests.

I would think that you could likely move in as early as tomorrow."

Gabriela frowned.

"That quickly? How about the contents? Won't they need time to gather their belongings?"

Biermann arched his brows as he opened the door and walked back to open her door for her. He spoke as he offered a hand to assist her out.

"Their possessions are forfeit to the Reich. They get to pack a single suitcase each and they do that under guard...how long can that take."

The frown that had formed on Gabriella's forehead faded and she brightened considerably at the news.

She was getting tired of living in the cramped confines of a hotel suite.

CHAPTER EIGHT

- April -

- Air Operations -

RAF Bomber Command makes seven strikes at Brest and also goes after targets in Mannheim, Emden, Wilhelmshaven and Kiel.

The Germans hit London with heavy attacks involving 700 bombers on the night of April sixteenth/seventeenth and nineteenth/twentieth. Over the month the Luftwaffe also sends raids on Birmingham, Coventry and Plymouth.

* * * * *

- Battle of the Atlantic -

The U-boat fleet has expanded to thirty-two operational boats, allowing the Germans to maintain approximately twenty on war patrols during the month. The Nazis also have eighty-one subs on sea trials or in training in the Baltic.

U-boats are tending to go farther afield in order to find unescorted targets and the British move to extend their convoy escorts range to more than halfway across the Atlantic, and are using fueling bases that have been established in Iceland to increase the range of convoy escorts.

Expansion of aircraft allotments for Iceland now allow for additional convoy protection. On the fifteenth of the month RAF Coastal Command is brought under the operational control of the Admiralty, a move which will assist their effectiveness against operational German U-boats.

U-boats sink forty-three ships for a total tonnage of two hundred and forty-nine thousand tons. Only ten of these ships are attacked while in convoys.

German aircraft have an excellent month, sinking one hundred and ninety-five ships for a total tonnage of six hundred and eighty-seven thousand tons.

* * * * *

- April First -

- North Africa -

To Rommel's surprise the British forces retreat, withdrawing from Mersa Brega and abandoning defensive positions after suffering losses at El Agheila in Libya.

Delighted the *'Desert Fox'* makes the decision to take advantage of the situation and continues his offensive drive.

* * * * *

- Iraq -

Pro-German Rashid Ali ,backed by the members of the *'Golden Square'* (Four Officers of the Iraqi Armed Forces) launches a military coup d'état with the aim of overthrowing the current regime of pro-British Regent "Abd al-llah.

* * * * *

- April Second -

- North Africa -

Rommel's forces take Agedabia in Libya with ease and he decides to continue with his offensive momentum. The German General splits his forces into three groups and strikes out across Cyrenaica in a wide sweep intent on taking Benghazi, using his scout plane to fly from group to group and direct the separate advances.

The British are ill prepared to defend against such audacious behavior on the part of the *'Africa Korps'* and are forced to split their forces in order to attempt to stop the German advance.

* * * * *

- Mediterranean -

The British carrier HMS *'Ark Royal'* delivers a small number of Hurricane fighters to Malta.

* * * * *

- USA -

Roosevelt orders the transfer of ten coastguard cutters to the Royal Navy. These ships are far superior to the corvettes the British are currently using on convoy duty.

* * * * *

- Hungary -

Count Teleki, Prime Minister of Hungary is against further collaboration with Germany and comets suicide rather than continue in his duties. The Regent, Admiral Horthy and the new Prime Minister Laszlo Bardossy, continue to work with the Germans.

* * * * *

- April Third -

- Iraq –

The coup is successful and a new pro-German government is put into place under the leadership of Rashid Ali.

The British, who need to maintain their Iraqi oil supply, quickly organize troops from India and the Middle East to send into Iraq to ensure access to the vital oilfields.

* * * * *

- East Africa-

British forces under General Platt take Asmara, the capital of Eritrea.

* * * * *

- April Fourth -

- USA –

Roosevelt formally agrees to allow British warships to be repaired in U. S. shipyards as well as to be refuelled when on combat missions.

* * * * *

- North Africa -

Rommel's new offensives are proceeding well. Benghazi, on the coast is taken. The *'Africa Korps'* is now approximately two hundred miles east of El Agheila and moving towards Tobruk and Egypt.

* * * * *

- April Fifth -

- Yugoslavia –

A *'Soviet-Yugoslav Nonaggression Pact'* is successfully negotiated but it is too late to affect German plans.

* * * * *

- North Africa -

Rommel's advance continues. Barce on the coast is taken and inland Tengeder falls and the *'Africa Korps'* begins to advance toward Mechili.

* * * * *

- April Sixth -

- Balkans -

Axis forces from Germany, Hungary and Italy move through Romania and Hungary and launch the *'Blitzkrieg'* invasions of Yugoslavia and Greece.

* * * * *

-North Africa -

Rommel's advance is sustained forcing the Australian Division on the coast out of Derna and back toward Tobruk. In a devastating blow to the British, Generals O'Connor and Neame are captured during the night by a German patrol.

* * * * *

- East Africa –

The British take Addis Ababa in Abyssinia. The port of Massawa in Eritrea is attacked with the support of British naval vessels.

* * * * *

- April Seventh -

-Yugoslavia -

The advancing German *'XL Panzer Korps'* enters Skopje.

* * * * *

- Greece -

After reaching Strumica in the advance into Yugoslavia the Germans move against Greece.

* * * * *

- April Eighth -

- East Africa -

Allied forces take the port city of Massawa in Eritea, capturing seventeen large Axis ships and many smaller military and civilian vessels.

Immediately after this success the 4th Indian Division, which had been the backbone of the successful campaign in Eritea, is prepared for shipment to Egypt.

All that is left for the East Africa campaign to accomplish now is to clear the road between Asmara and Addis Ababa.
This is being done by forces working from both ends.

* * * * *

- Yugoslavia -

The German offensive is expanded as Kleist's First Panzer group advances westward over the Bulgarian border destroying the Yugoslavia forces on the frontier and advancing as far as Nis.

* * * * *

- North Africa -

Under the command of the *'Desert Fox'* the *'Afrika Korps'* takes Mechili and Rommel immediately begins to organize his advance into Tobruk.

* * * * *

- Greece -

The German forcers take Saloniki.

* * * * *

- April Ninth -

- Greece/Yugoslavia -

The Greek *'Metaxas Line'* defensive front collapses. Thessaloniki is taken and the Greek Second Army surrenders.
   Monastir in Yugoslavia is taken and the Germans begin to move south through the Monastir Gap. German forces move south over the Austrian border taking Maribor and begin to seize bridges over the Drava River.

* * * * *

-April Tenth -

- Greenland -

With the approval of the *'Free Denmark'* government in exile, the USA occupies Greenland where it intends to builds airbases to assist in the escort of convoys.

* * * * *

- Yugoslavia -

The German advance is assisted by desertions from the Yugoslavian army by many of its Croat troops. Although the invasion is not complete, the Axis powers are confident enough to announce that the Kingdom of Yugoslavia has been split up and that the *'Nezavisna Drzava Hrvastska'* (NDA) (Independent State of Croatia) had been established under Ante Pavelic and his *'Ustase'* (Croatian Fascist Organization and Revolutionary Movement) which was fanatically Catholic and had been pushing for a *'pure'* Croatia for some time, actively promoting persecution and genocide against Serbs, Jews and Gypsies.

* * * * *

- North Africa -

The *'Africa Korps'* start to encircle Tobruk, Libya as they begin to set up a siege of the port city and they take Fort Capuzzo and Sollum, on Egypt's border.

* * * * *

- April Eleventh -

- USA -

Patrick Laughy

Although hanging firm to the position that the United States is still a *'Neutral'* in the conflict, Roosevelt advises Churchill that he has declared that the Red Sea is no longer considered as a *'Combat Zone'* thereby authorizing U.S. ships to deliver cargos to Egyptian ports and that the U.S. Navy will extend the *'American Defence Zone'* further into the Atlantic up to the line of twenty-six degrees West, thereby extending the range for U.S. naval forces to provide convoy duty.

* * * * *

- Yugoslavia -

The Axis invasion continues. The Italians advance along the Dalmatian coast and from Trieste toward Ljubljana. The German *'XLI Korps'* moves over the Rumanian border toward Belgrade. Hungarians advance from Szeged toward Novi Sad.

These forces suffer little resistance at the hands of the Yugoslav army but are steadily harassed by the civilian population.

* * * * *

- North Africa -

The complete isolation of Tobruk is now complete and the last of the Allied forces have retreated back to the Egyptian border. The British artillery and Australian infantry inside the city offer fierce resistance to Rommel's forces and hold them at bay.

* * * * *

- April Twelfth -

- Yugoslavia -

The city of Belgrade announces its surrender to the German forces under General Kleist who have successfully fought their way down the Morava valley from Nis.

* * * * *

- Greece -

German forces defeat the British Commonwealth troops who had been holding defensive positions north of the town of Amyntaion close to the Greek border.

* * * * *

- April Thirteenth -

- Moscow -

Japan and the Soviet Union sign a neutrality pact. This allows Stalin to free up forces and strengthen his border with Germany.

* * * * *

- Iraq -

A small British force is airlifted into the country to shore up their vital oil possessions.

* * * * *

- Greece -

British and Greek defenders pull back toward Thermopylae.

* * * * *

- April Fourteenth -

- Tobruk -

Rommel's troop make a strong attack but are repulsed by the defenders.

* * * * *

- Albania -

The *'1ˢᵗ SS Panzer Division Leibstandarte SS Adolf Hitler'* (**LSSAH**), originally Hitler's bodyguard unit, captures the strategic Kleisoura Pass and begins to cut off the line of retreat for the Greek army in Albania.

* * * * *

- April Fifteenth -

British Naval forces of four destroyers intercepts an *'Africa Korps'* convoy near the Kerkinnah Islands off the east coast of Tunisia and sinks all five transports along with the three covering Italian destroyers.

* * * * *

- April Sixteenth -

-Yugoslavia -

Pavelic is officially sworn in to head the new Croat republic. A systematic programme of genocide against Orthodox Serbs by the Roman Catholic *'Ustase'* party, which is now in power, begins.

A half a million Serbs will be presented with a choice

---

between re-baptism and death.

Many Jews are also killed.

Local Catholic priests will usually be present for these massacres.

* * * * *

- April Seventeenth -

- Yugoslavia -

The Italians enter Dubrovnik on the Dalmatian coast. The former Prime Minister Cincar-Markovic immediately signs an armistice with the Germans.

The Nazis have successfully overrun the country at a cost of only two hundred dead.

King Peter escapes to Greece and a government in exile is formed in London.

* * * * *

- April Nineteenth -

- Iraq -

A British convoy begins to land troops of the 20th Indian Brigade at Basra.

* * * * *

- London -

The initial registration of women for war work under a new *'Employment Order'* is commenced.

* * * * *

Patrick Laughy

- April Twenty-First -

- North Africa -

Three British battleships shell Tripoli on their return from escorting a convoy to Malta.

* * * * *

- Albania -

Their path of retreat cut off by the advancing Germans, two hundred and twenty-three thousand Greek soldiers are forced to surrender.

* * * * *

- April Twenty-Second -

- Greece -

Both British military and civilian personal begin to evacuate from Greece.

* * * * *

- April Twenty-Third -

- Greece -

King George and his government are evacuated to Crete which Churchill is determined to defend.

* * * * *

- April Twenty-Fourth -

- Greece -

All British and Australian forces leave Greece for Crete and Egypt.

* * * * *

- April Twenty-fifth -

- Berlin -

Hitler issues directive 28 authorizing *'Operation Merkur'*, the airborne attack on Crete.

* * * * *

- Egypt -

Rommel wins a decisive victory at the Halfaya Pass close to the Egyptian border.

* * * * *

- Greece -

Axis forces defeat the defending Allies at Thermopylae.

* * * * *

- April Twenty-Sixth -

- Egypt -

The 'Africa Korps' under Rommel is still unable to crack Tobruk, however it attacks the defensive line at Gazala in Libya and enters Egypt.

* * * * *

- East Africa -

Allied forces take Dessie in Ethiopia capturing eight thousand Italian soldiers.

* * * * *

- April Twenty-Seventh -

- Mediterranean -

The British carrier HMS *'Ark Royal'* delivers a further twenty-three Hurricanes to a besieged Malta.

* * * * *

- North Africa -

The *'Desert Fox'* has his detractors in the German Supreme High Command.

Sent by the OKH, General Paulus arrives on an inspection tour of Rommel's forces. He has been sent from Berlin in an attempt to sort out what is going on.

There is no doubt in anyone's mind that Rommel has been successful but questions have arisen with regard to his tendency to disregard orders not to go on the offensive and whether or not he is out of control.

Shortly after his arrival Paulus orders a halt on preparations that are under way for more attacks on Tobruk.

* * * * *

German reconnaissance units occupy the Halfaya Pass in Egypt.

* * * * *

- Greece -

German troops take Athens. Greece surrenders.

* * * * *

- April Twenty-Ninth -

- East Africa -

The 5th Indian Division makes contact with the north side of the Italian held position at Amba Alagi in Abyssinia.

* * * * *

- April Thirtieth -

- North Africa -

Rommel convinces Paulus that Tobruk must be hit again and an all-out effort takes place supported by artillery bombardment and Stuka dive bombers. A breach is achieved in the western sector perimeter around the Ras el Madauar hill but a strong defence eventually brings it to a halt.

CHAPTER NINE

- May -

- The Inner Circle -

Joseph Goebbels exercised a unique form of power within Nazi Germany.

He contributed little if anything to the forming of the policies of the Nazi government. Hitler held that power firmly in his grasp.

He lacked the absolute authority that Himmler possessed, that of arrest and deportation to concentration camps.

However, Joseph Goebbels did have the unequivocal power to decide what the German people could read, see, hear and think. Propaganda was something Goebbels thoroughly understood. He was extremely good at persuading and convincing his countrymen to think along the lines that he alone determined.

In the early years of the party Goebbels used hero worship and adoration of the new order to solidify the Nazi political position in Germany. It was his job to counterbalance what the party deemed as the necessary use of ruthless force to ensure its success. He did this by initiating balanced steps the general public found to be of an overall positive nature.

For example he'd introduced popular national holidays such as May Day and the *'erntedant'* (harvest celebration), holidays which he ordered to increase yearly in their flamboyance and showiness. He used them as opportunistic stages from which the Nazis could demonstrate to the people how fortunate they were to be living under National Socialism and then move on to hypnotically harangue captive audiences with the party line.

Over time most Germans began to believe that they had

been celebrating these wondrous nationalistic holiday festivities all their lives along with the stability, unity and national pride resulting from the achievements of the Nazi party.

Once the party had solidified its political hold over Germany the economy switched over to the mass production of military materials. The planning for Hitler's realization of *'Lebensraum',* for an expanded new Reich began and with it a new chapter in Goebbels's propaganda campaign.

The citizens of Germany now had to be convinced of the need to prepare for war and that the need for that war was totally justified prior to its implementation.

Goebbels took up the challenge eagerly. German newspapers began a diatribe against the injustice of the Treaty of Versailles and more attention was given to the *'cruel providence'* of the pan-Germans living in Czechoslovakia and Poland and the *'ancient unity'* of Germany and Austria.

The Propaganda Minister then turned his attention to the making of movies that would drive home these points to the citizens of Germany, commencing with *'Germany Awake'.*

This allowed the short, clubfooted Goebbels to use his unlimited power and resources to engage in romantic relationships with the female stars of his productions. One of these was with a young Czech actress named Lida Baarova.

Goebbels fell head over heels in love with the woman.

Soon the tales of these liaisons became common knowledge within the upper echelon of the German government and Goebbels found himself living separately from his wife and children.

At the time, Goebbels's wife Magda, who absolutely worshipped the Fuhrer, went to Hitler to ask for his permission to get a divorce from her philandering husband. Hitler asked her to allow him to intervene in the situation with the aim of reuniting the couple.

He called Goebbels in for a frank chat. Goebbels informed Hitler that he was in love with Baarova and wanted a divorce so he could marry her.

Hitler was adamant that no such divorce should take place.

It was out of the question that Goebbels, the Nazi Minister of Propaganda should get divorced. Goebbels responded that he had carefully thought the matter through and recognized that he would be unable to continue on in his current position if he divorced but he was in love with the woman and determined to marry her. It was his view that he could then be sent to Japan as the German Ambassador.

Hitler went ballistic, ranting on for several minutes and ending by shouting: *'Those who make history may not have a private life'*.

Goebbels was not the Minister of Propaganda because he was a poor negotiator.

He managed to make a deal with Hitler.

They agreed that there should be a period of re-examination during which Goebbels was not to see the woman and return to the responsibilities of his marriage for the period of one year and that if at the end of that time he was still determined to seek a divorce, Hitler would reluctantly agree.

Goebbels gave the Fuhrer his word of honour to abide by his end of the bargain. Hitler, doubtful the Propaganda Minister would not see the woman for the year, dismissed Goebbels and then promptly brought Himmler into the picture and ordered him to have the Gestapo keep Baarova's home under continuous surveillance over the period in question.

Himmler seriously doubted that Goebbels would keep his word to the Fuhrer and as was the norm within the inner circle he saw to it that word of the agreement soon got around.

Now that it had become common knowledge that Goebbels had displeased Hitler, the circling sharks among the Fuhrer's hangers on, tasted blood in the complex waters surrounding Hitler.

Individually, Himmler, Goering and von Ribbentrop rubbed their hands in glee and began to do their best to position themselves to absorb Goebbels's duties if the possible need for a replacement should arise.

They were disappointed when Goebbels did keep his word to Hitler and a frustrated Baarova finally gave up hope and left Berlin.

Goebbels, not unlike the others within the inner circle, sometimes disagreed with something Hitler determined as necessary if the Germans wished to retake their proper place in the world. Like the others, however, he would then simply bite his tongue and do what Hitler wanted him to do.

Once Hitler had shifted Germany's economy over to a military buildup, Goebbels, who held his Fuhrer in high esteem, had done as he had been instructed. He'd thrown himself wholeheartedly into the process of convincing the German people that war was a necessity, speaking out and writing aggressively to justify the need for war.

He did this despite his own personal beliefs.

At the time, Goebbels was probably the only member of the Nazi hierarchy who correctly adjudged what the end result of war would be for Germany.

He foresaw the length and the gravity of a decision for Germany to turn to military aggression. He considered that going to war at this time would force Germany to take unnecessary risks and was well aware that in a Germany at war, his own position of power would be weakened while that of the military grew.

Even after the astounding victories won during the early years of the war, Goebbels stated: 'We must not fool ourselves. It will be a long and difficult war. Its outcome will not depend on boisterous victory parties but on a determination to do one's daily duty.'

* * * * *

- Einsatzgruppen -

In May of nineteen forty-one, Reinhard Heydrich verbally passed on the order for the extermination of the Soviet Jews to members of the reorganized 'Einsatzgruppen' members at their NCO school in Pretzsch, where they were in training for the upcoming 'Operations Barbarossa'.

* * * * *

- The Enigma Machine -

The Enigma Machine was an electro-mechanical rotor cipher machine used for the encryption and decryption of secret messages. It was invented by a German engineer named Arthur Scherbius at the end of The Great War.

Early models of the machine were used commercially from the early nineteen twenties and adopted by the military and government services of several counties', including that of Nazi Germany, prior to World War Two.

In December of nineteen thirty-two German military texts were first broken by three Polish cryptologists working for Polish Military Intelligence.

Marian Rejewski, Jerzy Rozycki and Henryk Zygalski using *'reverse engineering'* and theoretical mathematics created mechanical devices that could be used to break the Enigma codes. They called these devices *'cryptologic bombs'*.

Their discoveries created the basic foundation of all further work, first undertaken in Poland and then moved to France and finally Great Britain, which was embarked upon to facilitate the decoding of ciphers from the Nazi utilized Enigma machines which were continually being improved and upgraded over time.

Five weeks before the outbreak of World War Two on the twenty-fifth of July nineteen thirty-nine, the Poles presented their Enigma-decryption techniques and two full sets of decrypting equipment, including special cryptologic *'Zygalski sheets'* and *'cryptologic bomb'* supported by a how-to-use lecture by their team, to both the French and British military intelligence representatives in Warsaw.

It was this gift from the Poles that provided the basis for the successful decryption of all future German secret communications encrypted by Enigma achieved by the British code-breakers at the famous *'Bletchley Park'* during the war.

Something that arguably shortened the war by a good two years.

* * * * *

- Rudolf Hess -

Rudolf Walter Richard Hess was born on April twenty-sixth eighteen ninety-four.

He enlisted in the 7th Bavarian Artillery Regiment as an infantryman at the outbreak of the Great War and was wounded several times.

Toward the end of that war he enrolled to train as an aviator but did not see any active air service before the war ended. He left the armed forces in December of nineteen-eighteen with the rank of `Leutnant der Reserve`.

In nineteen-nineteen Hess enrolled in the University of Munich where he studied geopolitics under Karl Haushofer, who was a proponent of the concept of `Lebensraum` for Germany.

This concept later became one of the pillars of Nazi Party policy.

Hess joined the Nazi party on July first nineteen-twenty and was with Hitler at the time of the failed `Beer Hall Putsch` in nineteen twenty-three.

He served time with Hitler in prison after the incident and assisted him in writing `Mein Kampf` in nineteen twenty-four which was later to become the foundation of the political platform of the Nazi Party.

When the Nazi's took power in thirty-three Hess was appointed Deputy Fuhrer and took up a post in Hitler's new cabinet. At that time he was the third most-powerful man in Germany, second only to Goring behind Hitler.

He often appeared on the Fuhrer's behalf at rallies and speaking engagements and it was Hess who signed into law much of the early Nazi legislation including the `Nuremberg Laws' of nineteen thirty-five which stripped the Jews of Germany of all their rights and made them non-citizens.

Once war commenced in nineteen thirty-nine however, Hess found himself sidelined from power as Hitler turned his attention toward foreign affairs and military planning and operations, areas where Hess was not directly engaged.

As a result, the Fuhrer had less interest in and reason to spend time with his old comrade; he had more important things on his mind.

Hess idolized Hitler and had recreated himself in the Fuhrer's image. Like the German leader, Hess was a non-smoker, a non-drinker and a vegetarian.

Beginning in the nineteen forties, as his usefulness to Hitler continued to slip further and further away he became very unhappy and despondent at the new position he found himself in among those of the Fuhrer's inner circle.

Seemingly unable to regain Hitler's side, he wilted both physically and mentally from this loss of ongoing contact and influence with his idol.

Now, Hess was desperately seeking to find a way to rise again in importance in Hitler's eyes and regain all the wonder of the position he'd lost since the start of the war.

* * * * *

- Bordeaux -

Upon its arrival in Bordeaux Eric's U-boat required some minor repairs as well as re-supply.

It was scheduled to sail again in two weeks' time.

He gave his crew leave and his father, who had just completed overseeing the transport of another contingent of Jewish scientists, medical researchers and engineers out of Germany to the French port by train, arranged to spend two days with him in the rented house before returning to Berlin.

After dinner on the first night, Eric dismissed the staff for the day and the two men sat together in the library with cigars and brandy and brought each other up to date on what each had been doing since they had last seen each other .

Eric did most of the talking as he brought the Count up to date on the scope of the extended family in South America and the astounding progress that had already taken place with regard to the creation of a small village and the construction of the mine.

The Count began to share in his son's excitement as he went on to describe the extent of the advanced state of development which had been accomplished on the vast underground research facilities and U-boat pens that had been hollowed out and were nestled beneath the mine at the coastline.

Shortly after one in the morning Karl von Staffer excused himself and retired.

The discussions has left Eric wound up and filled with enthusiasm. Despite the hour, he found that he was anything but tired.

He made a phone call.

Forty-five minutes later he was eagerly welcoming the giggling twins into a nearby hotel room with open arms.

Four hours later, tired but content, he returned to the house, slipped into bed for a few hours' sleep and feeling surprisingly rested, he joined his father for breakfast at eight-thirty.

By ten they are at the Krupp *'Germaniawerft A.G.'* shipbuilding yards on the harbour in Kiel where they are met by the manager who takes them on a tour and they spend some time viewing the second in the series of monstrous U-boats which is in the process of construction and has an estimated completion date of July first.

They return to the house for lunch after which they again retire to the library where the Count opens a large trunk which he has brought with him from Berlin.

Inside are copies of files, schematics, drawings and designs covering hundreds of cutting-edge research projects that are currently being developed in Germany and they begin to go through these systematically.

They break for dinner and then Eric dismisses the staff for the night and they return to the library and its trunk full of treasures.

Eric is blown away by many of these, especially those relating to the development of new weapons and his father smiles as he watches his son take them in.

"You will take these with you on the next trip and they will provide the basis for the initial work to be begun by our scientific, medical research and engineering people in Brazil.

The people we have recruited are already some of the best minds in Germany and we will be adding to those as we take new territory into the Reich. When you next sail you will note that there are foreign scientists, doctors and engineers among those you are transporting on board. These men are at the top in their chosen fields.

On each of your trips you will take more personnel and equipment to Brazil and in addition to consignments of valuables and gold, I will provide you with the updated progress reports on each project contained within this trunk and any new ones that occur. This will allow our people to have the benefit of any recent innovative advances or discoveries that have been made in Berlin. In time all four of the super subs will take part in these transfers to our holdings in Brazil.

If, as we believe, Germany loses this war, upon the collapse of the Third Reich our access to unlimited funds and the *'Operation Fatherland'* setup in Brazil will guarantee that we will, at that point, be at par or ahead of Berlin in all research in these areas.

At war's end, we will therefore be in a position to continue their successful development into the future, securely entrenched in our private, secret, and self-contained facilities in Brazil.

And if we are ahead of Berlin, we can't help but be far in advance of the rest of the world.

Out of disaster, we farseeing Germans will continue to

lead the world in scientific achievement, medical discoveries and engineering marvels in every field. With this power, we will steadily rise again to regain control of the Fatherland and will be soon able to proudly hold our heads high as we take our rightful position at the helm of the modern world. "

CHAPTER TEN

- May -

- Air Operations -

The British Bomber Command sends a total of two thousand six hundred and ninety sorties over Germany dropping two thousand eight hundred and forty tons of bombs. Targets include Cologne, Bremen, Hamburg and Brest. They lose seventy-six aircraft.

The Luftwaffe hits Liverpool in several heavy attacks. Eighteen vessels are sunk in the harbour and twenty five are badly damaged. Port facilities are reduced to seventy-five percent of their normal handling capacity. The ports of Belfast and Clyde are also hit. London is bombarded heavily and the Houses of Parliament are damaged in this attack. Late in the month Dublin is bombed by mistake.

* * * * *

- Battle of the Atlantic -

The British at *'Bletchley Park'* have their first very limited successes in the breaking of the German signal codes as a result of U-boat captures made during this month. The triumphant recovery of the enigma machines and code books from these U-boats makes this possible.

On each occasion it offers only a short window of opportunity however, in that the codes fed into these machines are changed daily and major mechanical alterations in the machines themselves are undertaken on a monthly basis.

U-boats setting sail on a war patrol are only provided the changes for a limited period of time, that to be slightly longer than their estimated period of patrol.

Captures of the machines and code books from U-boats that are successfully taken are therefore only of limited use and realistically these captures are few and far between.

* * * * *

A new Newfoundland Escort Force created for convoy duty and largely made up of vessels provided by the Canadian Navy is created after convoys HX-126 and OB-318 suffer heavy losses in mid ocean. This new force is designed to provide continuous protection for all eastbound convoys bound for Britain.

Convoys are now to be provided escort in stages from Canada, Iceland and finally from Britain.

U-boats sink fifty-eight ships for a total of three hundred and twenty-five thousand tons, over half of which is sunk by a group of six U-boats operating in the weakly protected waters off Freetown. Another eighty-one ships are sunk by other means.

* * * * *

- May First -

- Iraq -

Iraqi soldiers make a small probing attack on the British outpost of Rutba just west of Bagdad and establish positions around the Royal Air Force Habbaniyah airfield.

* * * * *

- North Africa -

Rommel's forces hammer at Tobruk in a renewed attempt to broaden and deepen their achieved salient through the defensive line. Once again the Australian forces largely contain this attack.

* * * * *

- May Second -

- Iraq -

British forces at Habbaniyah launch pre-emptive air strikes with their eighty obsolescent aircraft against the Iraqi forces encircling them and Anglo-Iraqi war begins.

Despite the age and condition of these ancient machines they achieve a good deal of success and allow the numerically small number of British troops to retain control of the airfield.

* * * * *

- North Africa -

The *'Desert Fox'* continues to hammer at Tobruk but no significant change in the battle lines results.

* * * * *

- May Third -

- Ethiopia -

British forces encircle and begin to attack at Italian defensive positions on the road between Asmara and Addis Ababa. The Italians are strongly positioned in caves located high in the steep and rugged hills.

* * * * *

- Iraq -

The British attack the forces surrounding Habbaniyah and launch an air attack on Iraq's Rashid airfield.

* * * * *

- May Fourth -

- North Africa -

Rommel calls off his attempts to take Tobruk and digs in for a siege of the city. Both sides of the engagement are in good position with regard to the receipt of supplies and reinforcement and it is difficult for the Germans to create deep defensive trenches as the ground is extremely hard.

Each side adopts a policy of offensive night patrolling which provides neither with any chance of respite or relaxation, similar to what was the case in the trench warfare of The Great War.

* * * * *

- Iraq -

British action is confined to air operations only.

They attack the airfield at Mosul which is being used by a small German force. The Nazis are receiving supplies from Syria, with the cooperation of the Vichy French authorities.

* * * * *

- East Africa -

The 29th Indian Brigade takes on the Italian defenders around Amba Alagi and force them from their positions on three hills along their western line of defence.

* * * * *

- May Fifth -

- East Africa -

Exactly five years from the day he was forced to flee from his country, Emperor Haile Selassie enters his capital Addis Ababa in triumph. In the ongoing battle at Amba Alagi the crucial middle hill position is taken from the Italians.

* * * * *

- North Africa -

Supplies for the besieged city of Tobruk are brought in by destroyer. Two destroyers are brought into daily evening missions to maintain supplies for Tobruk and one a week replacement troops arrive by the same means and the wounded are evacuated.

* * * * *

- May Sixth -

- Iraq -

With much of the Iraqi air force destroyed, British forces consolidate their hold on Habbaniyah airfield. The besieging Iraqi ground forces who are under steady air attack abandon their positions around the airfield and are driven back from Sin el Dhibban tower Fallujah. The 21st Indian Brigade arrives at Basra.

* * * * *

- Soviet Union -

The Presidium of the Supreme Soviet elevates Stalin from general secretary of the Communist Party to the position of President of the Council of the People's Commissars.

* * * * *

- Mediterranean -

After months of hesitancy and at Churchill's insistence, the British make an attempt to run a convoy containing five transports containing supplies and tanks though the Mediterranean from Gibraltar to Egypt.

Code named 'Tiger', this convoy is joined by one battleship, a carrier and a second battleship which is under orders to go on to join with the Mediterranean Fleet.

Accompanying these heavy naval units are four cruisers and seven destroyers. Six more destroyers join this fleet later in the day.

Two additional convoys leave Alexandria for Malta with an escort of five cruisers and three destroyers.

Admiral Cunningham takes out the entire Mediterranean Fleet in support, with three battleships, a single carrier, three cruisers and nineteen destroyers.

* * * * *

- May Seventh -

- Iraq -

Forty British planes attack two Iraqi columns they find in the open between Fallujah and Habbaniyah inflicting heavy casualties.

General Quinan takes command of British forces in the county.

* * * * *

- Iceland -

In a special operation set up for the purpose, the German Trawler *'Munchen'*, a weather-ship, is boarded northeast of Iceland and codebooks for the Enigma are captured.

* * * * *

- Mediterranean -

On the night of May seventh part of Cunningham's naval force shells Benghazi in Libya.

* * * * *

- May Eighth -

- Indian Ocean -

The British heavy cruiser HMS 'Cornwall' encounters the German raider *'Pinquin'* and sinks her. The German ship has been on a war patrol during which she has sunk twenty-eight ships for a total tonnage of one hundred and thirty-six thousand, five hundred and fifty.

* * * * *

- Mediterranean -

The Italians launch air attacks on both the eastbound and westbound British convoys, but the carrier in each dispatches their aircraft and beats them off with no serious damage resulting to the fleets.

* * * * *

- East Africa -

Indian troops take the Falagi Pass and three additional small mountain peaks south of Amba Alagi.

* * * * *

- May Ninth -

- Atlantic -

U-110 attacks convoy OB-318 east of Cape Farewell, Greenland and sinks two ships. One of the escorts, the British corvette, HMS *'Aubreita'* locates the sub with ASDC (sonar) and commences a depth charge attack supported by an accompanying destroyer, HMS *'Broadway'*.

The U-110 survives this attack but suffers serious damage and is forced to surface. HMS *'Broadway'* takes course to ram but instead fires two depth changes beneath the U-boat in an attempt to force the crew to abandon ship before the German crew can successfully scuttle her.

The U-boat Captain, *'Kapitanleutnant'* Friz-Julius Lemp, has the vents opened to fill the U-boat and sink her, then orders abandon ship and the crew floods out onto the deck.

The British believing that the crew were going to man the deck gun, opened fire raking the German sailors with gunfire. Many are hit before the British ships came to the realization that the crew is in the process of abandoning the U-boat and were surrendering.

Lemp, who assumed the sub would sink, ordered his radio operator to leave the codebooks and Enigma Machine in place and get out before he went down with the U-boat. When he realized that his ship was not going to sink he turns in the water and tries to swim back so he can climb back aboard and destroy the machine and its books but before he can reach the U-boat he goes under and disappears, never to be found.

The U-boat was then boarded by a party from HMS *'Bulldog'*. One of the sailors in the party was an ex-radioman and as soon as he got onto the sub, he made for the radio room and retrieved both the Enigma machine and the codebooks.

U-110 was put under tow in an attempt to get her back to Scapa Flow but she sank en route.

As mentioned earlier, these scoops of Enigma Machines and their codebooks had a limited value as changes in rotors and codebooks took place on a regular basis, but having the enemy's secret communications hardware went a long way to assisting the code-breakers at Bletchley Park in doing their jobs.

* * * * *

- Tokyo -

A peace treaty signed in the Japanese capital ends the French-Thai War.

* * * * *

- Mediterranean -

One of the transports in the *'Tiger'* convoy strikes a mine and sinks.

* * * * *

- May Tenth -

- Berlin -

Leaving a letter of explanation for Hitler with his adjutant, Rudolf Hess, the Deputy Fuhrer of the Nazi party and the man who assisted Hitler in the writing of `Mein Kàmpf` while he was imprisoned in the early years of the Nazi movement, sets off on a bizarre, self-appointed mission with the intent of single-handedly achieving a peace with the British.

Hess, who was by the mid nineteen-forties, feeling sidelined from the affairs of the nation and more importantly from Hitler's attention, has decided to fly to England and engage with pro-German Englishmen with a view to gaining a peace agreement between the two countries that would prevent Germany from having to fight a two-front war and thereby bring him back into Hitler's good graces.

Hess had been planning his strange mission for some time.

In October of nineteen-forty, he'd arranged training on the Messerschmitt Bf 110 under the instruction of the chief test pilot at Messerschmitt.

He became competent with this type of plane and over time found a specific aircraft that handled well. It was a Bf 110E-1-N, which from that point on, was held in reserve for his personal use.

Hess asked for a radio compass to be fitted, modifications made to the oxygen delivery system and large long-range fuel tanks to be installed on the plane. These requests were granted and completed by March of nineteen-forty-one.

After that time Hess made several unsuccessful attempts to make his bizarre trip to the British Isles, on each occasion having to turn back because of mechanical difficulties or bad weather.

On May tenth he took off at 17:45 hours from the airfield at Augsburg-Haunstetten. He was carrying a supply of money, toiletries, a flashlight, a camera, maps and charts and a collection of twenty-eight different medicines in addition to dextrose tablets to ward off fatigue and an assortment of homeopathic remedies.

Flying at high speed and low altitude he bailed out of the craft over Scotland. Once he had been identified and received medical care he was incarcerated.

Two British psychiatrists examined Hess and concluded

that he was not insane but was mentally unstable, with tendencies toward hypochondria and paranoia.

Hess was to attempt suicide on more than one occasion while in custody.

* * * * *

- Iraq -

Forces from the Jordanian Arab Legion, under British leadership, take Rutba.

* * * * *

- Mediterranean -

The naval forces under Cunningham, now on the return trip to home port, shell Benghazi again.

* * * * *

- May Eleventh -

- Berchtesgaden -

Hess`s adjutant delivers his superior's letter to Hitler at the Berghof around noon.

Upon reading it Hitler went ballistic, considering the Deputy Fuhrer`s flight to the British Isles as an act of insanity and a personal betrayal.

Worried that his allies would perceive Hess`s act as an attempt by him to secretly open peace negotiations with the British, Hitler ordered that all German radio broadcasts covering the crazy, unauthorized flight should openly characterise Hess as a madman, delusional and acting without any authority and without the Fuhrer`s knowledge.

He also ordered Hess to be shot if he returned to

Germany and promptly abolished the post of Deputy Fuhrer.

As Hitler's Minister of propaganda, Joseph Goebbels should have been the man to deal with the humiliating and damaging aftermath of the Hess situation. It should have been Goebbels who masterminded the damage control necessary after Hess's foolish flight to England.

But Goebbels wanted no part in the matter whatsoever. He could see no way for him to placate Hitler's rage over the incident and did not want his name associated with any part of it. He immediately ran for cover, telling his staff that he was unwell and quickly disappearing to his country estate.

It was left to his subordinate to attempt to put a brave face on Hess's misadventure.

Goebbels wasn't seen again in Berlin until the whole mess had blown over.

* * * * *

- May Twelfth -

- Moscow -

The soviet Union officially recognizes Rashid Ali's `National Defence Government` in Iraq.

* * * * *

- Mediterranean -

All three of the convoys ordered to sail by Churchill arrive safely at their destinations.

`Operation Tiger` has delivered two hundred and thirty-eight tanks and forty-three Hurricane fighters to Egypt, with the loss of only the fifty-seven tanks that were on the transport that was earlier sunk after hitting a mine.

* * * * *

- May Thirteenth -

- Berlin -

Hitler assigns all Hess's former duties to the ever omni-present and ambitious Martin Bormann who is given the newly created title of `Head of the Party Chancellery`.

* * * * *

- Iraq -

The German `Fliegerfuhrer Irak` (Flyer Command Iraq) arrives in Mosul to support the Iraqi government of Rashid Ali.

* * * * *

- May Fourteenth -

- East Africa -

South African troops advancing north from Addis Ababa join the Amba Alagi battle and move to attack the Italian Triangle position. The Italians promptly retreat.

* * * * *

- Syria -

The RAF is given the go-ahead to launch attacks against German aircraft stationed at Syrian and Vichy French airfields.

* * * * *

- May Fifteenth -

- Crete -

Germany launches a powerful air attack against the island in preparation for the coming landings and in hopes of subduing the garrison and forcing the RAF to withdraw the few aircraft it has on Crete.

* * * * *

- North Africa -

Fortified with the tanks from the Tiger convoy, General Wavell orders `Operation Brevity`. In this operation, forces which are being led by General Gort will move against the defensive positions at the Halfaya Pass and attempt to break through to the open area of the Cyrenaica Plateau.

* * * * *

- Yugoslavia -

The Italians establish the independent Kingdom of Croatia.

* * * * *

-May Sixteenth -

- North Africa -

`Operation Brevity` makes some gains at the Halfaya Pass but Rommel promptly launches counter attacks. The two sides begin trading alternating control of Fort Capuzzo and the Pass.

* * * * *

- May Seventeenth -

- Iraq -

British forces in the area of Habbaniyah begin an attack on Iraqi-held Fallujah.

* * * * *

- May Eighteenth -

- East Africa -

The Duke of Aosta, Viceroy of Italian East Africa surrenders his forces at Amba Alagi.

* * * * *

- Iraq -

The British force moving in to reinforce Habbaniyah airfield outflanks the Iraqi blocking force and successfully reaches the airfield.

* * * * *

- Syria -

Vichy French General, Dentz orders his forces to meet force with force as airfields in Syria are bombed again by the RAF.

* * * * *

- North Atlantic -

The German battleship `*Bismarck*`, under the command

of Admiral Lutjens, sails from Gydnia for an Atlantic war patrol in company with the heavy cruiser `Prince Eugen`.

* * * * *

- May Nineteenth -

- Iraq -

The fortified British forces at Habbaniyah capture Fallujah and the airfield is bombed by the German Luftwaffe.

* * * * *

May Twentieth -

- Crete -

The German invasion of the Island begins.

With massive support from Fliegerkorps VIII which has a strength of four hundred bombers and two hundred fighters which clear the way for the following troop landings, airborne troops of the 7th Paratroop Division from Fliegerkorps XI begin to drop from the skies.

The Germans attack with approximately twenty-three thousand elite troops to take on a garrison which consists of thirty-two thousand British and Empire troops and ten thousand Greek defenders.

British General Freyberg is in command of the defence and his forces are suffering from a shortage of equipment and heavy weapons.

* * * * *

- Iraq -

`Sonderstab F` (Special Staff F), the German military

mission to Iraq, is created to support the `Arab Freedom Movement` in the Middle East. This puts `Fliegerfuhrer Irak` and other German elements already in Iraq under a single operational umbrella.

* * * * *

- Straits of Denmark -

The `neutral` Swedish Navy reports the sighting of `Bismarck` and `Prince Eugen` at Kattegat in the Straits of Denmark to the British.

* * * * *

- Atlantic -

The U.S. Merchant ship `Robin Moor` is sunk by the German submarine U-69.

* * * * *

- May Twenty-First -

- Mediterranean -

The British aircraft carriers HMS `Ark Royal` and HMS `Furious` deliver forty-eight additional Hurricanes to Malta.

* * * * *

- USA -

U. S. President Roosevelt describes the sinking of the `Robin Moor` as an `act of intimidation` to which `we do not propose to yield`.

* * * * *

- Bergen -

British reconnaissance aircraft spot the `Bismarck `and `Prince Eugen` off the coast of Norway. The British battleship HMS `*Prince of Wales*` and the battle cruiser HMS `*Hood*` set sail from Scapa Flow to intercept.

* * * * *

- Ethiopia -

Despite the surrender, remnants of the Italian troops fight on.

* * * * *

- Crete -

The attacking Germans, realizing that holding airfields is crucial to winning the battle, rush reinforcements to the Maleme airfield, consolidating their hold on the only airbase they have successfully taken.

* * * * *

- May Twenty-Second -

- North Atlantic -

The British are very concerned about the `*Bismarck'* and the `*Prince Eugen*` attempting to break free out into the open Atlantic.

The Bismarck is the pride of the German fleet and a very modern and formidable warship which, if left unchecked, could create absolute havoc with British convoys plying the Atlantic.

Determined to increase his naval forces aligned against the two German ships and bring them to bear on the unique German warship, the Commander in Chief of the British Home Fleet, Admiral Tovey, sails for the Denmark Strait with the battleship HMS `King George V` and the carrier HMS `Victorious`. These ships are joined by the battle cruiser HMS `Repulse` later in the day

* * * * *

- Iraq -

Iraqi forces unsuccessfully counter-attack the British forces in Fallujah and are stoutly rebuffed.

* * * * *

- Crete -

There is little change in the allied positions but the Germans are growing in strength as troops pour into the airfield at Maleme and are making good use of their air superiority.

* * * * *

- May Twenty-Third -

- North Atlantic -

Using their advanced radar equipment, the patrolling British cruisers HMS `Suffolk` and HMS `Norfolk` sight the `Bismarck` and `Prince Eugen` in the Denmark Strait. Definitely out-gunned, the British ships do not engage but instead try to stay out of range of the Bismarck's large guns and shadow the German ships until reinforcements arrive.

* * * * *

- Crete -

The Maleme airfield is bombarded by Lord Mountbatten's 5th Destroyer Flotilla at the cost of HMS *'Kelly'* and HMS *'Kashmir'*.

* * * * *

King George of Greece is evacuated from the island and travels to Egypt.

* * * * *

- Berlin -

Hitler issues Fuhrer Directive No. 30 which outlines the Nazi support of `The Arab Freedom Movement in the Middle East` which he refers to as '*his natural ally against England*`.

* * * * *

- May Twenty-Fourth -

- HMS Hood -

HMS 'Hood' was the last battle-cruiser built for the Royal Navy.

Commissioned in nineteen twenty, she was the largest naval ship in the world between the two wars and during that time had been used to *'show the flag'* and effectively demonstrate to the world the superior power of the British navy to remove any doubt that *'Britannia ruled the seas'*.

Returning from her recent assignment with the Mediterranean fleet where she had been sent during the Spanish civil war *'Hood'* was headed to England in nineteen thirty-nine where she was due for a major refit scheduled for nineteen forty-one.

The ship was showing her age which in the modern era had reduced her overall usefulness and HMS *'Hood'* needed to be brought up to modern standards in many areas, one of which the need for heavier armour-plating on her decks in view of the advances in naval gunnery which had taken place since she had been built.

Unfortunately the outbreak of war in September of nineteen thirty-nine forced the massive ship back into active service without the benefit of the upgrades she so badly needed.

* * * * *

- North Atlantic -

The *'Hood'* and the *'Prince of Wales'* sight the *'Bismarck'* and *'Prince Eugen'* and immediately open fire on the German ships. The *'Bismarck'* returns fire and ten minutes after the first British salvo tore through the sky, a long-range, plunging shell from *'Bismarck'* strikes *'Hood'* aft, near her the ammunition magazines and in an area where the old ship was carries only light armour.

HMS *'Hood'* literally erupted in a single massive explosion and sank within three minutes. Of the crew of one thousand, four hundred and fifteen men only three survived the devastating blast.

HMS 'Prince of Wales' continues to exchange fire with the German ships for a short time during which she scores three hits on *'Bismarck'* one of which is a strike on the *'Bismarck's'* bow with a fourteen inch shell.

'Prince of Wales' is experiencing serious malfunctions with her main armament and quickly breaks off from the engagement.

In total, the *'Bismarck'* has been struck by three shells, and in addition to the bow hit which has breached fuel tanks, she has sustained damage to machinery below decks which has restricted her speed.

Admiral Lutjens aboard his flagship decides to take *'Bismarck'* in to Brest for repairs. He orders the 'Prince Eugen' to break off and make her own way.

The loss of the famous *'Hood'* in a matter of minutes strikes at the heart of English pride and is a horrific blow to British moral.

Churchill pulls out the stops, ordering the Royal Navy to sink the *'Bismarck'* at whatever the cost.

* * * * *

- Crete -

The Allied forces in the Canea area are now dug in around Galatas and the steady buildup of German troops continues at Maleme.

* * * * *

- East Africa -

Soddu in southern Abyssinia falls to the Allies.

* * * * *

- May Twenty-Fifth -

- Crete -

The expanded German forces begin their advance toward Galatas initiating intense fighting.

* * * * *

- May Twenty-Sixth -

- North Atlantic -

A reconnaissance aircraft from HMS *'Ark Royal'* locates *'Bismarck'* and begins to shadow her while the British Home Fleet rushes to the scene. The British ships are one hundred and fifty miles away from the point of contact and have no realistic chance to catch the German ship before she reaches the safe haven of protection offered by the Luftwaffe fighters based on the French coast.

'Ark Royal' launches fifteen Fairey Swordfish aircraft at long range in a frantic attempt to launch a torpedo attack to hopefully delay *'Bismarck'*, who has successfully shaken off her pursuers, from reaching safety in a French port.

The British cruiser HMS *'Sheffield'* is also shadowing the massive German ship while keeping well out of gunnery range and is steaming between the *'Ark Royal'* and the *'Bismarck'*.

The racing aircraft mistake the British cruiser for the 'Bismarck' and fire off torpedoes at HMS *'Sheffield'* before they realize their mistake. The torpedoes used in the attack are fitted with unreliable magnetic detonators which cause most to explode on contact with the water and the shocked *'Sheffield'* manages to avoid the rest.

The aircraft return to the *'Ark Royal'* and re-arm with contact-detonator warhead torpedoes and launch for a second attempt. The reach the *'Bismarck'* just before sunset and immediately attack. Three torpedoes hit the German battleship, two impacting forward of the engine room and the third striking the port steering room and jamming her rudder in a fifteen degree port turn.

'Bismarck' begins to sail in uncontrollable circles until a combination of alternating propeller speeds is found which will keep her on a reasonably steady course which, with the prevailing force eight wind and sea state, forces the German battleship to sail towards the pursuing British warships and leaves it with almost no manoeuvering capability.

The British naval forces steaming at high speed reach the German Battleship that evening and began to unmercifully pound the crippled *'Bismarck'* with their guns.

* * * * *

- Crete -

As the day comes to a close consideration is given to a pullout of Allied forces who are under heavy sustained attack from an ever growing German presence. Although confusing orders result from these discussions, the majority of the Allied force leave the island under cover of darkness

* * * * *

-May Twenty-Seventh -

- North Africa -

Rommel has brought up reinforcements to his troops on the Egyptian border and he retakes the Halfaya Pass using his two panzer regiments. He immediately makes defensive positions, digging in his big 88mm guns.

* * * * *

- Iraq -

British forces around Habbaniyah and Fallujah begin to advance on the capital of Baghdad.

* * * * *

- North Atlantic -

'Bismarck', the pride of the German Navy is sunk by Royal Navy forces at ten thirty-nine in the morning.

* * * * *

- Crete -

The Germans take Canea and Suda. The remaining Allied forces are now splintered and disorganized. They begin to retreat to Sfakia to be evacuated.

* * * * *

- May Twenty-Eighth-

- Iraq -

The 20th Indian Brigade advances from Basra to occupy Ur for the Allies but can push no further until repairs have been made to roads and railroad track.

* * * * *

- Crete -

Allied forces fight a rearguard action to cover their retreat to Sfakia.

Hitler's use of airborne troops in the attack has been a brilliant success but the casualties, primarily deaths, among these troops has been staggering and he determines that such large-scale attacks should not be repeated in the future.

* * * * *

- May Twenty-Ninth -

- Iraq -

The members of the German military mission flee Iraq.

* * * * *

-May Thirtieth -

- Iraq -

Rashid Ali and his supporters abandon Iraq.

* * * * *

- May Thirty-First -

- Iraq -

An armistice between the United Kingdom and Iraq is signed.

The British right to station troops in the country is confirmed and the Iraqis agree to take no further action that might in any way aid the Axis powers.

CHAPTER ELEVEN

- June -

- Bletchley Park -

The code-breakers adopted a new name for their projects in June of nineteen forty-one to reflect their progress. By this point in time they had not only broken the Enigma code but had also been successful with the Lorenz machines and the Japanese *'Purple'*.

The security designation for the work being done at Bletchley Park (BP) was that of *'Ultra Top Secret'* and from this time on all product resulting from their work there was referred to as *'ULTRA'*.

Over the month British forces, using intelligence provided by *'ULTRA'* encoded signals, sink nine German supply ships, seven of which had been sent out to support the *'Bismarck'* and two that had been supplying Merchant Raiders.

* * * * *

- Generalplan OST -

Prepared by Himmler, the Nazi outline for the *'Germanization'* of the *'Lebensraum'*, (Generalplan OST); the blueprint that would allow the new Reich make use of the newly conquered territory in the east for German resettlement, was adjusted in nineteen forty-one, when a decision was made by the Nazi leadership to completely destroy all of the Polish nation that was now under German occupation.

It was determined that it would take between ten and twenty years to accomplish this task. Within that timeframe, the territory in question was to be fully cleared of any ethnic

Poles and entirely re-settled by German colonists.

Most of the Polish indigenous political leaders, military chiefs and intelligentsia had already been removed from the territory by way of outright execution or through incarceration in concentration camps.

In order to reach the revised end goal of the absolute eradication of the Polish race in the occupied territory, new programs and systems would therefore have to be put into place.

Polish culture was to be eradicated.

Education was to be limited to a very basic level.

Older children were to be examined and evaluated as to the possibility of spotting any Aryan physical traits that might be present and then considered for possible Germanization.

Young children who demonstrated Aryan qualities were to be removed from their families and, after passing testing within the strict guidelines outlining Aryan characteristics, they would be cared for institutionally by the SS under an extension of the *'Lebensborn'* program with a view to their eventual Germanization.

Any children, young or old, who did not pass their 'Aryan' test, were now to be sent to a concentration camp.

It was envisioned that by nineteen fifty-two, all but approximately three to four million Non-Germanized Poles, would have been deported to regions in the east and scattered over as wide an area of Western Siberia as possible. They would then be assimilated into the local populations which would, over time, cause the Poles to vanish as a nation.

The three to four million remaining non-Germanized Poles (all of them peasants with low education) would remain as slave labour. These people were to either Germanize or they would be forbidden to marry. Medical services would be forbidden to all Poles living within the new Reich and eventually the race would cease to exist.

'Wehrbauer' (armed peasants or soldier peasants), would be settled in a fortified line along the new eastern German border to thwart any chance of a later threat from without.

* * * * *

- Germanization -

As Reich Commissioner for the Consolidation of German Nationhood, Himmler was deeply involved in the *'Germanization'* program for the East, particularly that of Poland.

As laid out in *'Generalplan OST'*, the aim was to remove all non-Germanic peoples from German *'Lebensraum'* and to reclaim any 'Volksdeutsche' (ethnic Germans) from Poland.

Hitler had declared that no drop of German blood was to be lost or left behind to mingle with an *'alien race'*. Although many Germans were hesitant to relocate there and despite negative effects on the war effort Himmler continued to fulfill his Fuhrer's plans to colonise the expanded territory in the east.

He designed a system for dealing with the problem and began with the *'Volksliste'*, the classification of people deemed to be of German blood. These were to include those who had collaborated with Germany before the war and also those who considered themselves as German but had been neutral prior to the outbreak of war. It was also to include those who were partially *'Pollinized'* but deemed to be *'Germanizable'* and all Germans who were of Polish nationality.

Himmler ordered that those of this latter group who refused to be classed as ethnic Germans should be deported to concentration camps and have their children taken away or be assigned to forced labour units.

Ironically Himmler believed that Balts or Poles who resisted Germanization were likely to be racially superior to the more compliant ones who did, commenting that *'it is in the nature of German blood to resist'*. Unfortunately, as already demonstrated, any resistance against a Nazi policy was inevitably immediately eradicated.

Himmler specified the necessity to determine and then act on any signs of positive racial characteristics, eloquently expressing his belief that *'Obviously in such a mixture of peoples, there will always be some racially good types. Therefore, I think that it is our duty to take their children with us, to remove them from their environment, if necessary by robbing, or stealing them. Either we win over any good blood that we can use for ourselves and give it a place in our people...or we destroy that blood'*.

The *'racially valuable'* children were to be removed from all contact with Poles and raised as Germans, with German names. The Reichsfuhrer-SS decreed *'We have faith above all in this our own blood, which had flowed into a foreign nationality through the vicissitudes of German history. We are convinced that our own philosophy and ideals will reverberate in the spirit of these children who racially belong to us'*.

These children were to be adopted by German families. Any of the children who did not pass muster after being initially tested were to be shipped off to concentration camps.

* * * * *

- Friedrichshafen -

Count Karl von Stauffer arrived by rail at the at the family's ancestral castle, shepherding fourteen Jewish scientists, engineers and medical research staff to see them safely aboard a line of empty freight cars that was about to leave for the return trip to France.

His public removal of what the party considered subhuman German nationals, was still officially looked upon with favour by the Nazis, but the overall burgeoning Jewish problem was gaining a great deal of attention in the upper echelon of the party of late; Karl realized that his ability to safely continue his policy of openly assisting these individuals in leaving the Reich would have to cease sooner rather than later.

Currently he had a system in place that was functioning smoothly, with safe houses within Germany and at Bordeaux, which he used for holding his evacuees on a short-term basis until travel could be arranged to ship them to France and then onward to the expanding mining complex and hidden research facilities in Brazil, either by the U-boat captained by Eric or on neutral commercial ships.

He hoped to complete the removal of all those party rejects that were of interest to *'Operation Fatherland'*, before emigration for Jews was no longer an option under the Nazis. He believed that he might just be able to safely accomplish that before Himmler pulled the plug and decided to impress Hitler by dealing with the growing problem in some other manner.

The Count dwelled on the complexities of the problem while he watched the small yard engine that had pushed his own cars into the original spur line to the castle, uncoupled and move over to link with the empty freight cars sitting on the new rail siding before beginning to haul its charges down the hill toward the main line at he bottom of the mountain.

As the last car slipped from view among the dense foliage of the trees covering the hillside he seated himself in one of the comfortable chairs located at the back of the observation platform at the rear of his private railcars and lit up a cigar.

He intended to enjoy it with a brandy while he waited for the little engine to deliver its cargo and make the return climb back up the hill to nudge the private cars the final few hundred feet upward and into their enclosure nestled deep under the castle.

A half hour later the cars were tucked securely within their tunnel-like barn and he left the private units and stepped out onto the small receiving platform where the Countess, Ursula and Major von Krueger awaited him.

While the Count had already given Ursula a briefing on the importance of keeping the *'Operation Fatherland'* components of artwork separate and private from the works coming in from France for storage under the castle, he had not as yet taken her into his full confidence as he had been unable to find sufficient free time available for a full and complete explanation of the entire concept of *'Operation Fatherland'* to her.

It was for this reason mainly that he had made this trip from Berlin, as he intended to take her into a full understanding of the nature of the special operation now that time permitted.

He was of course also eager to see Ericka and spend some time with his daughter and new son-in-law, as well as to take the time to see for himself how the storage arrangements for the artwork and valuables had been constructed and was being utilized.

CHAPTER TWELVE

- June -

- Air Operations -

The RAF hits Brest on five separate occasions. They also bomb targets in the Ruhr, Rhineland and German northwestern ports. Several fighter sweeps over Northern France are also conducted.

With preparations underway for the invasion of Russia the Germans make fewer attacks against the British Isles. Manchester takes the major hit during the month.

* * * * *

- Battle of the Atlantic -

U-boats sink sixty-one ships for a total tonnage of three hundred and ten thousand tons. Due to the amassing of the aircraft needed for the planned German invasion of Russia, *'Operation Barbarossa'*, the Luftwaffe plays only a small part in in the sinking of allied shipping.

Total Allied losses amount to four hundred and thirty-two thousand tons.

Four cutters from the US Coastguard begin patrol operations off the southern coast of Greenland.

* * * * *

- Atomic Research -

The *'Maud Commission'* in Britain reports to Churchill that they have come to the conclusion that it will be possible to make an atomic bomb using the isotope *'Uranium 235'*.

A formal research program is set up under the code name 'Tube Alloys'.

Research in this area, albeit at this point less committed, has also begun in the US.

* * * * *

- June First -

- Crete -

Commonwealth forces complete their withdrawal from Crete.

* * * * *

- Iraq -

British forces enter Bagdad. Regent Emir Abdul Illah, the uncle of King Faisal, returns to his country.

* * * * *

- England -

Clothes rationing is instituted.

* * * * *

- North Africa -

Air Marshal Tedder takes command of the RAF forces in the Middle East. The majority of the German 15th Panzer Division has now joined Rommel's strength.

* * * * *

- June Second -

- USA -

The African-American *'Tuskegee Airman'* pilots are formed. They begin training.

* * * * *

- North Africa -

The French Vichy government grants the Axis powers the use of the Port of Bizerta to unload non-military supplies for their forces stationed in North Africa.

* * * * *

- June Third -

- Iraq -

The British enter Mosul where they capture a small number of Luftwaffe pilots.

* * * * *

- June Fourth -

Kaiser William II, the former German Emperor, passes away at his home in Doorn, Holland.

* * * * *

- Iraq -

The British oversee the formation of a new Iraqi Cabinet

and move troops to establish themselves in key points throughout the country as well as beef up their presence on the Syrian border.

* * * * *

- June Fifth -

- USA -

The proposed `US Army Bill` for nineteen forty-two is introduced to Congress. It calls for appropriations of ten billion four hundred million dollars.

* * * * *

- June Sixth -

Additional fighters for air defence against Luftwaffe attacks are delivered by HMS `Furious` and HMS `Ark Royal` to Malta.

* * * * *

- USA -

A new law comes into force. It allows the government to take over foreign ships that have been laid up in the USA.

* * * * *

- June Eighth -

After weeks of reports of a German presence in Syria, a combined British, Australian, Indian and Free French force invades Vichy controlled Syria and Lebanon. The Germans had been using air bases in Syria during the Iraqi fighting but by this point in the conflict, had abandoned the country after being asked to leave by Vichy authorities.

The defending Vichy forces amount to forty-five thousand troops under the command of General Dentz. They outnumber the Allied attackers.

Moving in from positions in Transjordan and Palestine, the invaders face little initial resistance and the senior Free French commander, General Catroux is emboldened to issue a proclamation suggesting that the defenders change sides and join the Allies. The British fortify this offer by indicating that they would seek no territorial gains if the defenders agreed to the proposition.

* * * * *

- June Ninth -

- Finland -

After much sabre-rattling by the Russians, Finland initiates mobilization against an anticipated attack by the Soviet Union.

* * * * *

- Syria -

Allied forces are making good progress. They take Tyre, Marjayoun and El Quneitra. A brief naval battle off the coast involving four British destroyers and two Vichy destroyers leaves the British coming out on top but only after taking some notable damage.

* * * * *

- June Tenth -

- East Africa -

The last Italian held port in East Africa, Assab is taken by a landed Indian battalion. Fighting breaks out near Galla Sidamo southwest of Addis Ababa.

* * * * *

- Syria -

Australian forces advancing along the coast north of Tyre begin constructing crossings over the Litani River as they push the Vichy forces back.

* * * * *

- June Thirteenth -

- Vichy France -

The puppet Vichy government extends the anti-Semitic laws to include the expropriation of Jewish businesses and announces that more than twelve thousand Jews have been arrested and interred in concentration camps as a result of a *'Jewish plot'* to hinder Franco-German cooperation.

* * * * *

- Syria -

The Australian forces continue to push through the Vichy French defenses and begin the advance towards Beirut.

* * * * *

- Norway -

The German pocket battleship *'Lutzow'* is damaged by a

torpedo attack from a British aircraft off the Norwegian Port of Lindesnes and is forced to return to port.

* * * * *

- Russia -

The official Soviet news agency Tass issues a denial that there is growing tension between Germany and the Russians over the Soviet position on Finland.

* * * * *

- June Fourteenth -

- USA -

The United States freezes all German and Italian assets in the country.

* * * * *

- Mediterranean -

The British carriers HMS *'Ark Royal'* and HMS *'Victorious'* deliver forty-three additional Hurricane fighters to Malta.

* * * * *

- Russia -

The Russians deport ten thousand one hundred people from Estonia, fifteen thousand from Latvia and thirty-four thousand from Lithuania. All are sent to Siberia.

* * * * *

- June Fifteenth -

- North Africa -

In a move to relieve the siege of Tobruk, the British unleash 'Operation Battleaxe'.

The British have little in the way of tank support for their infantry. Rommel's dug in 88 mm guns make the attempted assault through the Halfaya Pass a hell on earth for the attackers and *the 'Desert Fox'* has no difficulty in holding his defensive positions against them.

* * * * *

- June Sixteenth -

- Syria -

Vichy forces, having spurned the offer to turncoat, counterattack and take El Quneitra back from the Australians.

* * * * *

- USA -

The US government orders all German and Italian consulates in the country closed and all diplomatic staffs are to be out of the country by July tenth.

* * * * *

- North Africa -

'Operation Battleaxe' is going poorly for the British. Rommel's forces are rebuffing all their attempts to break through to relieve Tobruk.

* * * * *

- June Seventeenth -

- Berlin -

Hitler makes the decision to launch his attack against the Soviet Union, *'Operation Barbarossa'*, on the twenty-second of June.

* * * * *

- Syria -

Australian troops take the city of Jezzine in Lebanon which is situated approximately halfway between the Lebanese border with Palestine and Beirut. The *'Habforce'* group, which had played a large part in the battle in Iraq, is ordered to begin an advance from Iraq due west along the main oil pipeline leading to the city of Palmyra in Syria.

* * * * *

- North Africa -

Rommel begins to organize his tank forces with the intention of striking out at the much weakened British armour facing his forces. Licking its wounds, the entire British force begins to retreat, signalling the failure of 'Battleaxe' to accomplish its mission to break the siege at Tobruk.

* * * * *

- June Eighteenth -

- Turkey -

Von Papen, the German ambassador in Ankara, concludes a ten year treaty of friendship between the two counties.

* * * * *

- June Nineteenth -

- Syria -

During heavy fighting outside Damascus the Vichy French forces cut off and eventually eliminate an Indian battalion.

* * * * *

- June Twentieth -

- Finland -

All reservists under forty-five years of age are called up.

* * * * *

- June Twenty-First -

- East Africa -

After crossing the Omo River, where they take four thousand prisoners, the British take Jimma, southwest of Addis Ababa, capturing an additional fifteen thousand prisoners.

Jimma had been Italian General Gazzera's base of operation but he and a small unit of men have managed to escape.

* * * * *

- Syria -

Allied forces take Damascus after the garrison of Vichy French evacuates.

The 'Habforce' enters Syrian territory from Iraq and begins to advance.

* * * * *

- June Twenty-Second -

- Eastern Front -

In a three pronged operation aimed at Leningrad, Moscow and the southern oil fields of the Caucasus, Hitler unleashes his *'Blitzkrieg'* attack on Russia. *'Operation Barbarossa'*, the German invasion of the Soviet Union, begins.

More than three million German soldiers, reinforced by half a million auxiliaries from Germany's allies, (Finnish, Romanian, Hungarian, Italian, Slovakian and Croatian and a contingent from Spain), attacked the Soviet Union across a broad front, from the Baltic Sea in the north to the Black Sea in the south.

With the consent of the Finns, German troops begin deploying in what had formally been neutral Finnish territory and moved against the Russians.

Romanian troops invade the south-western border of Russia in support of its German allies.

Hitler has repudiated his non-aggression treaty with the Soviet Union and therein opened Germany to the inherent perils of having to fight a two-front war for.

* * * * *

- London -

Churchill takes to the airwaves to announce that *'Any state who fights Naziism will have out aid...It follows therefore that we shall give whatever help we can to Russia'*, making it clear to the world that the British will help the Soviet Union defend against the Nazi attack.

* * * * *

General Auchinleck takes over command of the British forces in Libya and Egypt.

* * * * *

- Lithuania -

Approximately one year earlier the Russians, with tacit agreement from the Germans, had invaded Lithuania and established the puppet *'Lithuanian Soviet Socialist Republic'*, taking and holding power through political repression and terror. Now that Germany has turned on the Soviet Union, a diverse segment of the Lithuanian population is emboldened and rises up against the oppressive Soviet installed regime and, forming a short-lived Provisional Government, declares renewed independence.

* * * * *

- Syria -

Heavy fighting between the Vichy French forces and the Australians begins around Marjayoun.

* * * * *

- June Twenty-Third -

- Eastern Front -

Although Stalin has been receiving good intelligence on the German's intent to invade for an extended period of time, he has chosen to dismiss it out of hand and the German *'Operation Barbarossa'* invasion of the Soviet Union is taking the defending Soviet troops off guard and making astounding gains.

In the North, the Fourth *'Panzergruppe'* (Panzer Group) has advanced nearly fifty miles into Russian territory. The Third has punched even farther and taken bridges over the Niemen, and the Second has penetrated deeply on either side of Brest Litovsk.

In the South, Kleist's First Panzer Group has faced stiffer opposition but has gained ground.

The Luftwaffe continues to hammer the Red Air Force, catching much of it on the ground in early surprise attacks, and is also highly successful in its mandate to disrupt Soviet communications.

* * * * *

- East Prussia -

Late in the evening Hitler arrives at his headquarters located at Rustenburg in East Prussia. The bunker-like compound is codenamed *'Wolfsschanze'* (Wolf's Lair).

* * * * *

- Syria -

The advancing British force from Iraq reaches Palmyra and begins an attack on the Vichy-French held city.

* * * * *

- June Twenty-Fourth -

- Eastern Front -

The attack on Russia continues to make rapid gains. Kaunas and Vilna are taken and Brest Litovsk, now far in the rear of the advancing German units, is under assault.

* * * * *

- USA -

At a press conference Roosevelt announces that he shares Churchill's mindset and will be sending aid to a Soviet Russia.

* * * * *

- June Twenty-Fifth -

- Sweden -

The Swedish government announces that it will allow the Germans to move up to one division of troops from Norway through Sweden to bolster Finnish defenders.

* * * * *

- Eastern Front -

In the north the Germans take Daugavpils and begin skirmishing to take bridgeheads over the Dvina River. Army group center has advanced to the point where it can initiate the first of the pre-planned large-scaled encirclements of Russian troops.

* * * * *

- June Twenty-Sixth -

- Eastern Front -

The Soviet Union bombs Helsinki, Finland and the Finns declare war on the Russias.
Hungary and Slovakia declare war on the Soviet Union.

* * * * *

- Mediterranean -

HMS *'Ark Royal'* and HMS *'Victorious'* set sail with an additional fifty-seven Hurricanes for Malta.

* * * * *

- June Twenty-Seventh -

- Hungary -

The Hungarians declare war on the Soviet Union.

* * * * *

- June Twenty-Eighth -

- Albania -

Italian occupied Albania declares war on the Russians.

* * * * *

- Eastern Front -

Three hundred thousand Russian troops are now completely encircled by the German forces near Minsk and Bialystok.

* * * * *

- June Twenty-Ninth -

- Finland -

Finish and German troops begin *'Operation Artic Fox'* against the Soviet Union.

* * * * *

- Eastern Front -

The German forces under the command of Guderian and Hoth join up near Minsk to complete another encirclement of a large body of Russian troops around Gorodische.

* * * * *

- June Thirtieth -

- Eastern Front -

The German Second Panzer Group takes Bobryusk and forward operations begin to cross the Berezina River. Troops from Army Group South take Lvov while other advance units make deep thrusts toward Kiev.

* * * * *

- Moscow -

Stalin who had been absolutely blindsided by Hitler's attack despite the extent of his intelligence reports, which he had chosen to disregard, has finally awoken from his self-imposed incommunicado state.

He forms a new *'State Committee of Defence'*.

This committee will be made up of Stalin, Molotov, Voroshilov, Malenkov and Berian, with Stalin very much in charge.

- Part Two -

CHAPTER THIRTEEN

- July -

- Berlin -

For obvious reasons the planning and preparation for the attack against Russia had been kept a closely held secret among only the very highest ranking members of the Nazi party.

While that policy had proven effective in lulling Stalin into a false sense of security exactly as planned, it had also meant that it came as a great shock to the German population at large.

On the morning the attack went ahead the Berlin newspapers printed a single-sheet extra edition to announce that Germany was now at war with the Soviet Union.

Generally speaking, although taken completely by surprise at the announcement of a sudden attack against an ally, the German public breathed a sigh of relief since few had been able to understand why a treaty had been made with communist Russia in the first place.

Upon the launch of the German invasion, Hitler ordered Goebbels, as Propaganda Minister, to explain to the German people what had happened and sell the need for this war to the populace.

Goebbels immediately met with his subordinates and laid down guidelines for how this was to be done. He began by setting the stage.

'Now that the Fuhrer has unmasked the treachery of the Bolshevik rulers, National Socialism, and hence the German people, are reverting to the principals which impelled them ...the struggle against plutocracy and Bolshevism.

The Fuhrer has assured me that the Russian campaign will end within four months, but I tell you it will take only eight weeks'.

Within twenty-four hours of the invasion, German public interest had begun to wane. Generally speaking they chose to push the situation to the backs of their minds and get on with their day to day lives.

At shortly after noon on the second day of the war against Russia, Hitler boarded his personal train and he and his staff left Berlin for his new Eastern Front headquarters, *'Wolfsschanze'* (Wolfs Lair), which was located in the forest near Rastenburg in East Prussia.

* * * * *

- Moscow -

Taken by surprise - talk about understatement!

Within hours of the initiation of *'Operation Barbarossa'* the Russian Air Force frankly admitted they had already lost twelve hundred aircraft and the Soviet army acknowledged that infantry resistance was un-coordinated.

A still-disbelieving Stalin had in fact ordered his army to stay out of German territory and his air force to restrict raids to within ninety miles of the original border.

He was convinced it was all a mistake, kept the communication lines open with the Germans, and requested Japan to intervene and mediate any political and economic differences that might have arisen between Germany and Russia.

* × * * *

- The Vatican -

The Pope made no comment on the invasion; however, there was little doubt as to which side he was on, describing Germany's invasion of Russia as *'high-minded gallantry in defense of the foundations of Christian culture'*.

Several German Bishops went further, publicly supporting it, one classing it as *'a European crusade'*, referring to it as similar to that of the Teutonic Knights and exhorting all Catholics to fight for *'a victory that will allow Europe to breathe freely again and will promise all nations a new future'*.

* * * * *

- Wolfsschanze -

The decision to build the *'Wolfsschanze'* (Wolfs Lair), was reached in the autumn of nineteen-forty. The secret complex was to become the first of several *'Fuhrerhauptquartiere'* (Fuhrer Headquarters), which were constructed in various parts of occupied Europe.

The location selected for this facility was far from major roads and urban areas, in a densely wooded region about five miles from the small, East Prussian town of Rastenburg.

The two and a half square mile complex, which had been completed by June twenty-first, nineteen forty-one, consisted of thirty-seven buildings and was disguised by bushes, grass and artificial trees planted on the flat roofs. Camouflage netting was also erected between the buildings and the surrounding forest so that, from the air, the installation blended in with the unbroken woodland surrounding it.

The buildings themselves were constructed from three

different materials, dependent on their use, the most common being concrete and masonry buildings which were to be used by those of lesser rank and solid reinforced concrete buildings, to be used by Hitler and those of his inner circles, both Military and Political, as well as bomb shelters, and plain masonry buildings for things like the cinema.

The complex was well serviced by roads and there was a rail line with a special siding for Hitler's personal train and a nearby airfield.

The facility itself was contained within three concentric security zones and was built by the *'Organisation Todt'* specifically for use by the Fuhrer and his staff during *'Operation Barbarossa'*.

'Sperrkeis 1' (Security zone 1), was located at the very center of the Wolfs Lair. It was ringed by steel fencing and guarded by the *'Reichssicheheitsdienst'* (RSD), the SS security force that provided personal protection for Hitler and the important party leaders.

This security zone contained Hitler's personal Fuhrer Bunker and ten other camouflaged bunkers which had been constructed from six foot, seven inches of thick, steel-reinforced concrete. The additional shelters in this area were built to protect members of Hitler's inner circle and included facilities for Martin Bormann, Herman Goering, Wilhelm Keitel, and Alfred Jodl. Hitler's personal accommodation was on the northern side of the Massive Fuhrer Bunker as he did not like direct sunlight. Both Hitler's and Keitel's bunkers held additional rooms of a size that allowed military conferences to be held in them.

'Sperrkeis 2' (Security zone 2), surrounded the inner zone. This area housed the quarters of several of the Reich Ministers including that of Fritz Todt, Albert Speer and Joachim von Ribbentrop, and also the housing and living quarters for the personnel who worked in the Wolfs Lair. It also held the barracks used by the RSD personnel.

'Sperrkeis 3' (Security zone 3), consisted of the heavily fortified outer security areas which surrounded both of the two

inner zones. It was defended through the liberal use of land mines and the *'Fuhrer Begleit Brigade'* (FBB), a special armoured security unit from the Wehrmacht which fulfilled important protection duties such as manning guard houses, watchtowers and checkpoints.

Support troops could also be summoned from about fifty miles away where they were billeted.

The cost of building the complex was estimated at thirty-six million marks.

Approximately two thousand people worked at the *'Wolfs Lair'* at its peak.

* * * * *

- Hitler's View -

A few days after arriving at *'Wolfsschanze'* and settling in, confidence of achieving a swift victory over the Russians was running high among the staff.

A now cautious Hitler, appeared to be privately of two minds.

In a conversation with Jodl he stated: *'We have only to kick in the door and the whole rotten structure will come crashing down'*. A short while later he commented to one of his aides: *'At the beginnings of each campaign one pushes a door into a dark, unseen room. One can never know what is hiding inside'*.

Early German victories certainly appeared to tend toward the positive view.

German armoured units were hammering easily through the Soviet defensive lines and then quickly found themselves left free to roam at their leisure. Within two days of the launch of the German *'Blitzkrieg'* attack, masses of Russian prisoners had been taken and the majority of bridges needed to continue the assault had been taken intact.

Concerned that the German public receive only positive news about the situation on the Eastern Front, Hitler held off authorizing any releases until near the end of the month, when on a Sunday he turned his Propaganda Minister loose.

Hitler had personally recorded ten special communiques for public release on German radio and he instructed Goebbels to begin running them. These were spaced over the day and each was announced with great fanfare.

Goebbels had initially advised against such a long series of reports over the span of a single day and Hitler's Chief Press Officer, Otto Dietrich had supported that view. The Fuhrer dismissed their concerns, commenting to Dietrich that he was far more attuned to the mentality and emotions of the masses than: *'all the other intellectuals put together'*.

The broadcasts went ahead.

* * * * *

- The Fuhrer in Residence -

A normal day in Hitler's life when in residence at *'Wolfsschanze'*, would begin about eight or nine in the morning when he would take his dog for a walk. At ten-thirty he would peruse the mail which had been delivered either by air or courier train and at noon he would attend a situation briefing which might last for up to two hours.

He had his lunch at two in the afternoon in the dining hall, routinely sitting in the same seat between General Jodl and Otto Dietrich, his press chief, with Keitel, Martin Bormann and Goering's adjutant, Karl Bodenschatz sitting across from him.

After lunch the Fuhrer would deal with non-military matters for the rest of the afternoon. Coffee was served around five in the afternoon and this was followed by a second military briefing given by Jodl a six in the evening.

Dinner which could run anywhere up to two hours began at seven-thirty in the evening after which films were shown in the cinema. Hitler would then retire to his private quarters where he would give monologues to his entourage, including the two female secretaries who had accompanied him to the Lair.

On some occasions this little group would be treated to gramophone records consisting of Beethoven symphonies or selections from Wagner and other operas or occasionally German *'lieder'* (romantic poems set to music).

* * * * *

- Nazi Confidence Solidifies -

German successes seemed almost surreal.

Armoured spearheads into Soviet territory continually surpassed expectations and the sheer number of mass surrenders of Red troops was mindboggling, having reach half a million in total.

On July the third of July, General Halder recorded in his diary: *'It is no exaggeration to say that the campaign against Russia had been won in fourteen days'.*

A jubilant Hitler was no longer of two minds, stating to his entourage: *'To all intents and purposes the Russians have lost the war'*, following up with: *'How fortunate it was that we smashed the Russian armor and air force right at the beginning'.*

He was not alone in making that assessment. Thousands of miles away, in the US Pentagon, the guess was that the Red Army was likely to fold up in a month or so.

* * * * *

- Einsatzgruppen -

The main assignment for this special group, as they moved into Russia behind the attacking troops, was the same as it had been in Poland: to execute those civilians who might be a danger to the maintenance of good order within newly occupied territory, with specific attention given to Soviet Party

Commissars and Jews.

These four *'SS-Einsatzgruppen'* units, each consisting of three thousand men, were supervised by select officers, who for the most part were professional men. They included a Protestant pastor, a physician, a professional opera singer and numerous lawyers.

At first glance one might see these choices as poor in relation to suitability to their task. However, they soon demonstrated that Heydrich had been right to make his selections as he had. Despite some initial qualms these men became efficient executioners, as they brought their considerable skill and training into play, to swiftly complete the job.

In a letter dated July second of nineteen forty-one, Reinhard Heydrich instructed his *'Einsatzgruppen'* leaders that they were to expand these instructions to include all senior and middle Rankin Cominterm officials, all senior and middle ranking members of the central, provincial and district committees of the Communist Party, extremists and radical Communist Party members, people's commissars and Jews found to hold positions in any party and government posts.

In addition, open-ended instructions were given to execute: *'other radical elements, these to include saboteurs, propagandists, snipers, assassins, ad other agitators'.* Reinhard also suggested that any pogroms spontaneously imitated by the native occupants of the conquered territories were to be quietly but energetically encouraged.

On July eighth he announced that all Jews were to be regarded as partisans and gave the order for all male Jews between the ages of fifteen and forty-five to be shot. On the seventeenth of July he further ordered that the *'Einsatzgruppen'* were to kill all Jewish Red Army prisoners of war, plus all Red Army prisoners of war from Georgia and Central Asia, as they too might be Jews.

He then clarified what was to be termed by the *'Einsatzgruppen'* as a Jew. Unlike in Germany, where a Jew was defined as anyone with at least three Jewish grandparents, those in the case of the Russian campaign were to be considered as such, just as long as they had a least one Jewish grandparent.

This new evaluation was to be utilized regardless of whether or not the individual in question actually practised the Jewish religion.

In the first stages of the invasion pogroms did break out, particularity in Latvia, Lithuania and the Ukraine. Some were, as suggested, provoked by the German invaders and within a few weeks of the attack, forty pogroms had led to the deaths of approximately ten thousand Jews.

* * * * *

- Jews in Occupied France -

The restrictions on Jews in Paris began almost immediately after the German occupation. In October of nineteen forty the Germans blew up seven synagogues in central Paris.

Between then and nineteen forty-one the Germans arrested approximately ten thousand Jews in Paris and about the same number fled the city for the unoccupied zone in the South.

* * * * *

- Jews in the Occupied Low Countries -

Jews residing in the German occupied Low Countries, Luxembourg, Belgium and the Netherlands, faced Nazi instituted anti-Jewish laws and ordinances. Their civil rights were restricted and their property was confiscated as were their businesses. As well they were banned from certain professions, isolated from their fellow countrymen and forced to wear the yellow star-of-David on their clothing.

Patrick Laughy

* * * * *

Prior to the war approximately three thousand Jews lived in Luxembourg. More than a thousand of these were foreign and stateless Jews who had found refuge there after nineteen thirty-three.

In nineteen forty-one, the Jews were placed in the Fuenfbrunnen internment camp near the city of Ulflingen in northern Luxembourg. This camp was set up as a transit camp to hold individuals for future deportation.

Deportations from this camp were to begin in nineteen forty-one.

* * * * *

After the German invasion of Belgium in nineteen forty a Belgian government-in-exile, situated in London, worked with the Allies. King Leopold III had remained in Belgium however, and therefore the Germany military administration in place there coexisted with a civilian Belgian administration.

Despite that fact, the Germans definitely held sway and upon occupation they immediately took responsibility for all Jewish residents. There were approximately sixty-five thousand Jews in residence, the majority located in Antwerp and Brussels. Once again, the majority of these were foreign and stateless, those who had found refuge in Belgium directly after the Great War and between the wars.

Some of these were deported to the internment camps, such as Gurs and St. Cypien in southern France.

The remaining Belgian Jews were quickly rounded up with the intention of using them for slave labour. They worked primarily in the construction of military fortifications in northern France and in other construction projects, as well as in clothing, armaments factories and stone quarries within Belgium.

* * * * *

- Jews in the Netherlands -

Under occupation by the Germans, the Netherlands maintained its Dutch civilian administration, albeit under strict German supervision.

Amsterdam, the country's largest city had a Jewish population of about seventy-five thousand and of these nearly ten thousand were foreign Jews who had fled to Amsterdam in the nineteen-thirties.

Queen Wilhelmina and the government had fled to London and Nazi commissioner, Artur Seyss-Inquart was in charge. He insisted on strict compliance with anti-Jewish measures.

In January of forty-one all Jews were ordered to report for registration. More than one hundred and forty thousand complied with this order.

In February of forty-one, the Germans arrested several hundred Jews and deported them first to Buchenwald and then to Mauthausen concentration camp.

* * * * *

- Romanian Jews -

Romania had a prewar Jewish population of about seven hundred and fifty thousand, the third largest in Europe, following that of the Soviet Union and Poland.

On June twenty-eighth of nineteen forty, the Soviet Union occupied Romanian territory, seizing Bessarabia located between the Prut and Dniester rivers and northern Bukovina along the Carpathian Mountains in the northeast.

Hungarian and Bulgarian demands on Romanian territory were settled in the nineteen-forty *'Vienna Arbitration Awards'*, which had been sponsored by Germany and Italy. As a result Romania was forced to cede northern Transylvania to Hungary on August thirtieth of nineteen-forty and southern Dobruja to

Bulgaria on the seventh of September of that year.

Romania joined the Axis Pact on the twentieth of November nineteen-forty.

When Romania first came under Nazi influence, the power of the Romanian fascist political movement, the 'Iron Guard,' increased substantially in influence and the government began to introduce a string of increasingly punitive anti-Jewish laws.

Although the Romanian government did not follow the lead of other pro-German counties by deporting their two hundred thousand Jewish nationals and other undesirables to concentration camps, they did, in cooperation with *'Einsatzgruppen'* detachments, execute hundreds of thousands of Jews, mainly those who resided in Bessarabia, northern Bukovina and Transnistria, which were in the area of the Ukraine which had been transferred to Romania in nineteen forty-one.

As part of the Axis Pact, the Romanians participated in *'Operation Barbarossa'*.

Within days of the invasion Romanian authorities staged a pogrom in the city of Iasi, the regional capital of northwestern Romania and the base location of *'Iron Guard'* strength. As a result nearly one fifth of the cities Jewish population, eight thousand Jews, were killed, many in their own homes or in the streets. Thousands more were arrested and summarily executed in the courtyard of the Iasi police headquarters.

An additional four thousand Jews were deported in sealed freight cars to Calarasi and Podul Iloaei, more than half of these succumbing to the conditions of transport and dying during the trip. No nourishment or water had been provided and the train travelled for days in the heat of high summer.

'Einsatzgruppen' and Romanian units also roamed through Bessarabia, northern Bukovina and the southern Ukraine, randomly dispatching large groups of Jews. When Romanian troops entered the capital of Bessarabia they immediately began to execute any Jew they came across.

* * * * *

- Kiel -

The second super-U-boat, which had been scheduled under the initial building program of four of this class, had been recently completed.

Through the offices of his father, Eric had requested that his first officer be promoted in rank to take command of this new sub as it began its sea trials.

Upon notification that this request had been granted, Eric, without any input from his father, found himself being automatically promoted to the rank of *'Kapitanletnant'* (Lieutenant-Commander) in order to maintain the proper naval chain of command while working on the project.

The Count had been carefully reporting periodically to Hitler on the progress and development of this massive ocean-class U-boat and Eric's part in that process due to his position of naval advisor to the project, in his brief reports concerning advances in military hardware.

He now included information to the Fuhrer that although the initial submarine was ranked as *'still in the testing stages'*, the first sub, which had been under Eric's command, had successfully and covertly completed a cross-Atlantic shakedown-cruise and returned safely to Bordeaux where it would be undergoing further improvements, refinement and testing.

Hitler had replied specifically to this achievement by sending Karl one of his rare, personally-penned responses, expressing his delight as to the progress of the program and announced that, as a demonstration of his appreciation of Eric's accomplishment, he would immediately issue instructions to the Commander-in-Chief of the U-boat fleet to the effect that *'Kapitanleutnant'* von Stauffer was to be promoted to the rank of *'Korvettenkapitan'* (Commander) and placed in full and sole charge of the further, top-secret development of this special class of U-boats.

In a matter of three weeks, Eric had advanced two ranks and had received Adolf Hitler's personal stamp of approval to oversee the future development of this particular class of super U-boat.

Now that Hitler had become even more personally involved, Grand Admiral Karl Donitz, who had earlier in the program for the development of these craft expressed curiosity and interest in exactly what they were designed for, suddenly lost his very recently renewed interest in what the project entailed.

He had received the message that Hitler wanted this project separate from the Kriegsmarine and Donitz had no intention of raising the subject again unless asked to do so by the Fuhrer himself.

Life suddenly got simpler for Karl when it came to keeping the entire program under wraps and he found that any new requests for specific U-boat staffing needs he might have (all of whom would first be cleared by *Operation Fatherland's* security staff) were handled rapidly and efficiently, with no questions originating from the Admiral or his staff being asked.

The first super U-boat was currently being re-provisioned and undertaking minor repairs and would be laid up in port for approximately one month.

Newly promoted, Eric took advantage of that fact by joining the new crew of the now completed second U-boat to observe and assist with the beginnings of the sub's first sea-trials, which served to keep him in Kiel and consequently well within range of the delicious skills on offer from the delightfully inventive blond twins he had grown so fond of.

* * * * *

- Oslo -

Gabriella was well entrenched in the upper society of the

German occupying forces of Norway.

The first house she had looked at had proven to be as enchanting inside as it had been out and she and Konrad had indeed been able to move in the day after her viewing of the property.

The previous occupants - she had only met the wife briefly but there had apparently been six in the Jewish family - had been gone when she brought Konrad around the next evening to get his stamp of approval.

Remarkably all the furnishing had indeed remained and although she'd informed Konrad at that time that some of the furniture and finishes would have to be replaced or updated, the fact that Konrad had his own resources and both she and Ursula had received large cash payouts from their family trust upon marriage made anything possible.

Her new access to substantial funds allowed her to fulfill whatever new desire overtook her. Added to this wonderful situation was the fact that she had just recently had medical confirmation that she was pregnant and as a result Konrad had encouraged her to stop assisting him in the setup of the Norwegian SS Lebensborn clinics and instead take up her duties as a good German wife and see to the running their new household.

As eager as she had been to take part in the expanding Lebensborn programme, the challenge of running a large household and giving full attention to improving her social position appealed to her strongly and she eagerly accepted Konrad's suggestion, throwing herself into her new role.

Himmler, as always personally interested in the developments within the Lebensborn program, had been following their progress and soon got wind of the fact Gabriella was expecting. The Reichsfuhrer sent Konrad a personal telegram of congratulations in which he lauded the example the young SS couple was setting in occupied Norway and expressed his appreciation by immediately promoting the Major to the rank of SS-Obersturmbannfuhrer (Lieutenant Colonel).

Gabriella was ecstatic and immediately went about organizing a fitting dinner party to celebrate the promotion, which would of course include the attendance of all the German elite currently quartered in Oslo.

* * * * *

- Friedrichshafen -

The Countess Erika was of two minds.

She missed the social life of Berlin which could simply not compare with the very limited possibilities for social exchange offered by Friedrichshafen. She also missed Karl.

The flipside was the much reduced threat of the chance of an air raid over castle von Stauffer, versus one above the large house in Berlin, plus her newfound enjoyment at spending a great deal of time with Ursula and her husband.

The news of Gabriella's pregnancy had been a wonderful surprise and it had offered her yet another stimulus for promoting a similar condition in the case of her older daughter - something that she was determined to bring to fruition - which had been made abundantly clear to both Ursula and Friedrich. She had no intention of letting up on the topic, as she had been emboldened to do so by her son-in-law, who had offered tentative, if reserved, support of her initial suggestion.

She had fortified that initial thrust for her plea by pointing out that the party was strongly in favour of large families and that Ursula had a duty to help meet the need for new German blood to fulfill the requirements of a vastly expanded new Reich.

Ursula had responded to that remark by pointing out that she was currently fulfilling her duty to the needs of Germany by undertaking her current responsibilities and that having a child before those responsibilities had been complete was not compatible.

Ericka had tut-tutted any such suggestion.

After all she was available to assist with the care of

grandchildren and they would certainly have access to the necessary new staff to reopen the nursery if that should come about.

All in all and for the time being she was satisfied with the idea of spending her time at Lake Constance.

* * * * *

Ursula was enjoying her new duties immensely and was very pleased that she and Friedrich could spend a part of each day and every night together.

Her father had brought her up to speed on the concept of *'Operation Fatherland'* on his last visit and she was delighted that the Count had seen fit to allow her to take responsibility for a large part of reaching its goals.

Hitler's ordered invasion of Russia and the resulting two-front war had strongly served to fortify the commitment of the original members of *'Fatherland'* and those among Germans who were bright enough and had the opportunity to see the writing on the wall were beginning to swell the ranks of the conspirators, one of these being Friedrich who had expressed his shock upon learning of the invasion, blurting out in disbelief.

"My God, this is a disastrous decision, we have neither the equipment nor manpower to fight an extended two-front war."

When Ursula had told her father of this outburst, Karl had given her permission to share the concept of *'Operation Fatherland'* with her husband and *'IF'* he appeared to be of a mind to support its ideals, to include him in her duties directly and make him aware of their aims and goals.

As a result, she and her husband now spent the vast majority of their days working together and this additional closeness had, at least so far, only served to make the nights in their apartments that much more interesting and enjoyable.

CHAPTER FOURTEEN

- July -

- Air Operations -

The RAF bomb targets during this month were in the Ruhr valley and the Rhineland as well as Berlin. In addition several operations were also sent against ports in France and Germany. Bomber Command dropped four thousand, three hundred and eighty tons of bombs while flying over thirty-eight hundred sorties and lost one hundred and eighty-eight aircraft.

The Luftwaffe was far too busy elsewhere to continue its attacks on England.

* * * * *

- Battle of the Atlantic -

German U-boats sink only twenty-two ships for a total tonnage loss of ninety-four thousand, two hundred tons. A further twenty-six thousand, eight hundred tons are sunk by other means.

There are now sixty-three operational U-boats on patrol and a further ninety-three are currently in training. Twenty new U-boats will join the fleet during this month and only one will be lost.

German U-boats have up to this time been replenished by German ships sheltering in the Canary Islands but diplomatic pressure has finally forced the Spanish government to put a stop to it.

The allied convoy patrol armada has been increased substantially.

'Ultra' code breaking intercepts of U-boat traffic play a large role in raising the threat of surprise attack against U-boats from Allied resources.

* * * * *

- July First -

- North Africa -

A frustrated Churchill removes General Wavell from his command and replaces him with General Auchinleck.

* * * * *

- Middle East -

The British win the Battle of Palmyra against the French.

* * * * *

- USA -

All American males over twenty-one are required to register for the draft.

* * * * *

- Eastern Front -

The German Army Group North takes Riga while other German troops to the south have already pushed well beyond the Dvina as they rush toward Ostrov. West of Minsk the Berezina River is crossed and the *'Blitzkrieg'* into Russia continues.

* * * * *

- Newfoundland -

US naval aircraft commence flying anti-U-boat patrols from their new bases in Newfoundland.

* * * * *

- July Second -

- Eastern Front -

After regrouping, Hoeppner's Fourth Panzer Group attacks with renewed vigor toward Ostrov. To the south the Rumanian Third and Fourth Armies, in company with the German Eleventh Army, begin full-scale attacks.

* * * * *

- July Third -

Stalin orders a scorched-earth policy for retreating Soviet forces.

* * * * *

- East Africa -

Italian forces in southern Abyssinia surrender seven thousand troops to a Belgian unit. Additional Italian surrenders take place in the northwestern Gondar area around Debra Tabor.

* * * * *

- Syria -

Deir el Zor falls to the 10th Indian Division and the Vichy French fort at Palmyra surrenders to *'Habforce'* after a long siege.

* * * * *

- July Fourth -

- Poland -

German troops in Lwow undertake the mass execution of Polish scientists and writers.

* * * * *

- July Fifth -

- Tobruk -

British torpedo planes sink an Italian destroyer.

* * * * *

- Eastern front -

German troops reach the Dnieper River.

* * * * *

- July Sixth -

- Eastern Front -

Rumanian forces take Chernovtsy and are warmly welcomed as liberators by the civil population upon entering the city

* * * * *

- July Seventh -

British and Canadian troops who have been billeted in Iceland are replaced by American troops freeing them up for other duties.

* * * * *

- July Eighth -

- Yugoslavia -

Germany and Italy formally dissolve Yugoslavia into component parts making Croatia, which has a pro-Axis government in place, a separate entity. The province of Ljublana, part of Dalmatia, and some of the Adriatic islands are to be annexed by Italy. Bosnia is to be under Italian protection and Germany takes Montenegro, Carinthia and Cariola. Hungary is also provided some territory.

* * * * *

- Eastern Front -

The German forces successfully isolate Leningrad from the remainder of Russia.
Hoeppner's Fourth Panzer Group take Pskov.

* * * * *

- Syria -

Head to head slogging begins just inland from Sidon at Jezzine and Mazzrat-ech-Chouf.

* * * * *

- Russia -

Britain and Russia sign a mutual defense agreement, promising not to sign any form of separate peace agreement with Germany.

* * * * *

- July Ninth -

- Eastern Front -

The encircled pockets of Russian troops have now been wiped out by the German Army Group center. Three hundred thousand prisoners have been taken and in excess of forty Soviet divisions have been eliminated.

The Second and Third Panzer Groups have united to form the Fourth and have now crossed both the Dniepr and the Dvina Rivers and taken Vitebsk. They race on with the intent of encircling Smolensk.

* * * * *

- Syria -

Australian troops advancing north along the coast take Damour and there is now no obstacle blocking their advance to Beirut. Homs Salon falls to the allied advance and General Dentz asks for an armistice on behalf of the Vichy French forces.

* * * * *

- July Tenth -

- Eastern Front -

Guderian's Panzers take Minsk and the Germans advance farther into the Ukraine.

Kleist's Panzer Group hold against a heavy Soviet Fifth Army counter attack southwest of Korosten.

The first units of the Italian Expeditionary Corps in Russia begins to arrive. A legion of the Independent State of Croatia is part of the Italian corps.

* * * * *

- July Eleventh -

- Syria -

Ignoring orders from the Vichy French government which have forbidden him such action, General Dentz accepts the Allied armistice terms he's been offered. The cease fire begins at twenty-one hundred hours.

* * * * *

- Eastern Front -

The First Panzer Group begins a renewed advance on Kiev and reaches to within fifteen miles of the city.

The Soviet Defense Committee creates three new command areas for the Red Army. Marshal Voroshilov is to command in the *'Northwest Front'*, Marshal Timoshenko the *'Central West Front'* and Marshal Budenny the *'Southwest Front'*.

* * * * *

- USA -

President Roosevelt appoints William Donovan to head a new civilian intelligence agency with the title of *'Coordinator of Defense Information'*. This agency will eventually morph into the *'Office of Strategic Services'* (OSS) the precursor of the CIA.

* * * * *

- July Twelfth -

- Moscow -

An agreement between the British and Russians is signed. It provides for mutual assistance and forbids either country from making a separate peace with Nazi Germany.

* * * * *

- Eastern Front -

The city of Moscow is bombed by the Luftwaffe for the first time.

* * * * *

- North Africa -

Italian General Bastico replaces General Gariboldi as Commander in chief of their forces in North Africa. On paper, this position also directs the German forces fighting in North Africa as well, however, it is something that German General Rommel has, in the main, ignored to date.

* * * * *

- July Thirteenth -

- Serbia -

Royalists in Serbia begin an uprising against the Axis powers and communist-hatched plans instigate a parallel uprising and civil war in Montenegro.

* * * * *

- July Fourteenth -

- Mediterranean -

Suez is attacked by a formation of German Ju 88 bombers from their bases in Crete. Two ships which were unloading cargo at the time of the attack are damaged as are port facilities.

* * * * *

- Eastern Front -

The advancing Germans reach the Luga River.

* * * * *

- July Fifteenth -

The Red Army begins a counter-attack against the Germans near Leningrad in order to gain time to build up defenses around the threatened city.

* * * * *

- Newfoundland -

The Argentia naval air base is set up in Newfoundland. It will serve as an important transfer station for the Allies in the future.

* * * * *

- July Sixteenth -

- Eastern Front -

Finnish troops attack north of Lake Ladoga and take Sortavala, reaching the lake southeast of the town. Retreating Russian forces manage to get some of their troops to safety by boat.

German Army Group South surrounds a pocket of Russian troops south of Uman.

With Moscow in their sights, Guderian's panzers drive into Smolensk.

* * * * *

- Berlin -

Hitler, Goering, Bormann and Rosenberg meet to work on plans for the exploitation of the territory already captured by the Russian. Rosenberg is put in charge of a new ministry, with the task of organizing the new Reich *'Lebensraum'* in a manner that will provide increased economic return to the German state and begin eliminating the Jewish and Communist pockets in the areas now under German occupation.

* * * * *

- Vichy France -

General Weygand is appointed Governor General of Algeria.

* * * * *

- Japan -

The opening moves are made to remove Matsuoka from the Foreign Ministry. Prince Konoye resigns and re-forms his Cabinet.

Matsuoka had been arguing that Japan should abandon the Neutrality Agreement with Russia and join the Nazis in the attack against Russia.

* * * * *

- July Seventeenth -

- Eastern Front -

The Germans develop an important bridgehead over the Dniepr.

* * * * *

- Mediterranean -

The Luftwaffe undertake repeated air attacks against Malta.

* * * * *

- July Eighteenth -

- London -

The Benes government is formally recognized by the British as the legal provisional government of Czechoslovakia and a friendship and a mutual-assistance agreement is signed between them.

The 4th Reich

* * * * *

- July Nineteenth -

- Atlantic -

The US Atlantic Fleet forms TF1 which it designates as being responsible for the protection of American forces on Iceland and as support for convoys bound there. The USS *'Wasp'* delivers a cargo of P-40 fighters to the island.

The US navy commits up to twenty-five destroyers to the Iceland operation as well as heavier support forces with the mandate to provide escorts for ships of all nationalities sailing to and from Iceland.

* * * * *

- Eastern Front -

Once Guderian has completed the occupation of Smolensk, Hitler orders him to move his force south to join in on the attack against Kiev. Guderian argues against the southern shift in thrust, suggesting that it would be far more effective if he were to continue forward and take Moscow.

As had many before him, Guderian quickly finds out that one does not argue with the Fuhrer once he has made up his mind about something.

* * * * *

- V for Victory -

The BBC has been introducing their broadcasts to Europe with the Morse code designator for the letter *'V'* for some time and on this date it is unofficially adopted as the Allied signal, along with the motif of Beethoven's Fifth Symphony.

Churchill had also been using the V-sign publicly and on

this date *'Colonel Britton'* while broadcasting to Europe, urges the creation of resistance forces within the occupied Axis territories and suggests that they identify themselves with the *'V'* sign.

Shortly thereafter, *'V'* signs begin appearing on walls and German posters throughout occupied Europe.

* * * * *

- July Twenty-First -

- USA -

Roosevelt asks Congress to extend the draft period to thirty months from one year and to make the same change in the service of those enlisting in the National Guard.

* * * * *

- Eastern Front -

The Luftwaffe repeats a heavy bombing attack on Moscow.

The Russians withdraw their defensive forces from the line of the Dniestr River.

* * * * *

- Mediterranean -

A major convoy designed to take relief to Malta forms up and leaves Gibraltar.

Covered by *'Force H'*, which has been specifically reinforced for the occasion, this convoy consists of seven transports.

The enhanced *'Force H'* fleet now contains its normal compliment of the carrier HMS *'Ark Royal'*, the battle cruiser

'Renown', a cruiser and eight destroyers; plus the battleship HMS *'Nelson'*, three cruisers and nine destroyers which have been furnished by the Home Fleet.

* * * * *

- July Twenty-Second -

- Mediterranean -

An Italian reconnaissance plane spots the convoy sent to replenish Malta and reports the sighting. The Italians decide, figuring it is only another carrier ferrying planes, to stay in port and therein miss their opportunity to intercept the convoy.

* * * * *

- July Twenty-Third -

- Mediterranean -

An Italian aircraft formation finds the Malta resupply fleet and sinks one destroyer and hits one cruiser and three destroyers.

* * * * *

- July Twenty-Fourth -

- Mediterranean -

One of the transport ships is hit just before reaching Malta.

* * * * *

- Tokyo -

The Japanese present an ultimatum to representatives of the Vichy French government on the nineteenth, giving the Vichy six days to provide them with bases in southern Indochina or suffer the consequences. On this date they succumb to the demand.

* * * * *

- Atlantic -

A force of fifteen Halifax bombers attacks the battleship *'Scharnhorst'* which is anchored in the port of La Pallice. The ship is hit five times and seriously damaged.

With *'Prince Eugen'* having been hit earlier in the month and *'Gneisenau'* already undergoing repairs, the Germans now have no functioning capital ships in the Brest area.

* * * * *

- July Twenty-Sixth -

- USA -

Responding to the Japanese occupation of French Indochina, President Roosevelt orders the seizure of all Japanese assets in the United States. The British take the same action in England.

* * * * *

Roosevelt orders the incorporation of the entire Philippine army into the US army and appoints General MacArthur to command the US forces in the area.

* * * * *

- July Twenty Seventh -

- Eastern Front -

Using a pincer movement the Germans cut off the Russian forces around Smolensk.

* * * * *

- July Twenty-Eighth -

- Indochina -

Japanese forces occupy southern Vichy-French Indochina. They allow the Vichy colonial government to continue to administer Vietnam, tolerating the French repression of the country to continue. Vichy agrees to the occupation of the bases in Indochina, despite the fact that there is little doubt the Japanese intend using them as jumping off points for an invasion of Malaya, the East Indies and/or the Philippines.

Japanese assets in the Dutch East Indies are frozen and all existing oil deals are cancelled.

* * * * *

- Baltic States -

The Germans solidify their presence and the *'Einsatzgruppen'* begin their task of *'special handling'* for the native Jewish population.

* * * * *

- July Twenty-Ninth -

The Japanese freeze Dutch assets. Three-quarters of Japan's foreign trade is now at a standstill and ninety percent of its oil supplies have been effectively cut off.

* * * * *

- July Thirtieth -

- China -

The US gunboat *'Tutiula'* is damaged by a Japanese bombing run on Chunking. Japan apologizes for the incident.

* * * * *

- Norway -

Using aircraft from the carriers HMS *'Victorious'* and *'Furious'*, the British commence an attack on German shipping and installations near Kirkenes and Petsamo. They lose fifteen aircraft to German anti-aircraft and German fighters. Little damage results from the attack.

* * * * *

- July Thirty-First -

- Eastern Front -

The sixteenth army from German Army Group North advances to the south side of Lake Ilmen. In the south, Finnish troops cross the border and begin their attacks toward Viipuri and Vuosalimi.

* * * * *

- North Africa -

Axis forces are reorganized.

General Cruewell is put in command of the *'Afrika Korps'* with Rommel in charge of the new Panzer Group Africa.

Rommel now commands two Panzer Divisions and one light infantry division as well as seven Italian divisions.

* * * * *

- Berlin -

Acting on instructions from Hitler, Goering orders SS-General Reinhard Heydrich to: *'submit to me as soon as possible a general plan of the administrative material and financial measures necessary for the carrying out the desired final solution of the Jewish question'.*

CHAPTER FIFTEEN

- August -

- Hitler's Health -

In late July Hitler had become ill.

He had been suffering from reoccurring stomach pains for some time. This condition was being treated by his personal physician, Doctor Morell.

His system was now showing signs of rebelling against the up to one hundred and fifty anti-gas pills he had been taking each week as well as the ten injections of *'Ultraseptyl'* which was a strong sulfonamide.

He had succumbed to a bout of dysentery which was a common enough malady in the swampy surrounding of the *'Wolfsschanze'*. His symptoms were pronounced. A victim of diarrhea, nausea and aching limbs, he would break out in a sweat one minute and be shivering the next.

Toward the end of the month he and von Ribbentrop, who had been against the invasion of Russia from the start, got into a heated argument when the Foreign Minister again raised his objections to the move against the Soviets.

By this point in time, Hitler was rarely challenged on anything and von Ribbentrop had definitely stepped over the line on this occasion. It had been an unexpected exchange and suddenly Hitler visibly paled and broke off mid-sentence, clutching at his heart and sinking listlessly into a chair.

There was a frightening moment of strained silence in the room and then in a wavering voice Hitler whispered: *'I thought I was going to have a heart attack. You must never again oppose me in this manner'.*

When he heard of the incident, Morell urged Hitler to have an electrocardiogram which he then forwarded to

Professor Dr. Karl Weber, who was director of the Heart Institute at Bad Nauheim and a leading authority on heart disease.

He did not identify the patient that the electrocardiogram had been taken from, simply labeling it as that of a highly stressed diplomat.

The diagnosis was: *a rapidly progressive coronary sclerosis, a virtually incurable heart disease.*

It is doubtful that Dr. Morell told Hitler of the true diagnosis, but he did start The Fuhrer on some additional medication. Hitler was now instructed to also take a heart tonic, *'Cardiazol'*, a harmless solution used for circulatory weakness, fainting and exhaustion and *Sympathol 3 one percent.*

* * * * *

- Einsatzgruppen -

Since The Soviet Union was an ally the Nazis, they had therefore made little if any mention of the anti-Semite atrocities that had taken place prior to the opening of hostilities between the two countries. This meant that the Jews residing in Russia had no previous knowledge in regard to Hitler's views on *'racial cleansing'.*

It is not surprising therefore that many of the Jews welcomed the German invaders as liberators from Soviet repression. They saw no reason to conceal themselves or flee and were easily located and picked up by the advancing Germans.

The extermination process went ahead rapidly. It was handled by those in charge as a tidy businesslike operation, as if the *'Einsatzgruppen'* teams were picking apples rather than executing human beings.

Their methodical work was very rarely marked by any resistance from their quarry. One commander reported that: *'Strange is the calmness with which the delinquent's allow themselves to be shot and that goes for non-Jews as well as Jews. Their fear of death appears to have been blunted by a kind of indifference which has been created in the course of twenty years of Soviet rule.'*

Not everything was going smoothly for the teams conducting the *'Special handling'* however. The physical task, while demanding, was feasible, but it was the mental aspect of the operations that was beginning to raise concerns.

The psychological effects on those actually carrying out the executions was leading to some of the enlisted men having nervous breakdowns and others turning to excessive drink just to manage to keep functioning from day to day. A number of the lower ranked officers were developing serious stomach and intestinal ailments.

Despite Himmler's orders that the exterminations were to be conducted as humanely as possible, there were early signs that the demoralizing and dehumanizing effect of the daily mass murders was causing many of those directly involved to use excessive enthusiasm in carrying out their duties by sadistically beating prisoners for the fun of it.

Heydrich's most pressing problem was quickly becoming one of finding a means for coping with the excessive effects the hands-on shooting of the victims was causing within the members of his *'Einsatzgruppen'* troops.

He determined to raise the issue with Himmler.

* * * * *

- Drancy Transit Camp -

In August of nineteen forty-one a transit camp was established in the northeastern Parisian suburb of Drancy in occupied France. This camp was initially set up as an internment camp but it soon morphed to become the major transit camp the Germans would use for the deportation of Jews from France.

The camp was housed in a multistory U-shaped building

that had served as a police barracks before the war. The entire building and courtyard were now enclosed and surrounded by barbed-wire and guarded by French police who were ordered by the Germans to maintain early control of the camp.

* * * * *

- Natzweiler-Struthof Concentration Camp -

This camp was constructed near Natzweiler, a town about thirty-one miles southwest of Strasbourg, the capital of Alsace in eastern occupied France. Construction was completed in May of nineteen forty-one.

A small camp, it was built to hold fifteen hundred prisoners. Inmates were used as forced labour in nearby granite quarries, on construction projects and in the construction and maintenance of the camp itself.

* * * * *

- Bialystok Ghetto -

According to the terms of the German/Soviet Pact of nineteen thirty-nine, Bialystok, a city in northeastern Poland, was assigned to the Soviet sphere of influence and occupation. Soviet forces entered the city in September of nineteen thirty-nine and held it until, as a result of *'Operation Barbarossa'*, it was forcibly occupied by the Germans.

Bialystok was then named the capital of the Bezirk Bialystok district of Reich occupied Poland.

As ordered, '*Einsatzgruppen*' detachments followed the army into the city and quickly organized the rounding up and execution of thousands of Jewish inhabitants.

In August of nineteen forty-one the occupying Germans ordered the establishment of a ghetto in Bialystok.

Approximately fifty thousand Jews from the city and the surrounding areas were then confined in a small area within the city of Bialystok. This new ghetto had two sections, divided by the Biala River.

The majority of the inmates at Bialystok were then put to work in forced-labour enterprises, primarily in huge textile factories which had been established within the ghetto boundaries, although some were employed as slave labour to work outside of the secure enclosure.

* * * * *

- Kovno Ghetto -

Prior to the outbreak of World War II, Kovno (Kaunas) was the capital and largest city in Lithuania. Its Jewish population was about forty thousand, approximately one quarter of the city's total residents. Under the terms of the German/Soviet Pact, the Russians had occupied the city in nineteen-forty. Shortly before and immediately after the Germans overran and took the city on the twenty-fourth of June nineteen forty-one, organized Lithuanian mobs had begun to attack the Jews of Kovno in their ethnic enclaves, primarily along Jurbarko and Krisciukaicia streets. Several hundred were killed in these sporadic rampages.

In July of forty-one, *'Einsatzgruppen'* and Lithuanian auxiliaries began the cleanup of the remaining undesirables through systematic massacres of the Jews who were holed-up inside the several forts around the city.

These forts had been constructed by the Russian tsars in the nineteenth century for the defense of the city, and the majority of the remaining Jews had taken up residence inside, taking advantage of the protection offered by the surrounding battlements.

The *'Einsatzgruppen'* and their supporters summarily execute all the found, which ran into the thousands.

In August, the Germans established a ghetto in the Slobodka suburb of Kovno in order to concentrate any Jews who still remained in the city. This newly created ghetto had two parts, a small section for those who seemed unlikely candidates for forced labour and the larger, for those who did.

* * * * *

- Inner Circle -

With Hitler's determination to personally take charge of `Operation Barbarossa`, his inner circle had grown to include the hierarchy of the German Military machine. `

In fact the top military leaders now absorbed by far the majority of the Fuhrer's personal attention and time.

The original members of Hitler's political inner circle were not pleased by this new development and each, in his own way, personally detested it. However, it might have been a comfort to them to know that the top Generals who now made up his new *'military'* inner circle were far more displeased with this change than they were and would have been glad to have The Fuhrer out of their hair.

* * * * *

- Himmler -

Himmler continued to strive to improve his position in Hitler's good graces by being the man to provide the answers for the Fuhrer's need for a specialist in *'special handling'* problems.

As a result, the Reichsfuhrer-SS was deeply concerned about the report he'd received from Heydrich.

He immediately felt obligated to personally witness an execution to see what action could be taken to improve the situation. To that end, while making a visit to Minsk he asked the commanders of *'Einsatzgruppen B'* to arrange for him to view the firing-squad execution of one hundred prisoners.

As the firing squad raised their rifles, Himmler noticed that one young man being herded into position for execution looked to be, what he considered, a true Aryan. The lad had blond hair and blue eyes.

He asked the officer in charge of the execution if this man was a Jew. The response was positive. He then asked if both parents had been Jews and was told that they had been. He asked if the man had any antecedents who were not Jewish and was given a negative reply.

Himmler then stamped his boot and looking over at the young man said: *'Then I cannot help you'*.

The man was added to the line and the squad opened fire. Himmler, who had specifically ordered the viewing, did not watch the actual execution, instead he shuffled uncomfortably and carefully studied his boots.

When a second volley was fired into the writhing bodies and the Reichsfuhrer continued to avert his eyes.

When Himmler finally looked up he observed that two women were still alive and shouted *'Don't torture these women! Get on with it, shoot quickly'*.

The man responsible for the *'special handling'* groups in the Russian area, the senior SS and police commander for Central Russia, Obergruppenfuhrer von dem Bach-Zelewski, was present and standing near to Himmler. He quickly took this opportunity to impress upon Himmler the seriousness of the reaction registered on the faces of the members of the firing squad.

He asked Himmler to take note of how deeply shaken by the incident the men were, then said: *'They are finished for the rest of their lives. What kind of followers are we creating by these things? Either neurotics or brutes.'*

An obviously deeply upset Himmler ordered that everyone involved gather round and he gave them an impromptu speech which included the following:

'Yours is a disgusting task, but as good Germans you should not expect to enjoy doing it. Your conscience, however, should be in no way affected because you are soldiers who have to carry out every order without question. I alone, before God and the Fuhrer, bear the terrible responsibility for what

has to be done. Surely you have noticed that this bloody work was as odious to me and moved me to the depth of my soul. But I too was obeying the highest law by doing his duty.'

When Himmler returned to Berlin he met with SS-Brigadefuhrer, Artur Nebe, who he had placed in command of *'Einsatzgruppen'* B, the unit which had been detailed to follow Army Group Center during *'Operation Barbarossa'*.

He outlined his concerns to Nebe regarding the distress the mass shootings were having on the men in the field and assigned him the task of finding new and less hands-on methods that could be used to accomplish all future *'special handling'* tasks.

* * * * *

- Rosenberg -

Rumours of the atrocities being carried out by the SS had reached Rosenberg, who had been ordered by Hitler to draw up the initial blueprint for the occupation of the conquered Eastern territories.

Hitler had originally suggested to him that the establishment of *'weak socialist states'* would be the model for Russian lands occupied by the German attack. As a result, Rosenberg had personally envisioned the creation of a degree of self-rule for the conquered. At the time he had presented his plan at the special conference on the subject that was held at the *'Wolfsschanze'* on the sixteenth of July, Rosenberg had been led to believe that Hitler had accepted it in principle and that it would be adopted as written.

That had not been the case.

At that meeting Hitler stated; *'It is essential that we do not proclaim our views before the whole world. There is no need for that but the main thing is that we ourselves know what we want'.*

Rosenberg was astonished at what Hitler said next.

'This need not prevent our taking all necessary

measures - shooting, resettlement, etc. - and we shall take them. In principle we must now face the task of cutting up the giant cake according to our needs in order to be able; first, to dominate it; second to administer it; third to exploit it. The Russians have now given an order for partisan warfare behind our front. This guerrilla activity again has some advantage to us; it enables us to exterminate everyone who opposes us'.

A deflated Rosenberg left that meeting with the new title of *'Reich Minister of the East'*.

He was not a happy camper.

Privately he bemoaned the fact that his dream of the occupation of the east had been eviscerated by the fact that Hitler firmly believed the false conception for the Slavs, which had been formed in his early days in Vienna as a result of his ingesting the inflammatory pamphlets, that had described them as lazy primitives, and as a whole, a second class race.

He found himself shocked that Hitler completely misunderstood the structure of the Soviet Union. He knew that the Ukrainians and other tribes, that now found themselves under the yoke of the Russians, could reasonably be considered as potential allies of the New Reich and if handled reasonably might well be expected to form a bulwark against Bolshevism and could easily be given a good measure of self-rule.

He realized that Hitler had been supported by both Bormann and Goering in the determination that these peoples were enemies who should either be turned to slaves, or eradicated.

He resolved to challenge Hitler at the first opportunity and force him to see reason. The fact was however, that when he walked out of the meeting and had already failed to take any such step. This seemed to be moot point, in that he knew only too well that he would never do any such thing.

Just being in the same room as Hitler left him a trembling, bumbling fool and he had accepted that fact a long time ago.

* * * * *

- Brauchitsch and Halder -

Field Marshall Alfred Hermann Walther von Brauchitsch and General Franz Halder, Chief of the OKH General Staff, had been seriously considering the overthrow of Hitler since early in November of nineteen thirty-nine.

From the beginning of the Nazi takeover of government they had acted in tandem to influence Hitler against his wish to turn to militarism, at least until the German army was fully prepared. Hitler had brushed their concerns aside, publicly and resolutely criticizing both in the process and forged his way ahead, and by way of his successes, had brought them into line publically, if not privately.

Now that Hitler was laid up with medical problems, they took the opportunity that this situation provided, to subtly sabotage the Fuhrer's military plans as to the day to day mechanics of fighting the war and did their best to sabotage The Fuhrer's decision that Moscow should not be an immediate target.

As part of the plot to shift control of *'Operation Barbarossa'* from Hitler to senior Military officers, Halder began to use his personal influence with Wehrmacht General Jodl, Chief of the Operation Staff of the OKW, to gain his support for their plans to take over the planning and direction of the German military machine.

* * * * *

- Concentration Camp Medical Experiments -

- Dachau -

The use of concentration camp inmates as guinea pigs in the guise of medical research began in the nineteen-forties.

A major study on this question, presided over by Professor Ernst Holzlohner and Luftwaffe Doctor, Sigmund

Rascher was undertaken in Dachau in forty-one.

In nineteen thirty-six Rascher, a medical student, had denounced his father to the authorities and joined the SA. He transferred to the SS in nineteen thirty-nine. He had then been conscripted into the Luftwaffe.

Shortly thereafter he married a former singer who was acquainted with Himmler, possibly a past mistress, and from then on he was on good terms with the SS-Reichsfuhrer.

While a captain in the Luftwaffe's Medical Service, Rascher suggested that high-altitude/low-pressure experiments be carried out on human beings.

At that time, he had been taking a course in aviation medicine at Munich and he'd written Himmler a letter in which he said that his course included research into high-altitude flight. This research had expressed regrets that tests with humans had been impossible as such experiments were highly dangerous and as a result, no one had seen fit to volunteer for them. In the letter Rascher asked Himmler to place human subjects at his disposal to advance this current research, stating quite frankly that the experiments might prove fatal, but that previous tests using monkeys had been decidedly unsatisfactory.

Himmler believed the project had possibilities and he had instructed his personal administrative officer, Rudolf Brant, to answer the letter and advise Rascher that prisoners would be made available to him for this purpose.

Ecstatic, Rascher wrote back to Brant, asking for permission to carry out the experiments at Dachau.

* * * * *

- Hitler -

In mid-August, The Fuhrer began to recover from his illness. Back in harness, it did not take him long to figure out what Brauchitsch and Halder had been up to while he was under the weather.

He noted that neither his own plans for the fight on the Russian Front, nor that of Halder had been put into effect. Instead a compromise between the two was now in progress.

Hitler was furious and on August twenty-first he moved to rectify the situation by issuing an order that could not possibly be misunderstood by anyone. In part it read: *'The most important objective to be reached by winter is not Moscow, but the Crimea. An attack on Moscow will not begin until Leningrad has been isolated and the Russian Fifth Army in the south has been destroyed.'*

Still fuming, Hitler retired to his office and angrily began to dictate a lengthy memorandum, a stern lecture on how to wage a campaign, in which he charged that unnamed commanders were driven by *'selfish desires'* and *'despotic dispositions'* and characterized the army high command as *'a gathering of minds fossilized in out of date theories.'*

Needless to say, senior career army commanders were stunned and outraged at being belittled and accused of inept performance.

Halder was aghast and incensed.

The next day he spent hours with Brauchitsch complaining about Hitler's continual interference in army affairs, in the end suggesting that the two of them resign and be done with it. The Field Marshall, now in his latter years and obviously despondent, kyboshed the suggestion. He sighed and shook his head.

'It wouldn't be practical and would change nothing.'

In the days that followed Brauchitsch actually did his best to reduce the animosity Hitler's memo had stirred up among the senior officers, assuring all who would listen that the Fuhrer had personally promised him that, once the victory was certain in the Ukraine, all available forces would be thrown into the attack on Moscow.

Diminishing grumbling among senior officers continued for a week or so, then died out completely.

* * * * *

Patrick Laughy

- Mussolini Visits *'Wolfsschanze'* -

On August twenty-seventh nineteen forty-one Benito
Mussolini arrived at *'Wolfsschanze'* for a pre-planned and
much publicized visit to the Eastern Front.

'Il Duce' intended to use the trip to encourage Hitler to
agree to an enlargement of the small Italian Expeditionary
Force currently fighting on the Russian front, with a view to
sharing in the glory of the crushing of Communism.

Having recently lost his son Bruno in an air crash,
Mussolini was still in mourning and not at his best.

Hitler and his extended entourage waited on the
platform of the small railway station at the *'Wolfsschanze'* as
'Il Duce's' special train came into sight and puffed slowly into
the station.

The skies were clear, and a high level of pomp and
ceremony had been laid on by the Fuhrer who was feeling
much better health-wise and riding high on an adrenalin-rush
over the continued successes being won by his attacking
'Barbarossa' forces. He was eager to make the most of photo-
ops provided by the visit of Italy's leader for later domestic
consumption.

Hitler was buoyant and talked incessantly, dominating
the conversation from the get go. The Fuhrer's topics ranged
from the marvelous successes of his *'Blitzkrieg'* against the
Russians to the stupidity of France and Spain and the unsavory
Jewish elite that dogged Roosevelt's heels.

A harangued Mussolini was finally able to get a word in
edgewise.

Bereft of any military successes of his own to belabour,
he escaped into a reliving of the triumphs of ancient Rome who
had also fought in the regions the two fascist leaders were
going to inspect later in the day.

When Mussollini finished, he made his offer of more
troops to Hitler. and the Fuhrer, who was far from impressed
with the performance of Italian forces so far in the war,

promptly changed the subject and began to natter on again about the extent of the German achievements against the Soviets.

In the late morning they boarded Hitler's personal plane, a Focke-Wulf Condor D2600 all-metal four-engine long-range airliner at the airport near *Wolfsschanze'* and began their flight to Uman in the Ukraine.

Here they took the lead car in a motorcade, climbing into a Mercedes-Benz type G4 (2 series-W31) and began their inspection. The two leaders reviewed an Italian division and as the *'Bersaglieri'* roared past on their motorcycles in their steel helmets with the attached fancy feathers flipping about in the breeze, they shouted *'Duce, Duce'* as they swept past Hitler's staff car.

Mussolini's somber temperament immediately perked up at this display, but his dominance of the scene quickly evaporated as the motorcade entered into the smoking ruins of Uman and it was the Fuhrer who was wildly cheered as the motorcade began to sweep by his grinning soldiers.

Those in the motorcade were served lunch in the field and when they had finished eating Hitler took his leave of Mussolini and went on a walk-about among the German soldiers in the area of the field kitchen.

'Il Duce' felt slighted by this move; he had been hoping to join Hitler and share in the adulation of the troops, but it was not to be.

On the return trip to *'Wolfsschanze',* Mussolini went forward in the aircraft and engaged Hans Baur, Hitler's personal pilot, in conversation and after sharing comments on their mutual interest in flying, asked if he could pilot the plane.

Hitler was caught completely off guard by the suggestion and agreed to the request.

He immediately regretted having given his assent as Mussolini happily cavorted playfully around with the controls causing Hitler to fidget uneasily until the irritating episode was over.

After Hitler saw Mussolini's train off, 'Il Duce' sank

into a cloud of depression.

He had been unable to get Hitler to agree to allow a large contingent of Italian troops into the fight with Russia. It appeared to him that the war would be extensive and the glory of victory was something in which he would now be unable to share.

Back at *'Wolfsschanze'* Hitler settled in for tea with his secretaries and entourage and began to quietly contemplate the large map affixed to the wall across from him. Seemingly out of nowhere to those around him, he thusly came to the epiphany that it was now time to attack Moscow.

He spoke in a deep resonating voice.

'In several weeks we will be in Moscow. There is no doubt of it. I will raze that damned city and I will construct in its place an artificial lake with central lighting. The name of Moscow will disappear forever.'

* * * * *

- Wilhelm -

In January, Himmler had ordered Wilhelm to prepare an in-depth report for him in relation to the current situation with the *'Lebensborn'* project'.

Himmler was dissatisfied with the numbers of babies being produced and wanted an explanation as to why this was the case, and suggestions of ways to improve the output of pure *'Aryan'* children.

The hands-on evaluation required Wilhelm to travel to clinics across Germany and while it had offered him certain delightful fringe benefits, was otherwise uneventful and had taken him nearly five months.

Interspersed between his trips to the various clinics and the preparations of his report to the Reichsfuhrer, he had been kept busy with fulfilling his responsibilities as Himmler's liaison officer with his father.

Wilhelm returned to his office at SS-headquarters in

Berlin in July where he had begun to work on the final report and his recommendations for expansion and improvement of the *'Lebensborn'* system.

He was working on it at his desk when Himmler's senior aid, SS-Hauptsturmfuhrer Joachim Peiper stuck his head through the doorway and after spotting Wilhelm, stepped in and pulled the door closed behind him.

"Have you ever heard about something called *'Operation Fatherland'*?"

Wilhelm who had been writing didn't look up immediately. He caught his breath, laid down his pen and managed a smile as he responded.

"No...no I don't think so, but there are a lot of code names floating around lately...why?"

Peiper had a single sheet of paper in his right hand and he crossed to drop it on the desk in front of Wilhelm, who picked it up to read it.

"Some bloody Untersturmfuhrer in France has sent in a report, something about an art shipment from Paris being improperly consigned apparently.

A Luftwaffe NCO has been taken into custody and is being questioned.

"They've no doubt been torturing the poor bastard and he's probably making up tales to make them stop...something about an 'Operation Fatherland'...anyway, can you look into it, I'm up to my neck in trying to help *'Brigadefuhrer'* Nebe solve this damned *'Einsatzgruppen'* moral situation the boss is all wound up about..."

He broke off and smiled.

"Well that's nothing you're aware of, or have to be concerned with at any rate, but the point is I'm up to my neck at the moment and I don't have the time to get this particular foolishness sorted out."

Joachim shrugged.

"I have to say that I'm not particularly surprised the Luftwaffe is involved in it!"

He then stepped closer to Wilhelm's desk and lowered

his voice conspiratorially.

"The good Reichsmarschall, Herr Goering, has been grabbing everything of value he can find in France and having it hauled to his estate. There is nothing surprising about an improperly consigned shipment under the circumstances, I'd say."

He frowned and looked Wilhelm squarely in the eyes.

"If that is the case, for Christ's sake keep us out of it. We don't want to give the Reichsmarschall any reason to go running to Hitler with a complaint."

Wilhelm felt sweat beginning to form between his shoulder blades as he finished reading the brief incident report. He took a deep breath and did his level best to maintain his disinterested expression as he nodded his head absently.

"Sure, leave it with me. I'll do a follow-up and get back to you."

Obviously pleased to be rid of the offending document, Joachim smiled and spun back toward the door to pull it open, then quickly disappeared down the hall in the direction of his own office.

Wilhelm set the letter down on his desk and waited for a minute before he got up and crossed to his door to close it. He then went back to his desk and picked up the phone and was quickly put through to his father's secretary. He promptly set up an appointment to see the Count immediately.

CHAPTER SIXTEEN

- August -

- Air Operations -

Bomber Command hits targets in Karlsruhe, Berlin, Hamburg, Mannheim, Frankfurt and Hanover. Sweeps are made by fighters and fighter bombers over the regions of France and the Low Countries. A study to evaluate the effectiveness of the night bombing runs, is completed and indicates that there is only a seven percent accuracy being achieved.

Germany's aircraft are kept busy on the Eastern Front.

This month the Russians begin to bomb Berlin with a small force. They hit the city on seven occasions.

* * * * *

- Battle of the Atlantic -

Patrolling U-boats manage to sink twenty-three ships for a total tonnage of eighty thousand, three hundred. Three U-boats are sunk.

The U-boat fleet is operating closer to the British Isles now in order to allow the smaller boats to complete longer patrols.

The over-all number of ships lost to the Allies is forty-one, for a total of one hundred and thirty thousand, seven hundred tons.

* * * * *

Patrick Laughy

- August First -

- USA -

The US announces an oil embargo against *'aggressors'*. Export of oil and aviation fuel will be allowed for only the British Empire and the countries of the Western Hemisphere.

As designed, this decision hits Japan very hard as they have no oil of their own and now find themselves with only very limited stocks. The Japanese are left with one of two choices, change their foreign policy radically, or go to war and try to gain access to the oil on tap in the East Indies.

* * * * *

- Vietnam -

The Japanese occupy Saigon.

* * * * *

- Eastern Front -

The areas near Vitebsk and Orsha experience ferocious fighting. The Soviets attack along the northern edge of the Pripet Marshes due west of Gomel with the intent of slicing deeply into the German rear areas. For the most part the Germans easily repel these attacks.

- August Second -

- Norway -

The German occupation force confiscates all civilian radios.

* * * * *

- US -

Lend lease aid begins to flow to the Russians.

* * * * *

- Eastern Front -

The German forces in the north attack Staraya just south of Lake Ilmen as they swing right toward Leningrad.

* * * * *

- August Third -

- Eastern Front -

In an encircling move, German troops enclose Pervomaysk on the River Bug.

* * * * *

- August Fifth -

- Vichy -

Admiral Darlan is promoted and placed in charge of policy in North Africa. General Weygand will be his subordinate.

* * * * *

- Eastern Front -

The fighting around Smolensk comes to an end. Of the seven hundred thousand Russian troops involved in the defense of the city, three hundred thousand prisoners are taken and the

Patrick Laughy

rest are dead or unaccounted for.

The city of Orel is taken by the Germans.

* * * * *

- August Sixth -

- Thailand -

Diplomatic efforts on behalf of the British and the US warn the Japanese not to invade Thailand.

* * * * *

- Tokyo -

The Japanese present proposals to the US wherein they would agree to provide some concessions in both China and Indo China. In return for these they want an end to the freeze on Japanese assets.

The US rejects this suggestion out of hand and in response the Japanese suggest that Prime Minister Konoye and Roosevelt meet to discuss the issues at stake. The US makes no immediate response to this offer.

* * * * *

- August Ninth -

- Newfoundland -

Churchill and Roosevelt meet at Placentia Bay with their staffs. They discuss the situation in both Europe and the Far East. They agree to send strong warnings to the Japanese that America will enter the war if Japan attacks British or Dutch possessions in the East Indies or Malaya.

They send a joint message to Stalin proposing a

meeting in Moscow to make formal arrangements for the provision of supplies to the Soviet Union.

The two leaders create and sign the *'Atlantic Charter'* and release it to the world press. This document is a basic statement of the principles governing the policies of Britain and America that all countries should have the right to hold free elections and be free from foreign pressure.

* * * * *

- Eastern Front -

German Army Group South, supported by forces from eleventh and Seventeenth Armies, begins to attack along the River Bug.

* * * * *

- August Eleventh -

- Malta -

A British relief convoy sails into Malta.

* * * * *

- China -

Chungking, the nominal capital of Nationalist China, located on the Yangtze River, is bombed heavily by the Japanese.

* * * * *

- Eastern Front -

Finnish forces attack the Russian defenders south of

Lake Ladoga and take Vuosalmi.

* * * * *

- August Twelfth -

- Wolfsschanze -

Hitler issues Directive 34 in which, against the advice of his top Generals, he orders Army Group Center to halt and send troops from the Moscow front to shore up the Leningrad and the Crimean offensives.

* * * * *

- Vichy -

In a radio broadcast, Marshall Petain announces new measures for the suppression of political parties and the creation of a stronger police force, the creation of special courts and that Admiral Darlan is to be appointed to the Ministry of Defense. During his speech he states that Germany is fighting: *'in defense of civilization in the war against the Soviet Union'*.

* * * * *

- North Africa -

A cruiser and two destroyers, supported by two fast minelayers begins to provide relief for the troops holding firm against the siege of Tobruk. Over the next six days they will manage to pull out five thousand beleaguered Australian troops and replace them with six thousand fresh Polish soldiers.

* * * * *

- August Fourteenth -

- Eastern Front -

The Russians begin to evacuate their Black Sea naval base at Nikolayev.

Eight destroyers of the Black Sea Fleet cover the operation as thirteen of the ships under construction which are far enough advanced to be towed away, are removed. One battleship and ten other vessels under construction in early stages are blown up.

* * * * *

- August Seventeenth -

- US -

The US presents a formal warning to the Japanese along the lines that were agreed upon at Placentia Bay. They make no mention of the suggested meeting between the Japanese Prime Minister and Roosevelt.

* * * * *

Eastern Front -

German Army Group South reaches the banks of the Dniepr at Dnepropetrovsk and captures the town.

In the northern sector of the fighting, Novgorod on the shores of Lake Ilmen is also taken.

* * * * *

- August Eighteenth -

In response to rising displeasure from the German

populace Hitler publically orders a halt to *'Action T4'*; the systematic euthanasia of the *'non-productive'* among the citizenry. He does this for three reasons. Firstly he wishes to lessen the public outcry. Secondly, with the full knowledge that the aims of the operation have been pretty well completed, and despite his public order, he intends to instruct those in charge of the program that they may privately continue the practice. Thirdly, Himmler had advised him that he would like to employ the knowledge and abilities of those involved in the system, by expanding them into the concentration camp system in order to erase the mounting pressure of the greatly increasing number of prisoners.

* * * * *

- Eastern Front -

Marshall of the Soviet Union, Seymon Mikhailovich Budyonny, Commander-in-Chief of the Soviet armed forces of the Southwestern Direction, facing the German invasion of the Ukraine, begins to withdraw as many of his troops as possible behind the line of the Dniepr.

In the north, the Germans take Kingisepp on the Luga west of Narva. Heavy fighting breaks out near Novgorod and in the center, fierce engagements between the two sides break out near Gomel.

* * * * *

- August Nineteenth -

- Artic -

A British naval operation evacuates the population of Spitsbergen, taking the Norwegian residents to Britain and the Soviets to Russia.

Other British naval operations take place this month in

the region.

The carrier HMS *'Argus'* arrives in the Soviet Union with a cargo of Hurricanes complete with Royal Air force pilots, who will fly them in combat for the first few weeks.

The carrier HMS *'Victorious'* initiates air attacks against the German installations in an around Tromso, Norway, in early September.

* * * * *

- August Twentieth -

- Eastern Front -

The new German 250th infantry Division, nicknamed the *'Blue Division'* is formed. It is made up of Spanish volunteers and now begins to move toward Poland.

* * * * *

- August Twenty-First -

- Eastern Front -

In the North the Germans take Chudovo which is northeast of Novgorod and in doing so they cut the rail link between Leningrad and Moscow. Further north Finnish troops take Kexholm. In the center sector the Soviets abandon Gomel.

* * * * *

- August Twenty-Second -

- Eastern Front -

German forces close in on Leningrad while its inhabitants frantically improvise fortifications.

* * * * *

- August Twenty-Third -

- Eastern Front -

Second Panzer Group and Second Army, which have been seconded from the German Army Group Center, begins attacks south to link up east of Kiev with the forces of Army Group South.

Most of Hitler's top Generals abhor this move but Hitler remains adamant.

* * * * *

- German Occupied France -

The German commercial raider *'Orion'* returns to the Gironde Estuary in southwestern France from a war patrol that has lasted five hundred and ten days. She has sunk six ships for a total tonnage of thirty-nine thousand and has also assisted her sister raider, the *'Komet'* in the sinking of seven other ships.

* * * * *

- August Twenty-Fourth -

- Eastern Front -

Soviet General Konev leads a Soviet counterattack in the Gomel area. He gains little ground.

In the north the Finnish troops continue to press forward.

* * * * *

- Mediterranean -

With the battleship HMS *'Nelson'* in support, *'Force H'* carries out another offensive operation launching aircraft from HMS *'Ark Royal'* to attack the Italian airfield at Tempio in northern Sardinia. The fleet also lays mines off Leghorn.

The Italian crosier 'Bolzano' is torpedoed by the British submarine *'Triumph'*.

* * * * *

- August Twenty-Fifth -

- Iran -

British and Soviet troops invade Iran to occupy the Abadan oilfields and the important railways and roadways to the Soviet Union which are needed to move war materials.

* * * * *

- August Twenty-Sixth -

- Eastern Front -

The Soviets launch a brief and unsuccessful counterattack against the German position near Velikiye Luki.

* * * * *

- Iran -

British forces take complete control of the Abadan area while the Soviets move down from the north and take Tabiz and bomb Teheran.

* * * * *

- August Twenty-Seventh -

- Eastern Front -

The Germans launch full-scale attacks against the Baltic port of Tallinn.

* * * * *

- Ireland -

A German U-boat is forced to the surface off the Irish coast and it's `Enigma' machine is captured.

* * * * *

- Atlantic -

U-570 operation south of Iceland surfaces right below a patrolling Coastal Command Hudson bomber and is captured. The sub is taken to Iceland and preparations begin to convert it so it can be eventually commissioned by the British as HMS `Graph'.

* * * * *

- Vichy -

Prime Minister Pierre Laval of Vichy and a prominent pro-German newspaper editor are shot and wounded near Versailles by a member of the resistance movement. The Vichy government uses this act as an excuse to round up and imprison many of its opponents, describing them as communists.

---

* * * * *

- August Twenty-Eighth -

- Iran -

Ali Furughi leads a new government which orders a cease fire and begins to negotiate with the British and the Russians.

* * * * *

- Eastern Front -

The Soviets announce that the massive dam over the Dniepr at Zaporozhye has been destroyed.

Russia begins a two day evacuation of its Tallinn garrison by sea. Several convoys attempt to get through to Kronstadt but air attacks and mines are severe and most of the transports are sunk along with a good number of the escorting vessels, which have been supplied by the Soviet Baltic Fleet.

German forces supported by Estonian volunteers, take Tallinn.

* * * * *

- August Twenty-Ninth -

- Eastern Front -

Finnish forces take Viipuri. As has been their intention from the start, they halt their advance when they have reached their former frontier positions. This fact immediately enhances the Soviet's chances of defending Leningrad be removing one flank of the overall Axis attack.

* * * * *

- Iran -

The war here comes to an end. Peace talks begin and final terms are agreed on by the Iranian government early in September.

* * * * *

- Yugoslavia -

Backed by the Germans, General Milan Nedic is appointed to lead the Serbian puppet regime.

* * * * *

- August Thirtieth -

- Eastern Front -

Near Leningrad, the Germans take Mga, cutting the last railroad link between the city of Leningrad and the remainder of Russia.

* * * * *

- August Thirty-First -

- Eastern Front -

The first indications of an intended *'siege'* around Leningrad appear.

CHAPTER SEVENTEEN

- September -

- Wolfsschanze -

On the afternoon of September fifth Hitler cornered Halder and said: *'Get started on the central front within eight to ten days.'*

By this stage in the Nazi regime, all the members who were in the political inner circle or revolved around the edges, were eager to learn whatever they could about Hitler's daily thoughts and intentions. In this way they could keep abreast of The Fuhrer's moods and perhaps more importantly, anticipate his wishes and meet them before having to be asked.

None of those who depended upon Hitler's good graces wanted to be left out of the loop.

That evening at supper Hitler was lighthearted and congenial with his guests. The Fuhrer's mood was noted by Werner Koeppen, Alfred Rosenberg's in-house liaison man at *'Wolfsschanze'*.

Rosenberg, who now held the position of Reich Minister for the Occupied Eastern Territories, had instructed Koeppen to circumspectly record and report to him on Hitler's table conversations during luncheons, the evening meals and late-night soirees.

Since early July, Rosenberg's liaison man had been making notes on his napkin during the daily repasts. After the meals he would transcribe them and then forward the original and a single copy to Berlin for Rosenberg.

Additionally, and unknown to Koeppen, a second man was diligently keeping notes of Hitler's remarks during the daily meals.

Shortly after taking up residence at *'Wolfsschanze'*,

Martin Bormann had offhandedly suggested to his adjutant, Heinrich Heim that he might want to pay attention to what The Fuhrer said at the lunch, dinner and the nightly tea gatherings. He'd indicated that Heim should take care that Hitler was unaware of such activity and that his adjutant should simply rely on his memory and jot down the basics after each meal.

Heim was concerned about relying on his memory as he felt that he might miss some important utterings and instead, on his own initiative, he decided to adopt a more reliable system. During lurch and diner he would sit at the table, with a stack of index cards in his lap and make copious notes, missing nothing as the meal progressed.

Because of the setting, this process was not possible at the evening tea sessions, which took place in the Bunker. At these, like it or not, he was forced to rely on his memory.

Bormann was amazed at the depth and volume his adjutant provided him and not a little paranoid that Hitler would notice what was going on and become upset. However, over time it became apparent to Bormann that the Fuhrer either didn't notice what was going on, or didn't care.

These recorded, spontaneous passages provide a comprehensive and insightful overview of Hitler's innermost thoughts - snippets of his frame of mind on a daily basis as the war progressed.

At dinner on September seventeenth for example, Hitler explained his concept of the spirit of decision, something he had determined was: *'In not hesitating when an inner conviction commands you to act. Last year I needed great spiritual strength to take the decision to attack Bolshevism. I had to foresee that Stalin might pass over to the attack in nineteen forty-one. It was therefore necessary to get started without delay, in order not to be forestalled, and that wasn't possible before June. Even to make war, one must have luck on one's side. When I think of it, what luck we did have!'*

He went on to advise his captive audience of attentive guests that the domination of the world would be determined by the seizure of Russian Territory: *'Thus Europe will be an impregnable fortress, safe from all threat of blockade. All this opens up economic vistas which, one might think, will incline the most liberal of Western democrats toward the New Order. The essential thing, for the moment, is to conquer. After that everything will be simply a question of organization. The Slavs were born slaves who felt the need of a master and Germany's role in Russia would be analogous to that of England in India. Like the English, we shall rule this empire with a handful of men.'*

On one occasion he spoke for some time about his plans to make the Ukraine the granary for all of Europe and how he would keep its people happy by providing them *with 'scarves and glass beads'.*

He then made a confession.

'While everyone else was dreaming of a world peace conference, he preferred to wage war for another ten years rather than be cheated of the spoils of victory'.

At dinner on September twenty-first Hitler was glowing with satisfaction when he told his guests of the capture of one hundred and forty-five thousand prisoners in a valley near Kiev.

At the noon luncheon on September twenty-fifth he revealed his fear of the sub-humans residing farther east. He told them that Europe would be endangered until these Asians had been driven back well behind the Urals Mountains.

'They are brutes, and neither Bolshevism nor Czarism makes any difference...they are brutes in a state of nature.'

Late in the evening on the same day he went on at some length extolling the virtues of battle, likening a soldier's first battle to a woman's first sexual encounter, as if he regarded each as an act of aggression.

'In a few days a youth becomes a man. If I weren't myself hardened by this experience, I would have been incapable of undertaking this Cyclopean task, which the building an empire means for a single man.'

He explained that it was with feeling of pure idealism that he himself had set out for the front in nineteen fourteen.

Patrick Laughy

'Then I saw men falling around me in thousands. Thus I leaned that life is a struggle and has no other object but the preservation of the species.'

Hitler's mind now never shifted far from the war in the east. He was currently obsessed with the seizure of Moscow.

Field Marshall von Bock suggested that with winter coming on, perhaps the German forces should spend the winter months in fortified positions rather than continuing on with the attack. Rested and refreshed, they could then return to the attack when the weather had improved.

Hitler replied:

'Before I became Chancellor, I used to think the General Staff was like a mastiff which had to be held tight by the collar to keep it from attacking anyone in sight.'

He went on to explain that in fact this mastiff had turned out to be anything but ferocious. It had opposed rearmament, the occupation of the Rhineland, the invasion of Austria and Czechoslovakia and even the war in Poland.

'It is I who have always had to goad on this mastiff.'

* * * * *

- Hungary -

At the beginning of *'Operation Barbarossa'*, officials in Hungary, allies of Germany, decided to deport foreign Jews living in Hungary to German occupied territory in Eastern Europe. These Jews were mostly of Polish and Russian decent.

Jews who were unable to establish citizenship were especially vulnerable to deportation and many of the native Hungarian Jews fell into that category and were included in the deportation orders.

By September of nineteen forty-one, approximately twenty thousand Jews had been removed from Hungary.

Added to these numbers were many of the Jewish communities in the Ukraine, like those in Transcarpathia, who were transported en masse after being unceremoniously loaded into freight cars and taken to Korosmezo near the prewar Hungarians-Polish border, where they were turned over to the Germans.

The Germans promptly force-marched these prisoners from Kolomyia to Karmenets-Podolski where *'Einsatzgruppen'* detachments and troops under the command of the *'Higher SS and Police Leader'* for the southern region carried out the mass *'special treatment'* operation which had been decreed as necessary for the proper *'Germanization'* of the occupied territory.

* * * * *

- Minsk Ghetto -

German forces occupied Minsk, the capital of the Belorussian Soviet Socialist Republic (SSR) in the Soviet Union, shortly after the start of *'Operation Barbarossa'*.

Once taken by the military, the SSR became part of the Nazi *'Reichskommissariat Ostland'* (Reich Commissariat Ostland). Within this German civilian administration, Minsk became a district capital with Wilhelm Kube appointed as the German General Commissioner of Belorussia.

Five days after the occupation, two thousand Jewish intelligentsia were executed by the *'Einsatzgruppen'* and from that point on executions of Jews were a common occurrence.

In late July of nineteen forty-one the occupying forces ordered the establishment of a ghetto in a small section of the northwestern part of the city of Minsk.

The Soviet census of nineteen twenty-six listed fifty three thousand, seven hundred Jews as living in Minsk, constituting approximately forty-one percent of the entire population of the city.

Jews were rounded up from the area surrounding Minsk and herded together into the new ghetto along with the Jewish occupants of the city. In total, approximately eighty thousand were crowded into the new holding area.

* * * * *

- Concentration Camps -

Heavy secrecy remains draped solidly over the operation of all Nazi concentration camps.

Prisoners, primarily transported by rail and crammed into cattle cars, often do not survive the trip. Those that do, arrived in a state of hunger and exhaustion.

Upon their arrival at the camps, any personal property they had been allowed to pack and bring with them, was seized and they were issued a set of clothing which included a navy and white-striped trousers and shirt; a spoon, a bowl and a cup.

Each prisoner was allotted space in the tiers of wooden bunks in huts which were by this point containing up to three times the number of persons for which the structures were originally intended.

The conditions surrounding a prisoner's daily life worsened as the war progressed.

The diet bordered on starvation. Health and hygiene conditions and lack of water aided the spread of disease and epidemics, especially outbreaks of typhus and spotted fever, which were regular occurrences.

Medical services were restricted to that of the camp doctor and his prisoner assistant(s). Little real medical help was realistically on offer from these practitioners.

By nineteen forty-one the problem of body disposal had reached a critical point. Initially the camp's dead were buried in common graves, but by this point in the war that was no longer a practical solution.

There were simply too many bodies.

For example, in the autumn of nineteen-forty-one several weeks after the start of Germany's war with the Soviet Republic, Russian prisoners of war were being assigned to Dachau in the thousands - this at a time when an ever-growing influx of political prisoners, anti-socials and Jews from captured territory were also being added to the soaring camp population.

Many of these prisoners were never officially registered and the actual numbers of unregistered deaths taking place on a daily basis behind the camp fences will never be known.

It is common knowledge that at this time the crematorium built in nineteen-forty in the north-west corner of the camp was operating night and day, the ovens glowed red and massive trenches were needed for the disposal of the accumulated ashes.

* * * * *

- Vilna Ghetto -

At the end of the Great War, both Poland and Lithuania had claimed Vilna (Vilnius), as their territory. Polish forces occupied it in nineteen-twenty and at the outbreak of World War II, Vilna was considered part of northeastern Poland.

Under the agreement Hitler had made with Stalin in the German/Soviet Pact, Vilna, along with the rest of eastern Poland, was occupied by Soviet forces in September of nineteen-thirty-nine. In October of that year the Russians had transferred the Vilna region to Lithuanian.

Once *'Operation Barbarossa'* was launched, the Soviets re-occupied Lithuania. In August of nineteen-forty, the Russians incorporated Vilna, along with the rest of Lithuania into the Greater Soviet Union.

The German army marched into Vilna three days after the start of their *'Blitzkrieg'.*

In early September of nineteen forty-one the Germans adopted a new policy with regard to ghetto construction. They established not one, but two ghettos in Vilna, one for those who could be used for slave labourers and the other, for those Jews who they considered as incapable of work.

Those in that second group, useless to the new Reich, were concentrated in ghetto number two.

In September of nineteen forty-one, the Germans set up a factory in the northeastern suburb of Lvov, on Janowska Street. It became part of the network of factories owned and operated by the SS which were called *'Deutsche Ausruestungswerke'*, or DAW (German Armament Works).

Jews working here were forced-labourers and worked primarily in carpentry and metalwork.

The Germans finished a camp to house them adjacent to the factory, in early October of nineteen forty-one.

* * * * *

- Lithuanian Jews -

The Jewish population of Lithuania had grown considerably as the Germans began to march into, and quickly occupy Poland in nineteen thirty-nine. Approximately two hundred and fifty thousand Jews now resided in Lithuania, their numbers having been bolstered by refugees who had fled Poland ahead of the invading Nazi troops.

As had the authorities in other German occupied territories; the Lithuanians carried out pogroms against the unwanted Jewish population, both shortly before and immediately after the arrival of the German forces.

The *'Einsatzgruppen'* who moved in after the occupation, were joined enthusiastically by Lithuanian auxiliaries, began executing the unwanted Jews. By the end of August nineteen forty-one, most of the Jews residing in in rural Lithuania had been dealt with.

* * * * *

- Einsatzgruppen -

- Babi Yar -

One of the largest organized executions perpetrated by

the *'Einsatzgruppen'* took place just outside of Kiev, at Babi Yar.

Babi Yar is the name of a large ravine situated just northwest of the Ukrainian capital city, Kiev.

German forces entered Kiev in September of nineteen forty-one.

During the first days of the occupation, several buildings which were being used by the German Army were blown up. Most likely this was done by the Soviet Secret Police (NKVD).

The Germans conveniently blamed the Jews for the explosions.

In a meeting, the military governor, Major-General Kurt Eberhard; Police Commander for Army Group South, SS-Obergruppenfuhrer Friedrich Jeckeln; and *'Einsatzgruppe'* C Commander, Otto Rasch decided to use this act of civil disobedience as an excuse to make a public example of what could be expected from the Germans in answer to any such act of open defiance.

They decided to demonstrate their displeasure by executing the entire Jewish population of the city.

At this time there were approximately sixty thousand Jews residing in Kiev.

In late September, the Germans posted notices requiring all Jews to report for resettlement outside the city of Kiev. Failure to report was made a capital offense.

Masses of Jews reported as ordered and were directed to proceed along Melnik Street toward the Jewish cemetery and Babi Yar. Once they were within proximity of the ravine and under guard, the Jews were directed to hand over all their valuables and to disrobe.

The lines of naked victims were then shepherded into the actual ravine where they were shot in small groups. The executions continued for two days. Approximately thirty-three thousand were killed in this single operation.

The actual executions were carried out by *'Sunderkommando'* *'Special Unit'* 4A, soldiers of

'Einsatzgruppen' C, aided by the *'Sicherheitsdienst des Reichsfuhrer's-SS'* (SD); SS-Police Battalions; who were enthusiastically backed by the local police.

In the months that followed, the ravine called Babi Yar was repeatedly used as an execution site and mass grave for thousands of additional Jews and many so called *'sub-humans'* including gypsies, Soviet POW's, Ukrainian Nationalists and civilian hostages.

An estimated total of one hundred, to one hundred and fifty thousand additional victims, met their end at Babi Yar.

* * * * *

- Albert Widmann -

Albert Widmann was born in Stuttgart on the eighth of June nineteen-twelve.

He studied at the Stutgart Technical institute and received his certificate in chemical engineering in nineteen thirty-six and his doctorate in September of nineteen thirty-eight.

Shortly after graduation Widmann was hired by Walter Heess, the chief of the *'Kriminaltechnisches Institut'* (KTI) (Technical Institute for the Detection of Crime), who had previously employed him as a temporary consultant.

By nineteen-forty Widmann had been promoted to chief of the KTI's section for chemical analysis.

In his younger years, Widmann had not been particularly interested in politics, but along with some other students, he had in nineteen thirty-three, joined *the 'Nationalsozialistisches Kraffahrkorps'* (NSKK) (National Socialist Motor Corps). As a result he was incorporated into the Nazi party in May of nineteen thirty-seven.

When Widmann joined the KTI in December of nineteen thirty-nine he was transferred from the NSKK to the SS with the rank of *'SS-Untersturmfuhrer'* (Second Lieutenant).

When the euthanasia program (Action T4) was

contemplated, Widmann became immediately involved. Although not directly employed in the operation, he and his KTI office provided the program with the needed support service and he took part in the early discussions about killing methods.

In this capacity he took part in the early gassing experiments at the *'NS-Totungsanstalt Brandenburg'* (Brandenburg Euthanasia Center), an old jail that was officially known as the *'Landes-Pflegeanstalt Brandenburg a. H.'* (Brandenburg an der Havel State Welfare Institute), which was established in nineteen thirty-nine as an euthanasia center.

His job there was to instruct and teach the proper gassing method, for example how to measure the correct dose of carbon monoxide.

It was Widmann who submitted the paperwork for the carbon monoxide gas need for the T4 killing centres and the *'medicines'* needed for the euthanasia in children's wards and *'wild'* euthanasia hospitals that operated within the T-4 program.

It was to Albert Widmann that SS-Brigadefuhrer Artur Nebe turned when he needed to satisfy Himmler's order to find ways to minimize the psychological impact that *'special - handling'* teams experienced during mass killings.

Widmann eagerly stepped in to offer his expertise in the area and discussed with the director of the Criminal Police Technological Institute, Dr. Hess; methods for using carbon monoxide gas from vehicle exhaust for a killing operation in the east, based on the experience gained from the euthanasia programme.

Widmann headed for Minsk to meet with Nebe; with four hundred kilograms of explosive material and a selection of metal pipes, that would be required for planned experiments in using carbon monoxide.

They tried the explosives first. Locking twenty five mentally ill people into two bunkers in a forest outside Minsk they set their explosives.

The first explosion killed only some of them and it took

much time and trouble until the second explosion managed to kill the rest.

The two of them decided that the use of explosives in any practical operation of mass killing would be completely unsatisfactory.

They moved from there to a local lunatic asylum located at Mogilev. Here they placed between twenty and thirty of the inmates into a room that they had sealed hermetically and had two holes driven thought the outer wall and pipes run through.

They then parked a car outside and used one of the metal pipes that Widmann had brought to connect the exhaust of the car to one of the pipes sticking out of the wall.

The car was started and the carbon monoxide began seeping into the room. After eight minutes, the people in the room were still alive. Widmann and Nebe then had a second car connected to the other pipe and with the two cars operation simultaneously, all those in the room were dead within a few minutes.

After these experiments, Nebe came to the conclusion that what was needed was a truck equipped with a hermetically sealed box which could be moved from location to location to be utilized as a mobile gas chamber. Once such a vehicle had been filled with its human cargo, the exhaust could then be piped directly into the box.

Nebe ironed out the technical aspects of the idea with Dr. Heess and together they brought the proposal to Heydrich, who immediately adopted it.

At Heydrich's order, The Technical Department of the Reich Security Main Office, headed by SS-Obersturmbannfuhrer, Walter Rauff, developed the concept of a special vehicle to be used for the purpose of mobile euthanasia. His resulted in two basic vehicles being slated for construction, a small one and a large one.

The small model could handle about fifty persons in a single operation and the larger approximately seventy.

The 4th Reich

* * * * *

- Action 14f13 -

Hitler's chosen Head of the T4 program had at the time been the head of his Chancellery, Reichsleiter Phillipp Bouhler.

Bouhler had been given the task of overseeing the euthanization of Germany's mentally ill, disabled, and inmates of hospitals and nursing homes who the party had deemed as unsuitable for citizenship in the new Reich.

With the demands for the services provided by the T4 rapidly lessening as the unwanted domestic population had already been effectively dealt with, Bouhler had suggested to Himmler that he could use the same type of process to relieve the crowded conditions now facing the concentration camps.

They reached an agreement and the set up for such an operation using T4 staff began in April of Nineteen forty-one. The first known inmate selection for the process was conducted at Sachsenhausen concentration camp in that month.

This pilot project worked well, with at least four hundred prisoners being *'retired'* by summer.

* * * * *

- Sonnenstein Euthanasia Center -

As part of T4 program, six death institutes had been set up across Germany in nineteen forty and forty-one. These institutes were responsible for gassing seventy thousand mentally ill and mentally retarded patients gleaned from psychiatric institutions, old people's homes, nursing homes and hospitals.

One of these institutions was located in Pin-Sonnenstein. Initially it functioned under the direction of doctor Horst Schumann and subsequently by doctors Kurt Borm, Klaus Endruweit, Curt Schmalenbach and Ewald Wortmann.

Patrick Laughy

In the spring of nineteen-forty the Berlin headquarters of T4 took control of a complex of four buildings on the site of Pin-Sonnenstein which had originally been a mental institution of some repute. They screened off these four buildings from the rest of the hospital, surrounding it with a wall on the sides facing the Elbe River and the car park and on the remaining side put up a high board fence to shield its operation.

In the cellar of one of these hospital buildings, they installed a gas chamber and an attached crematorium.

By the end of June in nineteen-forty the institute had begun operations. In the years nineteen-forty and nineteen forty-one the program employed approximately one hundred, consisting of doctors, nurses, drivers, carers, office workers and police.

This was Germany, and an efficient and effective procedure for the operation of the facility had been properly mandated prior to the doors opening for business.

Like clockwork, several time per week, patients were brought in from mental and nursing homes in busses with blacked out windows. After passing the entrance gate to the institution, which was guarded by a police detachment, the patients were taken to the ground floor of Block C 16 where they were separated, by sex, by care workers and then placed into separate reception rooms. From here they were individually taken to another room where they were presented to a panel of two doctors from the institute. It was these doctors who decided on *'what the listed cause for the death would be'* and then issued a corresponding death certificate.

Following this *'examination'*, the patients were asked to disrobe in yet another room in preparation for *'showers'*, under the supervision of nurse and carers.

Once twenty to thirty had been gathered from this process, they were led into a gas chamber fitted out like a shower room with several shower heads located in the ceiling. The staff then closed the steel hermetically sealed door to the gas chamber. A doctor then opened the cock on a carbon monoxide cylinder and observed the death process which took up to thirty minutes.

After another twenty minutes the gas was extracted from the room and the corpses were collected from the gas chamber by *'stokers'* and cremated in two coke ovens supplied by the firm of Kori from Berlin.

Before cremation, selected patients were dissected by the doctor and any gold teeth removed. After cremation, the ashes were dumped on the institute rubbish dump or shovelled over the bank of the River Elbe behind the building at night.

To complete the process, the Sonnenstein Registry Office would send the victims' families a death certificate and a standard *'letter of condolence'*.

As a result of T4's offer to assist Himmler, the organization morphed easily, seemingly naturally dovetailing its operation to meet the Reichsfuhrer's new need to deal with his camp crowding issues.

Over the summer of nineteen forty-one; over one thousand inmates from concentration camps also went through this process at Pima-Sonnenstein, courtesy of the now expanded T4 program.

Individuals from Sachsenhausen, Buchenwald and Auschwitz, all camps which had no gas chambers of their own at the time, met their end at the Sonnenstein Euthanasia Center.

* * * * *

- Zyklon B -

The cyanide-based pesticide called Zyklon B was invented at the Kaiser Wilhelm Institute for Physical Chemistry and Electrochemistry in Berlin in early nineteen twenty-two by Walter Heerdt.

It was a very effective product for use in fumigation and was used worldwide after its creation. It was being produced in Germany when the Nazis came to power and is still being produced in the Czech Republic.

At Hitler's rise to power, Zyklon B was being produced

by the massive IG Farben Company.

The product was currently being used in the concentration camps to fumigate lice ridden clothing and buildings, for which purpose, it produced excellent results.

On September third, nineteen forty-one, an experiment involving the use of this product for an additional function was conducted at Auschwitz concentration camp.

Six hundred soviet prisoners and two hundred and fifty sick, Polish prisoners, were used in the experiment.

As explained by Rudolf Hoess, the commandant of Auschwitz at the time, two hermetically sealed rooms were used in this trial run.   Bunker number 1 held eight hundred men and Bunker number 2 held twelve hundred.

Once the two chambers were full and the doors securely closed, solid pellets of Zyklon B were dropped into the chambers through pipes in the side walls thus releasing cyanide gas when the product got wet. About one third of those inside the gas chambers died almost immediately and the remainder over a period of twenty minutes.   The speed of death was dependent on how close the specific person was to a gas vent.

SS doctor, Johann Kremer, who oversaw the gassing, would later testify that the: *'shouting and screaming of the victims could be heard though the opening and it was clear that they fought for their lives'*.

The experiment was considered by those observing, as a clear success.

* * * * *

- Blitzkrieg Russia -

In September of nineteen forty-one, German forces were at the gates of Leningrad in the north, Smolensk in the center, and Dnepropetrovsk in the south.   They were on the Road to Moscow.

The news was all good.

Two factors were about to raise their ugly heads and

would now begin to affect the campaign.

Geography and weather.

Moscow is approximately one thousand miles from Berlin.

Winter was coming in Russia.

The German army in the east was far from home. It was tired. Its supplies lines were hampered by the sheer distance both men and material had to travel in order to reach the front.

Under Hitler's leadership, the Military leaders of the Nazi forces had envisioned a rapid surrender from the Russians, two to four months at the most. Consequently the invading German troops had been neither militarily equipped, nor dressed, for winter fighting.

* * * * *

- Count von Stauffer -

Karl had arranged for an immediate meeting with SS-General Dieter Bichler, his man in charge of *'Operation Fatherland's'* security unit, as soon as Wilhelm had shown him the report that Himmler's chief aide had earlier presented to him.

After setting up a meeting for lunch with the General by phone, the Count had his secretary make a copy of the document for his own use and returned the original to his son.

They shared a coffee and briefly discussed some family matters, then Wilhelm left the matter in his father's hands and returned to his duties at SS headquarters.

Just under an hour later, Karl von Stauffer was sitting with the General at a small table tucked away in the corner apart from the main eating area, at a small café located near his office.

Once their order had been taken the Count withdrew the folded report from his inner tunic and opened it before spreading it flat on the table and pushing it across toward

Bichler.

The General placed his monocle in his one good eye and began to read the document. When he had finished he replaced his eyepiece in his pocket and refolded the document before slipping it into his pocket.

He looked up at the Count and inclined his head slightly.

"If you will excuse me for a few moments General; I don't think this should wait…I will see if I might use the house phone to make a call."

* * * * *

- Gabriella -

It was a beautiful sunny day and Gabriella was as excited as a child about to be given a promised new toy.

Her car had been shipped from Berlin and she was impatiently awaiting its scheduled arrival. She stood on the platform of Oslo's main station beside her husband's aide, Hans Biermann, who had driven her to the station, eagerly watching as the freight train slowly puffed its way into the rail yards and began to shunt onto a branch line some distance from where they stood.

It was a fairly large freight, consisting primarily of flatcars containing light military vehicles destined for use by the occupying forces.

As the last few of these came briefly into view from behind other stationary lines of standing freight cars, Gabriella spotted a much smaller tarp covered vehicle sitting all on its own in the centre of a flatcar.

She jumped up and down breathlessly, looking more than a little ridiculous in consideration of her state of advancing pregnancy, and Hans broke into spontaneous laughter as she shouted.

"That must be it, daddy did it… my beautiful baby is really here!"

She beamed as she turned to the young SS officer.

"Quickly Hans, see to the unloading…and have them be careful…I can hardly wait to get behind the wheel and drive her again."

CHAPTER EIGHTEEN

- September -

- British Air Operations -

Selected targets for Bomber Command include Stettin, Hamburg and Cologne. Northern German ports and Brest are hit again due to their naval value but these do little damage to the German fleets.

The now regular fighter and fighter bomber attacks over northern France also continue.

* * * * *

- Naval Operations -

There is an increase in Allied shipping losses. Eighty-four ships for a total of two hundred and eighty-five thousand, nine hundred tons go to the bottom. U-boats account for fifty-three of the ships for two hundred and two thousands, eight hundred tons. Some U-boats are shifted into the Mediterranean.

* * * * *

- North Africa -

Italian agents steal the *'Black Code'* book from the US embassy in Rome. Possession of this document gives the Italians a clear window into the plans and dispositions of the British Eighth Army.

* * * * *

- Yugoslavia -

Tito's Partisans begin active resistance operations in southwest Serbia.

* * * * *

- September First -

- Eastern Front -

With the assistance of the Finnish armies in the North, the attacking German forces are now within artillery range of Leningrad. To the east of city the advance is nearing the south shore of Lake Ladoga.

* * * * *

- Serbia -

In Serbia, a pro-German *'Government of National Salvation'* is created under Milan Nedic.

* * * * *

- USA -

The US Atlantic Fleet forms a *'Denmark Straight'* patrol supplied by two heavy cruisers and four destroyers. The US navy is now ordered to escort convoys in the Atlantic comprising ships of all nations provided that at least one American ship is present in the convoy.

* * * * *

- September Third -

- USA -

The Japanese are *'officially'* advised that the US is not interested participating in the Japanese proposed meeting between Roosevelt and Konoye.

* * * * *

- September Fourth -

- Battle of the Atlantic -

Operating in a convoy protection action, the US destroyer *'Greer'* is attacked by a German U-boat after being called into action by reports from a British aircraft. The German U-boat Captain mistakes her for a British warship and fires a torpedo and the USS *'Greer'* replies with a depth charge attack.

In a public reaction to the incident, President Roosevelt holds it up as an example of German aggression. Tension between the two nations is ramped up and the US commits to conducting convoy duties between the Western Hemisphere and Europe.

* * * * *

- September Fifth -

- Eastern Front -

German troops occupy Estonia.

* * * * *

- September Sixth -

- Tokyo -

Prime Minister Konoye gives in to military pressure

and agrees that, in view of declining oil stocks, war preparations should be completed by mid-October and if no agreement can be reached by then which will provide oil to Japan; the *'rising sun'* should go to war to get it.

* * * * *

- Occupied Europe -

Heydrich orders that all Jews over the age of six are to wear a distinguishing yellow *'Star of David'* badge.

* * * * *

- September Seventh -

- Berlin -

Bomber Command hits the German capitol in a heavy attack.

* * * * *

- September Eighth -

- Eastern Front -

Finnish forces cross the Svir River and take Lodenoye Pole, cutting the railroad track south from Murmansk to Leningrad. The siege of Leningrad begins.

Stalin orders that all *'Volga Deutsche'* be deported to Siberia.

* * * * *

- Mediterranean -

The transport of a further sixty-nine Hurricane fighters to Malta by *'Force H'* begins, using first, HMS *'Ark Royal'* and then both she and HMS *'Furious'*.

* * * * *

- September Ninth -

- Eastern Front -

A Spanish volunteer force, the *'Blue Division'* begins service on the Leningrad Front in support of the German forces.

* * * * *

- September Tenth -

- Eastern Front -

Guderian's attack southward east of Kiev reaches Konotop and Kleist's First Panzer Group begins to break out of their bridgehead over the Dniepr around Kremenchug.
The German armies have now nearly surrounded Kiev.

* * * * *

- September Eleventh -

- USA -

Still fuming over the USS 'Greer' incident, Roosevelt orders the US Navy to shoot on sight, if any ship or convoy being escorted is threatened.

* * * * *

- September Twelfth -

- Norway -

The German puppet *'Quisling'* government bans the Boy Scouts and other youth organizations. All boys of age are now obligated to join the youth sections of the Nasjaonal Samling Party.

* * * * *

- Eastern Front -

Guerin and Kleist link up near the town of Lokhvista, encircling a huge Soviet force between there and Kiev, one hundred miles to the west. The pocket contains over six hundred thousand Russian troops.

North of Kiev, Chernigov, on the banks of the Desna River, is evacuated as the German Second Army attacks.

* * * * *

- North Africa -

A renewed series of relief operation is undertaken for Tobruk. The first transports begin the task of bringing in sixty-three hundred men and a huge quantity of supplies, while taking out six thousand of the Australians.

The replacement troops this time are coming from General Scobie's 70th British Division.

* * * * *

- September Fifteenth -

- Estonia -

The German military administration sets up a puppet *'self-government'* under their chosen man. Hjalmar Mae.

* * * * *

- USA -

The US Attorney General rules that the Neutrality Act does not prevent US ships from carrying war material to British possessions.

* * * * *

- Eastern Front -

German forces capture Schlusselburg on the south shore of Lake Ladoga, east of Leningrad. This isolates the city completely from overland contact with the rest of the Soviet Union.

While some supplies may still be able to be moved by boat across the lake, the city has on hand only stores for about one month and that only after strict rationing is put into place.

Leningrad is now under siege and faces a bleak future indeed.

* * * * *

- September Sixteenth -

- Iran -

Dissatisfied with the Shah, who they feel has not seriously undertaken the removal of all Axis nationalists from the country, the Allied forces decide to occupy Teheran. The Shah abdicates in favour of the Crown Prince, Mohammad Reza Pahlavi and British and Soviet troops move into the capital.

---

* * * * *

- September Seventeenth -

- Atlantic -

The US Navy again increases its commitment to escort Atlantic convoys. It begins to take over responsibility for some of the Halifax to UK convoys and also most of the Iceland traffic.

The much-expanded Royal Canadian Navy is now escorting all other convoys as far as 22 degrees west to the point where the British Navy can relieve them from their duties and take up the responsibility for convoy protection onward to British ports.

* * * * *

- Eastern Front -

German forces at Kiev begin heavy attacks and gain some ground into the outskirts of the Ukrainian capital.

* * * * *

- September Eighteenth -

- USA -

President Roosevelt asks Congress for an additional five billion, nine hundred and eighty five million dollars for Lend-Lease projects.

* * * * *

- September Nineteenth -

- Eastern Front -

Kiev falls to the Germans after more than forty days of fighting. The Russians have lost in excess of five hundred thousand men to the German's loss of one hundred thousand.

* * * * *

- Yugoslavia -

Tito and Mihajljovic meet to discuss joint resistance against the Germans.

They quarrel however, Mihajljovic seeing Tito as an anti-Royalist troublemaker who wants to muscle in on the Serbian territory that Mihajljovic regards as his own preserve. In turn Tito sees Mihajljovic as a bourgeois representative of an already discredited officer corps.

They agree to meet again on the twenty-sixth of October, but their supporters soon begin fighting openly with each other.

* * * * *

- September Twentieth -

- Mediterranean -

The Italians send midget submarines into the Harbour of Gibraltar and succeed in sinking two ships.

* * * * *

- Atlantic -

An aircraft launched from the British escort carrier HMS *'Audacity'* shoots down a German convoy-shadowing FW Condor in the first success by one of these new type of escort vessels.

It is good news for those with high hopes for the new class of ships. However, the celebrating is short-lived in that, in the end, the convoy, designated OG-74, loses six of its twenty seven ships before it reaches port.

* * * * *

- September Twenty-Third -

- USA -

President Roosevelt announces that the US is considering the arming of its merchant shipping against possible German attacks.

* * * * *

- September Twenty-Fourth -

- Mediterranean -

The first of six patrolling German U-boats manages to slip past Gibraltar and break out into the Mediterranean.

'Operation Halberd' is launched by the British in a major effort to carry supplies from Gibraltar to Malta. Escorted by three battleships, one carrier, five cruisers and eighteen destroyers; nine transports make up the convoy.

* * * * *

- Eastern Front -

Advance tank forces of German Army Group South reach to within forty miles of Kharkov.

* * * * *

- London/Washington -

Fifteen governments sign the Atlantic Charter. They include the UK, USA, USSR, and the countries of the British Empire and many of the now exiled governments of Europe.

* * * * *

- September Twenty-Fifth -

- Eastern Front -

Having now isolated the Soviet forces in the Crimea, the Germans, with support from parachute troops, launch attacks near Perekop.

* * * * *

- September Twenty-Sixth -

- East Africa -

The Italian garrison at Wolchefit surrenders to the besieging 15th East Africa Brigade. Four thousand prisoners are taken.

* * * * *

- Mediterranean -

Italian Admiral, Iachino, leads a fleet of two battleships, six cruisers and fourteen destroyers out of port to intercept the British convoy en route from Gibraltar to Malta.

* * * * *

- USA -

The US Naval Command orders an all-out war on Axis shipping in American waters.

* * * * *

- Czechoslovakia -

The German governor of Bohemia and Moravia resigns his post. Reinhard Heydrich is chosen to replace him.

* * * * *

- USA -

The first batch, consisting of fourteen so named *'Liberty ships'* is launched. Another three hundred and twelve are on order.

* * * * *

- September Twenty-Seventh -

- Greece -

The *'National Liberation Front '*(EAM), the main group of Greek resistance fighters, is founded.

* * * * *

- Mediterranean -

Both the British and the Italian fleets send out air reconnaissance in order to try to locate the other. Neither side has any success.

Patrick Laughy

* * * * *

- September Twenty-Eighth -

- Ukraine -

German *'Einzengruppen'* troops exterminate over thirty thousand Jews at Babi Yar.

* * * * *

- Greece -

The first resistance uprising in the Drama region against the Bulgarian occupation begins.

* * * * *

- Czechoslovakia -

Heydrich imposes martial law on six districts.

* * * * *

- Moscow -

The conference suggested at Placentia by Churchill and Roosevelt takes place. Harriman is the US representative and Beaverbrook leads the British delegation.

* * * * *

- September Twenty-Ninth -

- Czechoslovakia -

Heydrich has Prime Minister Elias arrested and imposes

many more strict measures, very quickly building himself a vile reputation within the country.

* * * * *

- Artic -

Convoy PQ-1, consisting of ten ships, safely passes from Iceland to the Russian port of Arkhangelsk (Archangel) under the protection of one cruiser and two destroyers. In the same time period, QP-1 sails unmolested from Arkhangelsk to Scapa Flow.

* * * * *

- September Thirtieth -

- Easter Front -

As Hitler had demanded, Bock launches the attack on Moscow in force.

The operation is codenamed *'Typhoon'*.

With the battle for Kiev won, Guderian's Second Panzer Army begins to move north again where it is to form the right wing of the German attack upon on the Soviet capital.

The plan of attack uses sixty-nine divisions to destroy the central Soviet forces with a drive that is aimed to use a double tank envelopment with the pincers meeting eighty miles behind the Red Army before advancing on Moscow itself.

CHAPTER NINETEEN

- October -

- Inside Hitler's Mind -

- Wolfsschanze/Berlin -

The launch of a major offensive so late in the year, with the Russian winter setting in, was simply unconceivable to those in the Soviet High Command.

It came as such a shock that Guderian's Second Panzer Army was able to slice through the Soviet lines like a hot knife through butter. His armour easily ploughed its way through defensive positions and managed to travel an astounding fifty miles toward its target in the first twenty-four hours of the offensive, causing the infantry to race to keep pace and mop up the small, demoralized Russian pockets of crumbling resistance.

After reading the initial reports of the operational successes being achieved and confident of a swift victory in *'Typhoon'*, a delighted Fuhrer decides, on October the second, to board his private train and return to Berlin.

On the afternoon of October third, after months of making no public appearances, Hitler speaks at the *'Sportspalast'* at an event organized to appeal for support for the *'Kiegswinterhilfswerk'* (Wartime Winter Assistance Program).

In his opening speech, speaking quietly, enunciating carefully, slowly and concisely, and confidently for the most part, he offers the Massive German audience his reasons for the war against Russia.

Hitler was an astoundingly proficient orator.

Part of that speech.

The 4th Reich

'Always in an effort to limit the scope of the war, I decided in nineteen thirty-nine to do something...that you, my dear party comrades, know firsthand how difficult it was for me to do. I then sent my Minister to Moscow. That meant the most bitter triumph over my feelings. But at such a moment, one man's feelings have to subside, when the welfare of millions are at stake. I tried to reach an understanding. You know best of all how honest and frankly I've kept our obligations and commitments. Neither in our press nor at our meetings was a single word about Russia mentioned. Not a single word about bolshevism. Unfortunately, the other side did not observe their obligations from the beginning. This arrangement resulted in a betrayal which at first liquidated the whole northeast of Europe. You know best what it meant for us to look on in silence as the Finnish people were being strangled. And how it felt for me as a soldier, to stand idly by as a powerful state tries to dominate a small one. Yet I remained silent. I took a decision only when I saw that Russia had reached the hour to advance against us...at a moment when we had only a bare three divisions in East Prussia... when twenty-two Soviet divisions were assembled there. We gradually received proof that on our frontiers one airdrome after another was set up...and one division after another from the gigantic Soviet Army was being assembled there. I was then obliged to become anxious for this is no excuse in history for negligence...like claiming afterwards that I didn't think it was possible, or that I didn't believe it. I now stand at the top of the Reich, and thus I am responsible for the present German people and its future. I was therefore compelled slowly to take defensive measures.'

At this point the audience broke out in wild spontaneous applause and Hitler had to pause slightly before he was able to continue the speech.

'But in August and September of last year one thing was becoming clear. A decision in the West with England which would have contained...the whole German Luftwaffe was no longer possible, for in my rear there stood a State which...was

getting ready to proceed against me at such a moment...but it is only now that we realize how far the preparation had advanced. I wanted once again to clarify the whole problem and therefore I invited Molotov to Berlin. He put to me the four well-known conditions. One. Germany should finally agree that, as Russia felt herself again endangered by Finland, Russia should be able to liquidate Finland. I could not help but to refuse such consent.'

Once again a round of applause broke out and the Fuhrer waited for it to die down before he continued.

'The second question concerned Rumania...Two. A question whether a German guarantee would protect Rumania against Russia. Here, too, I stand by my word. I do not regret it, for I have found in General Antonescu a man of honor who at the time blindly stood by his word.'

A heartfelt round of applause.

'The third question referred to Bulgaria. Molotov demanded that Russia should retain the right to send garrisons to Bulgaria and thus to give a Russian guarantee to Bulgaria. What this means we know from Estonia, Latvia and Lithuania. The fourth question referred to the Dardanelles. Four. Russia demanded bases on the Dardanelles. If Molotov is now trying to deny this, that is not surprising. If tomorrow or the day after tomorrow he will be no longer in Moscow, he will deny that he is no longer in Moscow.'

Sustained Applause and cheering.

'He made this demand and I rejected it. I had to reject it. This made things clear to me and further talks were without result. My precautions were called for'

Cutting him off, a voice from the audience cried out *'We thank our Fuhrer!'* The statement was then soundly applauded by all in attendance.

'After that I carefully watched Russia. Each division we could observe was carefully noted and counter-measures were taken'.

Polite applause.

'The position in May had so far advanced that I could

no longer dismiss the thought of a life and death conflict. At that time I had always to remain silent, and that was doubly difficult for me...perhaps not so difficult with regard to the German people for they had to realize there...are moments when one cannot talk if one does not wish to endanger the whole nation. More difficult...'

Applause.

'...was silence for me with regard to my soldiers, who, division by division...stood on the eastern frontier of the Reich and yet did not know what was actually going on. And it was just on account of them I could not speak. Had I dropped one single word I would not have changed Stalin's decision. But the possibility of surprise, which remained for me as a last weapon, would then not have existed. Any such indication, any such hint, would have cost lives of hundred thousands of our comrades.'

Applause.

'I was therefore silent until the moment when I finally decided to take the first step myself. When I see the enemy levelling his rifle at me I am not going to wait till he presses the trigger. I would rather be the first to press the trigger.'

Loud applause.

'This was the most difficult decision of my whole life for every such step opened up the gate behind...which secrets are hidden so that posterity will know how it came about and how it happened. Thus one can only rely on one's conscience, the confidence of one's people...one's own weapons and what one asks of the Almighty. Not that He supports inaction but He blesses him who is himself ready and willing to fight and make sacrifices for his existence. On June twenty-second, in the morning, the greatest battle in the history of the world started. Since then something like three and a half months have elapsed and here I say this: Everything since then has proceeded according to plan.'

Extended applause.

'That I can say now, I say it only today because I can say that this enemy is already broken and will never rise

---

again!'

Several minutes of shouts of support and cheers.

'Her power had been assembled against Europe, of which...unfortunately most had no idea and many even today have no idea. This would have been a second storm of Ghengis Khan. That this danger was averted we owe in the first place to the bravery, endurance and ...sacrifice of the German soldiers...'

Applause.

'...and also the sacrifice of those who marched with us. For the first time something like a European awakening passed through this continent. In the north, Finland is fighting, a true nation of heroes...'

Applause.

'...for in her wide spaces she relies on her own strength, her bravery and tenacity. In the south, Rumania is fighting.'

Applause.

'It has recuperated with astonishing speed from one of the most difficult crises that may befall a country and the people are led by a man at once brave and quick at making decisions.'

Applause.

'This embraces the whole width of this battlefield from the Arctic Ocean to the Black Sea. Our German soldiers are now fighting in these areas and with them in their ranks, Finns, Italians, Hungarians, Rumanians, Slovaks, Croats and Spaniards are now going into battle.'

Applause.

'Belgians, Netherlanders, Danes, Norwegians and even Frenchmen have joined.'

Hitler received a standing ovation at this point and then he began offering his delighted audience some impressive statistics.

Two million, five hundred thousand prisoners taken, twenty-two thousand captured or destroyed artillery pieces, eighteen thousand captured or destroyed tanks, the destruction of over fourteen thousand, and five hundred aircraft.

Over twenty fire thousand kilometres of Russian railway captured and now converted to the German narrow gauge; an advancement of one thousand kilometres into Soviet territory as the crow flies!

Tempering the elated response from his listeners, he went on to say.

'The war in the East is one of ideologies, therefore all the best elements in Germany must now be welded into one indissoluble community. Only when the entire German people becomes a single community of sacrifice can we hope and expect that Providence will stand by us in the future. Almighty God never helped a lazy man. Nor does he help a coward.'

The next day Hitler returned to *'Wolfsschanze',* and Koeppen noted that at supper he was in a very good mood.

* * * * *

At lunch on October sixth, Hitler's choice of topics was the underground activity taking place in Czechoslovakia.

He determined that the best way to deal with this problem was the: *'deportation of all Jews far to the East.'* He expanded on this topic by suggesting that since Jews were the source through which all enemy information was spread, they should also begin deporting Jews from Berlin and Vienna to the same locale.

During the day, Bryansk was taken by Guderian's forces, as they completed the encirclement of three entire Soviet armies. Hitler's mood, already heightened, had become bubbly by supper and there was no discussion of politics during that meal.

* * * * *

By the eighth, after repeated positive reports from the front, Hitler felt that the Red army could reasonably be considered as defeated, and he expected Moscow to fall within days. When that happened Hitler ordered that: *'The city be destroyed and complexly wiped from the earth'.*

* * * * *

After emerging from his military conference on the ninth of October, a supremely confident Hitler retired to his study in the bunker and began to stride vigorously as he dictated a victory statement which he had decided his press officer Otto Dietrich would deliver at a press conference to be held the next day in Berlin.

* * * * *

At supper on the seventeenth, Hitler's conversation was primarily aimed at the new and bright future that lay ahead, now that the *'Lebensraum'* necessary for the German people had been achieved militarily.

* * * * *

- Concentration Camps -

Over time, the selections for the camps had increasingly included non-Jewish individuals. Political adversaries or other individuals, whom those who administered the program looked upon with displeasure, were being rounded up far more frequently now than had previously been the case.

These were referred to as the *'asoziale'* individuals who, pursuant to the general guidelines issued by the Bavarian police on August first of nineteen thirty-six, were to be taken into *'protective custody'*.

In the instructions accompanying the selection process for those suitable for *'protective custody'*, this group should now include *'gypsies, vagrants, tramps, the work shy, idlers, beggars, prostitutes, troublemakers, career criminals, rowdies, traffic violators, psychopaths and the mentally ill'*.

---

* * * * *

- Auschwitz-Birkenau -

Construction of *'Auschwitz II'*, or *'Auschwitz-Birkenau'* began in October of nineteen forty-one.

Of the three camps established near the village of Brzezinka in southern Poland, *'Auschwitz-Birkenau'* held the most prisoners. It was divided into nine sections, which were separated by electrified barbed-wire fences and patrolled by SS guards and dogs.

The camp included individual sectors for women, men, gypsies and families of Jews who had been deported from the Theresienstadt ghetto.

In September of nineteen forty-one *'Zyklon B'* had been tested at *Auschwitz'* with success. It had then been adopted by the institution as the best choice for use against those who were, in the future required to receive *'special handling'* and be *'retired'*.

The conversion of two small farmhouses into chambers that could be hermetically sealed for this purpose was ordered.

* * * * *

- Majdanek Concentration Camp -

Two ghettos were established in Lublin Poland. The first had opened in March of nineteen forty-one with a population of more than thirty thousand Jews.

Construction on the Majdanek Concentration camp, also referred to as the Lublin-Majdanek camp, was begun in October of nineteen forty-one.   In its inception, it was designated for use as an SS prisoner of war camp.

As a result the camp was, unlike most concentration camps, built within sight of a major city, that of Lublin. It had four sub-camps within the Ghettos of Lublin itself, where

Patrick Laughy

prisoners worked in German armaments industries or on other forced-labour projects.

* * * * *

- Ghettos -

The setting up of ghettos to isolate and make use of the Jewish populations of newly occupied Reich territory was, by this time, an accepted practice.

* * * * *

- Warsaw Ghetto -

Beginning in the spring of nineteen forty-one, German manufacturers set up workshops or factories in the ghetto to make use of the Jewish forced labour that was available there. Due to the war, a good deal of what they produced was destined for the consumption of the German military machine.

Among the firms active within the Warsaw ghetto were Toebbens, Schultz, Roehrich, Hoffmann and Schilling. These firms produced textiles, armaments and other manufactured goods. The *'brush-makers'* area of the ghetto was a major center of brush manufacture for the Reich.

The Germans oversaw the movement of goods in and out of the ghetto through the *'Transferstelle'* (Transfer Office) which was housed at the *'Umschlagplatz'* (transfer point and major rail yard). The *'Umschlagplatz'* was located near the northern boundary of the ghetto and functioned as the main transfer point.

* * * * *

- Vilna Ghetto -

In September of nineteen forty-one, the Germans

established two ghettos in the city of Vilnius in Poland, number #1 and #2.

In October of nineteen forty-one, the *'Einsatzgruppen'*, aided by Lithuanian auxiliaries, destroyed ghetto #2. The inmates from that ghetto were taken to Ponary, a wooded area about eight miles southwest of Vilna, and shot.

In addition to those from #2, Lukiszki Prison, which had served as a collection centre for Jews, also provided prisoners for these execution squads. By the end of nineteen forty-one, approximately forty thousand Jews and others deemed to require *'special handling'* had been *'retired'* in this manner.

During this period of time, the Jews remaining in ghetto #1 were being used as forced labour in factories or on construction projects outside the ghetto, while others had been sent to labour camps located in the Vilna region.

* * * * *

- Kovno Ghetto -

On October fourth nineteen forty-one, the smaller of the two Kovno ghettos, was eradicated. Any occupants deemed fit for work were transferred to the large ghetto and the remainder were taken to Fort Nine where they were shot by the *'Einsatzgruppen'* and auxiliaries.

On October twenty-eighth approximately ten thousand Jews who had been housed in the large ghetto were also given *'special handling'* and retired.

* * * * *

- Count von Stauffer -

A light rain was falling as the Count's staff car swung into the curb in front of SS headquarters in Berlin and Wilhelm, who had been waiting under the protection of the eve of the building walked across to the car, opened the curbside rear door and slipped into the seat beside his father.

As the driver pulled back into the traffic flow, Karl von Stauffer smiled over at his son and patted the briefcase which was resting on the seat between them.

"You'll be pleased to know that that matter in France has been dealt with. I'll bring you up to date after dinner."

For a moment Wilhelm was unsure of what specific matter his father was referring to, but then he recalled the report of a problem with a shipment of art treasures from France, with a reference to *'Operation Fatherland'*, that Himmler's Chief Aide, SS-Hauptsturmfuhrer Joachim Peiper, had earlier asked him to follow up on.

He was instantly both curious as to what had transpired, and very much conscious of the SS driver in the front seat. He opened his mouth to speak but the Count raised his hand dismissively.

"We'll discuss it later, suffice to say that the matter is no longer of concern to us."

* * * * *

- Eric -

They were about two days out from the Brazilian shoreline and the successful and uneventful completion of their third trip to the family's holdings.

The massive U-boat was travelling on the surface under calm sea conditions and under a solid cloud cover. Eric was on the viewing deck of the conning tower and could just make out some of the passengers who were taking advantage of the good conditions to enjoy some fresh air and limited exercise on the deck stretching out in front and below him

As they had on each trip, they'd travelled under conditions of *'Radio Silence'*, submerged during the day and, barring extremely bad weather, on the surface during hours of darkness for the majority of the trip, the only exception being on clear, brightly moonlit nights when there was a chance of being spotted by aircraft.

Unlike other U-boats he had served aboard, the massive, streamlined craft he now captained was capable of travelling just as fast when submerged as it was when on the surface.

The U-boat was in no danger if spotted by a ship on the surface, in that it could outrun any ship afloat, but aircraft were another kettle of fish.

Eric had made the determination not to run on the surface in daylight. And, although this new type XXII U-boar was quite capable of running the entire trip submerged, he felt it important to allow both the crew and his assorted passengers the chance to enjoy surface travel on any evening when, due to moon and cloud, there was little or no risk of them being spotted from the air.

He smiled to himself at the thought.

I wonder what the hell they would think if they did spot it. This U-boat is so large and so far ahead of its time in both design and appearance, they wouldn't know what the hell to make of it if they did see it.

To date, with the strict observance of the conditions he had set for surface travel, the U-boat had avoided contact with all other marine and air traffic during the three crossings and Eric had no intention of making changes to those criteria.

He glanced at his watch and nodded toward his First Officer.

"Time to get them back inside, sun will be up in about an hour."

* * * * *

- Wilhelm -

They had finished their meal and retired to the Count's study and as the Count closed the door firmly behind them, Wilhelm went over to the drinks table and poured each of them a healthy whisky and helped himself to two cigars from the box resting next to the decanters.

His father was settling into one of the armchairs facing the brightly burning fireplace as Wilhelm crossed to him and offered a drink and cigar from the tray he was holding.

Curiosity had been torturing Wilhelm since the car ride and his father had been very much aware of the fact. Before Wilhelm could speak, his father drew a large manila envelope from his briefcase, smiled at his son and dropped it on the tray.

"I think your boss should be happy with this report."

Wilhelm set the tray down on the table beside the chair on the other side of the fireplace, picked up the envelope, opened it and began to read as he settled into the chair.

* * * * *

- Eric -

Eric was using his binoculars to sweep the sky as his First Officer approached him.

"All but the lookouts are below Captain."

Eric nodded and stuck his head over the companionway that led from the open watertight hatch down into the conning tower.

"Clear the bridge, dive...dive..."

The Claxton sounded and he waited for his lookouts and first officer to go down the ladder then followed them and pulled the hatch to and locked it into place.

As he climbed down the conning tower ladder and dropped into the bowels of the U-boat, he was thinking excitedly about the impending arrival.

Work on the underwater entry into the tunneled-out, man-made bay, leading to the U-boat pens nestled deep below the mountain on the shoreline was reportedly ahead of schedule and nearing completion. It was apparently far enough advanced that it would be ready to receive his U-boat for the first time.

He recalled the initial stages of the hollowing out of the massive chamber which he had observed on his first and second trips, and tried to envision in his mind what he could expect to find upon their arrival. He wondered how difficult it was going to be to maneuver his ship into the newly blasted opening that had, on his earlier visits, been a solid wall of rock separating the expanding chamber from the sea beyond.

Eric was very much looking forward to reaching the Brazilin shore in two days' time.

* * * * *

- Wilhelm -

The Count had remained silent while his son read through the report.

When Wilhelm had finished, he exhaled a cloud of smoke and reached to rest his cigar in the ashtray, then picked up his glass and took a swallow before placing the document back into the envelope and setting it down on the table beside his chair.

'Well it would seem that the matter was certainly thoroughly investigated. I'm sure Joachim will be pleased with the result. No loose ends here. Signed confession from the Luftwaffe NCO to the effect that he was simply trying to gain some of the French booty for himself, and when the opportunity was presented, he took it and then made up the *'Operation Fatherland'* reference to try and cover up, after he had been caught.

Convenient that he was shot while trying to escape, he can hardly change his story now."

The Count noted the sarcasm registered in his son's voice but as he responded, his facial expression didn't change in acknowledgement of the fact.

"Yes, his end is unfortunate of course, but as the report indicates, he attacked one of his guards while he was being transported and then tried to flee. They didn't have any other option apparently."

Wilhelm rubbed his forehead and released the breath he'd been holding.

"So it would seem."

CHAPTER TWENTY

- October -

- British Air Operations -

Bomber Command's main targets are Stuttgart, Hamburg, towns in the Ruhr Valley and the northern German ports. In excess of twenty-five hundred sorties are flown at the cost of one hundred and twenty-six planes lost.

* * * * *

- Battle of the Atlantic -

U-boat strength has now climbed to one hundred and ninety-eight, with eighty available for operational patrols. They sink one hundred and fifty-six thousand, five hundred tons of allied shipping out of a total loss of two hundred and eighteen thousand, three hundred tons.

This is a reduction from September but that is partially accounted for by the fact that a portion of operational U-boats are now being diverted to the Mediterranean theatre.

* * * * *

- October First -

- Eastern Front -

Finnish forces attacking west of Lake Onega, capture Petrozavodsk.

* * * * *

Patrick Laughy

- October Second -

- Eastern Front -

The German attack on Moscow, *'Operation Typhoon'* is officially launched.

German *'Central'* forces begin an all-out offensive against the Russian capital city. Hoth's Third and Hoeppner's Fourth Panzer Groups plus the Second, Fourth and Ninth Armies all support the advance, which has been initiated two days earlier by Guderian's forces on the right wing.

The Germans have an advantage in both numbers and equipment and the Luftwaffe predominates in the skies above the front.

Tank units are leading the attack and Guderian his already made considerable progress toward Bryansk and Orel while Hoth and Hoeppner are moving to execute a plan that is aimed at encircling the Soviet defenders by linking up at Vyazma.

The three German armoured leaders who are in command of the operation are considered to be the best on the entire Eastern Front.

* * * * *

- Australia -

As a result of the election, a new government is formed under the leadership of Prime Minister John Curtin of the Labour Party.

* * * * *

- October Third -

- India -

Mahatma Gandhi leads his followers in a show of passive resistance against British rule.

* * * * *

- October Fourth -

- Eastern Front -

Coming up from the south, Hoeppner's Panzer Group attacks near Vyazma while Hoth's units are attacking the remaining Soviet defensive line between Vyazma and Rzhev. On the right wing, Guderian is pressing hard at Orel and Bryansk.

A massive pocket of Soviet troops located west of Bryansk and Vyazma are in very real danger of being cut off.

* * * * *

- October Sixth -

- Eastern Front -

Kleist's attack in the south right flank reaches Berdyansk, on the Sea of Azov, cutting off more than one hundred thousand Soviet soldiers. The German Eleventh Army moves along the coast with the intention of linking up with Kleist's forces. All German lines are advancing steadily.

The Soviet defenders in the area of Vyazma and Bryansk are being overwhelmed. Large pockets are being isolated and then mopped up south of Bryansk and west of Vyazma.

Additional German units are now already attacking in force well to the east of both towns.

* * * * *

- October Seventh -

- RAF -

Large bomber night sorties hit Berlin, the Ruhr and Cologne, suffering considerable losses.

* * * * *

- October Eighth -

- Eastern Front -

Advancing German forces take Mariupol on the Sea of Azov.

In the battle for Moscow the ferocious battles for Vyazma, east of Smolensk, and Bryansk continues and approximately six hundred thousand Soviet troops are taken prisoner and a huge quantity of equipment captured. The Germans shift their focus and begin attacking in a northwesterly direction towards Tula and Kalugu in the south and Rzhev and Kalinin in the North.

The beginning of the Russian winter brings heavy rain all along the front and the German advance begins to face the forces of nature as well as that of the defenders as they find the fields and poorly constructed roads of the Soviet Union turning into muddy and often impassable quagmires.

* * * * *

- October Ninth -

- USA -

Roosevelt asks congress to repeal certain sections of the Neutrality Act so that US merchant vessels can be armed.

* * * * *

- October Tenth -

- Eastern Front -

Recalled from his command in Leningrad, General Georgi Zhukov, an experienced commander who has previously excelled in the conflict against the Japanese in the Russian Far East and at Leningrad, takes up command of the defense of Moscow.

* * * * *

- October Twelfth -

- North Africa -

Another relief operation is begun for Tobruk. Over the next several days seven thousand troops are taken into the city and eight thousand are taken out. During the operation, *'Laton*a', a minesweeper is sunk during a Stuka dive-bombing attack and one destroyer is damaged.

* * * * *

- Eastern Front -

Despite the worsening weather, German troops capture Kaluga and the Soviets are forced to evacuate the town of Bryansk while the fighting around the area continues.

* * * * *

- Mediterranean -

HMS *'Ark Royal'* delivers a full squadron of Hurricane fighters to Malta.

* * * * *

- October Thirteenth -

- Eastern Front -

Temperatures fall and the muddy ground begins to harden allowing the German attack to regain its momentum. Vyazma is taken and the nearby Soviet pocket is pulverized.

* * * * *

- October Fourteenth -

- Eastern Front -

The relief offered the Germans by the temperature drop is short-lived in that it continues to drop which results in the rain turning into a heavy snowfall which creates its own version of mobility constrictions. Despite this additional setback, the Germans move slowly ahead and reach Kalinin, northwest of Moscow. The Soviet defense forces between here and at Tula stiffen with determination to halt the German attack.

* * * * *

- October Fifteenth -

- Occupied Poland -

Occupation authority's decree that any Jews found outside the ghettos will be summarily executed.

* * * * *

- Eastern Front -

Over two days, the Russians evacuate Odessa, which has been holding out behind German lines for several weeks.

Three Divisions, encompassing thirty-five thousand men, are evacuated by sea using two cruisers. four destroyers and several smaller craft. A single transport is sunk by an air attack but the rest of the vessels reach Sevastopol safely.

Most ships of the Soviet Black Sea Fleet are now based in Sevastopol.

* * * * *

- October Sixteenth -

- Moscow -

Panic sets into the city, as foreign diplomats and much of the Soviet government staff are moved to Kuibyshev and many senior communist party members begin an exodus in cars and on the trains.

Stalin remains in Moscow.

The citizens of Moscow are organized and work frantically to build tank traps and other fortifications deemed necessary to face the imminent German siege of the city.

* * * * *

- Tokyo -

Prime Minister Konoye resigns and is replaced by Minister of War, Hideki Tojo, who now takes three offices, that of Prime Minister, War Minister and Home Affairs Minister. This change heightens the likelihood that Japan will decide to go to war to solve her raw material supply problems.

Patrick Laughy

* * * * *

- Vichy -

Petain orders the arrest of three former Prime Ministers, Blum, Reynaud and Daladier, charging that they were responsible for the French defeat.

* * * * *

- Atlantic -

During the night of the sixteenth/seventeenth a convoy, near Iceland, made up of Canadian, British and US ships is attacked and in the resulting exchange, the US destroyer *'Kearny'* is torpedoed by U-568, killing eleven sailors.

* * * * *

- October Eighteenth -

- Eastern Front -

Mozhauysk is taken in the continuing German advance on Moscow.

Red army troops from Siberia arrive to reinforce the Moscow garrison. Stalin receives written assurance that the Japanese will not attack the USSR from the east.

* * * * *

- Mediterranean -

A fly in by strike planes from Gibraltar is carried out in order to augment Malta's air forces.

* * * * *

- October Nineteenth -

- Eastern Front -

- Moscow -

Despite pressure to leave the city, Stalin announces that he will remain in Moscow although most of the government has left. He orders that the city be defended with every effort, and harsh punishments to be imposed on any looters and defeatists.

Work proceeds at a hectic pace on three fixed defensive lines around the city as word of the German advance along the coast of the Sea of Azov reaching Taganrog.

An official *'state of siege'* is announced for the city and it is placed under martial law.

* * * * *

- Luxembourg -

The German occupying forces declare Luxembourg to be *'Judenrein'* (Cleansed of Jews).

* * * * *

- October Twentieth -

- Eastern Front -

Near Moscow there is heavy fighting close to Mozhaysk and at Malayaroslavets.

To the south the advancing Germans capture Donetsk.

* * * * *

- Occupied France -

Resistance fighters shoot and kill Lieutenant Coronel Fritz Hotz, the German commander in Nantes. Hitler is furious over the incident and orders the fifty hostages be shot by the Germans, in reprisal.

This response to resistance to German administration in occupied territory will now serve as a model for all future incidents of a similar nature.

* * * * *

- October Twenty-First -

- Libya -

New Zealand troops land in Egypt and move to take possession of Fort Capuzzo, located in the colony of Italian Libya, near the Libyan-Egyptian border.

* * * * *

- USA -

Negotiations between the US and Japan, which have been underway for some time, seem stalemated after the change in the Japanese government and there is now little hope within the US capital that they will not end in dismal failure.

* * * * *

- Mediterranean -

Two each of British cruisers and destroyers arrive in Malta to add their efforts to the threat which Malta can pose to the Axis supply lines to Africa.

* * * * *

- October Twenty-Second -

- Occupied France -

On this date another French resistance attack, this time in Bordeaux against a Nazi official results in a reprisal similar to that which took place in Nantes earlier in the month.

* * * * *

- October Twenty-Third -

- Libya -

`Operation Crusader'* launched by the British, is thwarted near Tobruk during heavy desert fighting.

* * * * *

- Eastern Front -

The Soviet command structure is reorganized, placing Zhukov in charge of the northern half of the front and Timoshenko in the southern.

* * * * *

- October Twenty-Fourth -

- Eastern Front -

Kharkov, a strategically important mining and industrial center in the Ukraine, is taken in a joint attack by the German Sixth and Seventeenth Armies, from the Army Group South forces.

* * * * *

- October Twenty-Fifth -

Under the command of Admiral Phillips, the British battleship HMS *'Prince of Wales'* sails from Clyde for the Far East. The ship will be central to the formation of a new Far East Fleet which is to be created around the *'Prince of Wales'*.

* * * * *

- October Twenty-Seventh -

- Eastern Front -

Forces of German Army Group South reach Sevastopol and capture Kramatorsk in the Crimea.

The Northern forces find themselves seriously slowed or stopped by a sea of mud. The leading tanks have now reached the outskirts of Moscow.

* * * * *

- October Twenty-Eighth -

- Eastern Front -

Most of the German *'central forces'* attacking toward Moscow are being halted due to exhaustion of both men and equipment, coupled with worsening weather conditions. By day they are facing a muddy quagmire that grasps and envelopes both men and machine and at night severe frost conditions. The German troops have little in the way of winter uniforms and gear, their war-weary equipment is simply balking at the cold.

The powerful German Mark IV tanks become mired in the muddy roads while the wider-tracked and more maneuverable Soviet T-34's have far less problem with the conditions.

Hitler's easy victories of the past two years have been possible because of the superior mobility and firepower provided by massed Panzer attacks which have been closely supported by strong tactical air support.

Suddenly his superior armour is mired in a sea of mud and his air force is grounded due to low visibility. Having lost its mobility, his infamous *'Blitzkrieg'* machine is bogged down, and can make little if any progress.

Despite this situation Guderian's forces attack near Tula, but they gain little ground.

Further north and under terrible weather conditions, the struggling Germans manage to take Volokolamsk.

* * * * *

- Sri Lanka -

Both HMS *'Prince of Wales'* and *'Repulse'* arrive at Colombo.

* * * * *

- October Twenty-Ninth -

- Eastern Front -

The first of the Soviet reserve divisions that have been transferred in from Siberia now go into the Soviet defensive line west of Moscow.

* * * * *

- October Thirtieth -

Patrick Laughy

- USA -

President Roosevelt approves a total of one billion US dollars' worth of Lend-Lease aid for the Soviet Union.

* * * * *

- Eastern Front -

- Moscow -

The German offensive against Moscow comes to a halt in order to await the full set-in of the Russian winter and with it, the assurance of permanently hard frozen ground, which will allow them to move their tank forces freely again.

* * * * *

- October Thirty-First -

- Atlantic -

The destroyer USS *'Ruben, James'*, part of a convoy screen, is torpedoed and sunk by U-552 near Iceland, killing more than one hundred sailors. It is the first loss of an American *'neutral warship'*.

CHAPTER TWENTY-ONE

- November -

- The War -

The conditions of the progress of the war from the German perspective have certainly changed by the end of October and beginning of November of nineteen forty-one.

The German war machine had taken some setbacks over the two previous years, but these had been few and minor and had rarely seriously affected the outcome of German victory.

This new situation of near stalemate on the Eastern Front, which was currently facing the previously seemingly unstoppable German forces was, at this juncture, admittedly short lived. As such it could therefore not necessarily be considered as *'the'* turning point in the war by those on either side of the battle.

However, most participants on both sides, did pause and look at it as possibly the beginning of *'a turning point'*.

* * * * *

- The Military Inner Circle -

Armed with the wonder of hindsight, those who made up Hitler's military inner circle, now found time to access the current problems facing *'Operation Typhoon'*, the taking of Moscow.

The causes of the stalemate were certainly obvious: a more numerous and determined Soviet defense coupled with the mud and freezing rains of late fall.

Finger pointing by those at the top of the German

military machine had begun however.

It was generally postulated by that tight circle, that it was Hitler's refusal to launch the attack a month earlier than he had that was responsible. They readily agreed among themselves that if Hitler had listened to their advice in the first place, Moscow would be by this point in the war, a mass of rubble and the Soviet government and the Red forces would be defeated; the war on the Eastern Front would be over.

Only one member of the military inner circle held another point of view and that was Hitler's naval liaison officer, Rear Admiral, Karl-Jesco von Puttkamer.

Von Puttkamer placed the blame for the now mired German invasion on the Eastern Front solidly at the feet of Brauchitsch and Halder, who had taken advantage of Hitler's illness to sabotage the Fuhrer's basic plan for the taking of Moscow.

Finger pointing aside, by the end of October the sleet had turned into snow and the mud froze. Conditions facing the German troops were unbearable. There had been few advances along the entire line and those made were hard earned and minimal.

The situation was so grave that Hitler ordered one of his architects, Herman Giesler, who had been working on the redesign and reconstruction of major German cities, to stop all work on these projects. He was to immediately turn his attention to the task of organizing the transport to the Eastern Front of all his workers, engineers, building materials and machinery and begin work on highway construction, railway line repair and the construction of rail stations and locomotive sheds that would then facilitate the rapid resupply of the German forces at the front.

* * * * *

- Hitler -

If Hitler was currently overly concerned about the state

of the Eastern Front, he demonstrated no such feelings during his meals.

He appeared to those joining him to be serenely confident of a victory against Moscow and on the eve of his departure to attend the annual celebration of the November Munich Putsch, much-brightened at supper, with jokes and recollections.

Hitler arrived for the celebration in Munch on the afternoon of the eighth of November. There he made an impassioned appeal to a convocation of Reichsleiters (National Leaders - the second highest political rank of the Nazi Party) and Gauleiters (Party Leaders of a regional branch of the Nazi Party) and later delivered a speech at the Lowenbraukeller (beer garden where the members of the unsuccessful Putsch had met in the early years of the party) which included a warning to President Roosevelt that if an American ship opened fire on a German vessel.

'It will do so at its own risk'.

His delivery at the Lowenbraukeller was noted by those close to him however, as less than inspiring and to them demonstrated that the Fuhrer was at least somewhat depressed by the current situation on the Eastern Front.

This impression was confirmed when Hitler, on the next day, reminded his staff of what had befallen Napoleon's army in Russia.

'The recognition that neither force is capable of annihilating the other will lead to a compromise peace'.

German Field Marshal Moritz Albrecht Franz Fedor von Bock, who had served as the commander of Army Group North during the invasion of Poland in thirty-nine and commander of Army Group B during the invasion of France in forty, currently held the command of Army Group Center. He was a man considered to be a brilliant theoretician and possessed of a strong sense of determination. He dismissed such pessimism.

He urged Hitler to continue pushing the offensive against Moscow. Interestingly he was supported by both

Brauchitsch and Halder. So much so, that Halder was the picture of optimism as he announced on November the twelfth that, in his opinion, the Russians were on the verge of collapse.

Hitler's outlook on the situation was instantly improved by these urgings and on the fifteenth of the month he ordered that the push for Moscow was to be resumed.

Over the next few days, due to improved weather, Hitler clung to that renewed confidence, but then the weather worsened, and once again ice, mud and snow began to turn the battlefield into a quagmire.

A few days later the Japanese ambassador to Berlin, General Oshima, dropped in to *'Wolfsschanze'* for a visit.

General Oshima was a career member of the Japanese Army, who had been appointed to the position of Japan's military attaché in Berlin in nineteen thirty-four, when he was a Colonel. He now had a close relationship with both von Ribbentrop and Hitler.

Oshima had been recalled to Japan in nineteen thirty-nine. By that time he had been promoted to Lieutenant General and had in October of thirty-eight gone into the Japanese Army reserve when he'd taken up his new post as that of Japanese ambassador to Berlin.

At the insistence of the Nazi government, Oshima, now holding the rank of Major General, had returned to Berlin in February of nineteen forty-one, where he once again took up the post of Japanese ambassador to the Reich.

On the occasion of this visit to see Hitler at *'Wolfsschanze',* Hitler confidently discussed the situation on the Eastern Front with him, explaining that winter had come much earlier than his weather experts had predicted.

Then, in the strictest confidence, he told Oshima that it was doubtful that, under the circumstance, they could take Moscow this year.

It was an indication to those present that Hitler had concluded that little was going to be accomplished against Moscow until good weather had returned to Russia. This was reflected by the fact that during meals the Fuhrer had lost interest in the previous confident banter and in a general sense, simply had much less to say.

Requests for seats at his table, previously much valued, began to decrease accordingly.

A deep freeze set in on the front and this situation brought about rumblings of complaints about Hitler's edict prohibiting the issuing of winter clothing at the beginning of the operation.

On the twenty-first of November, Gordian phoned Halder to report that his troops had reached the end of their endurance and that he was going to visit von Bock with a request that the orders he had just received be changed since he could: *'see no way of carrying them out.'*

Under direct pressure from Hitler, von Bock would not listen to Guderian's appeals and ordered the attack on Moscow to be continued.

Short, fitful, advances were accomplished as a result, but soon ground to a halt again.

A frustrated von Bock moved up to an advanced command post and took personal charge of the operation, ordering another assault on the twenty-fourth of November while the front was under extreme winter conditions.

Under fierce resistance from the Soviet defenders and the horrid weather conditions, this frantic attack was also doomed to failure.

Vexations over the situation on the Moscow front were then compounded on the twenty-ninth of the month when a crisis arose in the south. Field Marshal von Rundstedt was forced to evacuate Rostov, which he had captured only a week previously, causing the German's to lose the gate to the Caucasus.

Hitler ranted and raved at such a reversal. His German forces did not retreat, not even these thirty miles. He immediately ordered von Rundstedt to hold where he was.

The Marshall was both shocked and affronted at the order. It questioned his ability to assess the situation correctly and make logical decisions based on current first-hand intelligence. He was being second guessed by a politician who possessed little if any experience in the art of war, and from a great distance away from where the battle was being fought.

Von Rundstedt made his feelings clear to his staff as he read the offending telegraph message and ordered an immediate response. The message was drawn up by one of his subordinates. It read:

'It is madness to attempt to hold. First, the troops cannot do it and second if they do not retreat they will be destroyed.'

The dispatch was given to the Marshall for review prior to being sent and an irritated von Rundstedt added a final line to it before it was transmitted to Hitler.

'I repeat that this order must be rescinded or that you find someone else.'

Hitler was aghast at such response to his direct order.

Without consulting the Commander-in-Chief of the Army, he lashed out at von Rundstedt with a final wired exchange:

'I am acceding to your request. Please give up your command.'

Hitler replaced von Rundstedt with Field Marshal von Reichenau, who was one of the few of his military inner circle who still dared, by this point in the war, to frankly offer his honest opinions to the Fuhrer when and if asked for them.

Hitler then boarded his personal plane and flew to Mariupol in southeastern Ukraine, where he intended to get a firsthand view of the current military situation at the front. Here he sought out his trusted commander of the *'SS-Leibstandarte'*, Sepp Dietrich, in whose opinion, the Fuhrer had implicit faith.

To his mortification, Hitler was bluntly informed by Dietrich and his senior officers that they were in full agreement with the decisions taken by von Rundstedt and that, in their combined opinion, had the Marshall not ordered a retreat when he did, the entire German force would have been destroyed.

After hearing this assessment, Hitler gave Reichenau

orders to do exactly what he had had so recently specifically told von Rundstedt not to do.

He then instructed von Rundstedt to report to him.

The Field Marshall did as he was bid, expecting perhaps that Hitler might be about to offer him an apology, but that expectation was quickly dispelled.

He opened the meeting by telling von Rundstedt that in future he would not tolerate any additional applications to resign a command. To bolster has statement Hitler said.

'I myself, for instance, am not in a position to go to my superior, God Almighty, and say to Him, I am not going on with it, because I don' want to take the responsibility.'

* * * * *

- Minsk Ghetto -

Beginning in November of nineteen forty-one the Germans began to deport what would become, between that date and October of nineteen forty-two, over twenty thousand Jews from Germany and the Protectorate of Bohemia and Moravia, to the Minsk ghetto.

Many of these were provided *'special treatment'* when they arrived at Maly Trostinets, a small village situated about eight miles to the east. The remainder were housed in a separate ghetto in Minsk which segregated German Jews from local Belarussian Jews.

Little contact between these two ghettos was allowed.

These new Jews were used as forced labour for factories both inside the ghetto and outside the ghetto, especially in the Shiroka Street labour camp and the opera house which was being used by the occupying German forces as a warehouse for the sorting and storage of seized Jewish private property.

* * * * *

Patrick Laughy

- Riga Ghetto -

In late November the Germans began to move approximately twenty-eight thousand prisoners from the fenced-in area of the ghetto which they then *'retired'* in operations in the Rumbula Forest, near the Rumbula railway station which was five miles southeast of Riga along the Riga-Dvinsk railway and the Riga-Salaspils road.

Those that remained were fenced into what then then became known as the *'small'* or *'Latvian'* ghetto. Riga was also the destination for approximately fifteen thousand Jews who were deported from Germany, Austria, and the Protectorates of Bohemia and Moravia.

When these new Jews arrived in Riga, they were then housed in the spaces which had been, prior to their arrival, occupied by those who had recently been liquidated at Rumbula. This ghetto was then referred to as the *'big'* or *'German ghetto'*.

* * * * *

- Belzec Concentration Camp -

Construction on this new camp began in November of nineteen forty-one as part of *'Operation Reinhard'*, the SS plan to deal with all Jews resident in the newly occupied territory now being administered by the *'Generalgouvernement'*.

Although new camp construction was underway and expansion of current camps was ongoing, the fact of the matter was that the camps were bursting at the seams. Something had to be done to relieve the pressure being put upon them.

The Belzec camp was the second *'special treatment'* centre to go into operation and the first of its kind to be constructed in the *'Operation Reinhard'* area.

It was built at Belzec, in an area where there were good rail connections and which was situated near the centre of the large Jewish populations of Lvov, Krakow and Lublin regions.

Under construction on the Lublin-Lvov railway line, the camp was only sixteen hundred feet from the Belzec railway station and was easily connected to the main line by a short siding.

The SS guards who were to eventually man the site were to live in a separate compound to be constructed near the Belzec railway station.

The camp was designed to be divided into two facilities. Each side of the camp was to measure eight hundred and eighty-six feet. Upon completion, plans included having branches woven into the barbed-wire fencing and trees planted around the perimeter fencing to serve to camouflage the site.

The first facility in the two part camp, was an administration/reception area and the second was the *'special handling'* compound. A narrow enclosed path was to connect the two and was referred to as the *'tube'*.

The reception area held the railway siding and a ramp. The *'special handling'* compound, included gas chambers and mass grave facilities. Rail tracks would run from the gas chambers to the burial pits.

Although referred to as a *'concentration or internment camp'*, Belzec had not been designed, nor was it destined to be used, as a place to concentrate enemies of the state.

No, Belzec, with long demonstrated German efficiency, had been solely envisioned to serve as an escape valve for use as a method to avoid the serious problem of camp overcrowding.

* * * * *

- Genetic Research -

At the start of the Second World War, Germany led the world in the field of genetic research.

In eighteen eighty-five, Friedrich Leopold August Weismann, a German evolutionary biologist and professor of zoology and comparative anatomy at the University of Freiberg, theorized that the genetic information of a cell would diminish as the cell were through differentiation.

Three years later, Wilhelm Roux, a German zoologist and pioneer of experimental embryology, tested this germ plasm theory for the first time. One cell of a two-cell embryo was destroyed with a hot needle. The result was a half-embryo, supporting Weismann's theory.

In eighteen ninety-four, Hans Adolf Eduard Dreisch, a German biologist isolated blastomeres from two and four-cell sea urchin embryos and observed their development into small larvae.

These experiments were regarded as refutations of the Weismann-Roux theories.

Seven years later, in nineteen-one, Hans Spemann, a German embryologist, split a two-cell newt embryo into two parts, resulting in the development of two complete larvae and a year later Walter Sutton, an American geneticist and physician, published a paper entitled *'On the morphology of the Chromosome Group in Brachyotola magna'* in which he hypothesized that chromosomes carry the inheritance and that they occur in distinct pairs within a cell's nucleus. Sutton also argued that how chromosomes act when sex cells divide was the basis for the *'Mendelian Law of Heredity'*.

In that same year German embryologist Hans Spemann split a two-celled salamander embryo and each cell grew to adulthood, solidifying the position that early embryo cells carry necessary genetic information.

This experiment disproved Weismann's original theory that the amount of genetic information in cells decreases with each division.

In nineteen fourteen, Spellman conducted an early nuclear transfer experiment. In twenty-eight he conducted a series of successful nuclear transfer experiments and published the results of the transfers, which involved salamander embryos, in a book entitled *'Embryonic Development and Induction'*. Spemann went on to argue that the next step for research should be the cloning of organisms by extracting the nucleus of a differentiated cell and putting it into an enucleated egg.

In nineteen thirty-five, Spemann was awarded a Nobel Prize in Physiology or Medicine.

* * * * *

- Karl von Stauffer -

The Count sat across the table from family friend and co-conspirator the Baron, Doctor Heinrich von Kleist. They had finished eating and were seated next to a window, upon which the insistent drizzle that had settled over Berlin for the past few days, bombarded causing tiny rivulets to cascade downward and obstruct the view of the street beyond.

Both the weather and the time of day had discouraged patrons and there was only one other party eating in the small restaurant. That couple was at the back of the room, well away from the windows.

Nursing their second beers, both men were relaxed and, being able to converse without being overheard, had been discussing various topics without concern.

The Count was reflecting on the current situation on the Russian Front, having better access to what was going on than did the Baron, who, buried in the field of medical research, was shielded from military matters.

"...and it appears even Hitler has concluded that Moscow can't be taken this year. Not unlike Napoleon, our Fuhrer has had to come to terms with the Russian winter."

The Baron nodded and sucked in a deep breath.

"It would appear then that we are proven justified in determining to take another path in creating a separate long-term approach to the future of the fatherland."

Karl shrugged.

"I think Hitler's decision to take on a two front war was enough to confirm the rightness of our move to set up *'Operation Fatherland'*, although I would have to agree that this current stalemate situation in Russia certainly affirms our action. Germany cannot fight and hope to win a drawn out two-front war and this now has every chance of becoming exactly that."

Heinrich ground out his cigarette and shifted topics.

"I've been meaning to speak to you about something. You remember I told you that we had been conducting research into eugenics and genetics?"

Karl nodded and the Baron continued.

"Well, we've made some astounding discoveries of late and the possibilities are really interesting.

Without boring you to death by explaining the nuts and bolts of isolating and selecting individual genes, it seems likely that we will, in time, be able to duplicate a human being…to create a carbon copy if you like. This process could then be repeated over and over, with the result being that we could then produce a race of perfectly identical *'Aryan'* individuals, by using the genetic makeup of a single specimen that we had previously determined to be of an ideal eugenic makeup."

The Baron paused and waited for a reaction. Karl was trying to take it all in.

"You believe that you can create a genetically pure individual, with none of the normal flaws…and as many of them as you wish…is this really possible?"

Heinrich smiled.

"I think so. It's not a short term thing of course, it will take years of additional research and even when the process is perfected, well it's not like you would have instant adults…they would all be babies and would have to grow to maturity, before you would have a finished product."

The Count raised his hands and sat back in his chair.

"My God man, the whole thing sounds totally unbelievable. If it could be done, it would create a brand new world. But the ramifications…"

Heinrich nodded and toyed with his stein moving it around on the tabletop in small circles as he gathered his thoughts before continuing.

"There are bound to be many complications over the

acceptance of such a program for obvious reasons, but if it was to go ahead, the end result could end up with the world populated by a genetically superior human race.

It is an exciting prospect, but one that will require a good deal more excellent research to bring to fruition. As you know I worked with Gabriella's husband, Konrad, on this subject in the past and I was wondering if you think he would consider taking it up again. I know you wish them to reside in Norway and that he is doing important work there, but it occurred to me that he has all the facilities he would need to conduct research right where he is and he could perhaps take it on as a part time operation. If he did, we would have no difficulty in communicating with each other on a regular basis and keeping each other up to speed.

Then if things in Germany go as we expect, Konrad and I could carry on with the necessary research at the facility in Brazil after the war was lost. We would then be far ahead of any other research that is being done elsewhere in the world on the matter. Think of what it could mean for a resurrected Germany a few decades later!"

* * * * *

- Eric -

The massive U-boat was lying on the surface, stationary in a calm sea, with exhausts burbling quietly at the stern as it held position, bow-on to the Brazilian shoreline.

Eric stood in the conning tower as a signalman beside him, using a hand held light, flashed Morse code in the direction of the shoreline.

The soft clicking of the light seemed inordinately loud to him as his darkened ship, which was resting at a distance of two hundred feet from the towering cliff of the mountain, rolled gently in the swell.

There was a bright moon, but resting as they were, just below the massive wall of rock, they were in its shadow and surrounded by blackness.

As he waited for some response from the shore, he pictured in his mind an impression of what he knew of the hollowed-out interior behind and below the low tide mark of the sheer cliff face rising in front of him. He tried to imagine exactly where the newly blasted opening below the surface at the shoreline was placed and what it would look like.

He had been very excited at the knowledge that the opening had been completed. He knew it was now situated sixty feet beneath the water awaiting to receive the big U-boat. Impatience at getting to use it had filled him for several days.

Now that he stood looking toward the cliff however, he realized that he was becoming less excited and more concerned at just how complicated the whole operation of slipping in under the surface of the sea and through the opening which led into the new pens within the hollowed out core of the mountain was going to be.

His thoughts were interrupted by a series of steady flashes originating on the narrow beach and he lifted his binoculars to his eyes as he mentally read the message being sent.

When they had finished he lowered the glasses and turned his attention to the surface of the water between the U-boat and the shoreline. Two powerful underwater beams of light suddenly appeared just under the gently rolling waves, their parallel shafts shimmering beneath the ebb and flow of the water.

Between them he could see a small boat making its way out toward the sub and a few minutes later one of his crew accepted a hurled line and pulled the little craft fast against the side of the gently rolling U-boat.

He watched as a single figure clambered up onto the deck and the crewman tossed the rope back into the boat and it pulled away, heading back toward the shoreline.

The single figure who had left the boat gained the deck and began to cross the bow. Eric smiled as he recognized the shock of blonde hair and rugged build of his long removed cousin Hans Schultz.

He moved over to the edge of the conning tower that held the ladder leading down to the bow deck and used his flashlight to illuminate the rungs and assist Hans in his climb up.

When his cousin dropped down to the conning tower deck he briefly wrapped him in a bear hug and stepped back to look at him.

"You haven't changed a bit."

They both laughed and then hugged again.

* * * * *

- Wilhelm -

There was a single knock on his door and Wilhelm looked up as it opened a crack and SS-Hauptsturmfuhrer Joachim Peiper stuck his head in.

"Ah you are here…just got back from a trip to the Russian front. My God, what weather! Be damn glad you're not up there, let me tell you."

He stepped inside and closed the door behind him and spoke while still holding onto the doorknob.

"Just wanted to let you know that the boss was extremely pleased with the report you filled about that incident in Paris. I told him I had asked you to look after it and the report was your work. You're kind of below the radar with your current assignments and I think he had almost forgotten you existed. I just wanted to tell you that he had some kind words to say and it wouldn't surprise me if you found yourself being drawn closer into the center of the stuff going on around here."

Wilhelm looked up and flashed an uncomprehending stare for a second then nodded his head and smiled.

"Not much too it really. I just gathered up the relevant information and wrote it up"

And all I need now is to be hauled into the other stuff

going on around here.

Peiper grinned and opened the door to leave.

"It was a damn good report; keep up the good work."

The door closed behind him.

* * * * *

- Eric -

Hans stood beside Eric in the conning tower as Eric gave short crisp orders and the huge U-boat began to move slowly forward and to starboard, then back to dead ahead, moving first into the centre of the twin beams and then slowly forward toward the shoreline between them.

Hans, who had been watching carefully, turned toward Eric and nodded and Eric barked out another order.

The U-boat slowed to a stop and Eric ordered the conning tower cleared.

As the last of the lookouts dropped down he helped Hans find the ladder in the darkness and followed him down into the control room, pulling the hatch into place and tightening it down before dropping to the deck next to his grinning cousin.

The ship was already beginning to settle in the water and the apprehension in the compact room was strong. The sound of the ballast tanks blowing wasn't normally very loud inside the big U-boat, but in consideration of the fact that you could have heard the sound of a dropped pin due to the tension among all the members of the crew, it now seemed more like a rushing waterfall.

Eric issued a few crisp orders in a monotone, carefully keeping the U-boat perfectly balanced fore and aft as she settled and in no time at all a gentle shudder rolled through the big craft as it settled firmly into the massive steel cradle that had been constructed to receive it on the bottom.

Enclosed within the confines of the Big U-boat, unable to see what was happening below and around them and no longer in control of their surroundings, the crew fidgeted quietly.

A sharp look from their Captain brought the squirming to a halt.

Eric ordered the engines shut down and all ears strained to hear the next sound which came shortly thereafter. It was a loud hum that was accompanied by a soft jolt and an eerie sensation as the U-boat, sixty feet under the surface, began to move slowly but surely forward in the direction of the shoreline.

CHAPTER TWENTY-TWO

- November -

- British Air Operations -

Bomber Command hits Kiel, Hamburg and Emden. The serious losses of British aircraft previously being suffered have increased yet again. With the release of the *'Butt Report'*, sober questions are arising about the very practicality of maintaining the current bomber offensive against the Germans.

On the eighth of the month, the day after four hundred bombers were used in attacks on Berlin, the Ruhr, Cologne and Boulogne, thirty-seven, or a full ten percent fail to return. These concerns reach a pinnacle.

In response to these well-founded anxieties, Churchill, very much aware that the raids have led to more Bomber Command personnel being killed than Germans by these recent operations, orders the British bomber force to look to reducing the size of their missions until such time as both the weather conditions and the quality of aircraft improve.

* * * * *

- Maritime Warfare -

- Battle of the Atlantic -

Losses to Allied shipping are at their lowest peak since the beginning of the war. Just one hundred and four thousand, six hundred tons in total.

U-boats sink only thirteen ships for sixty-two thousand tons.

British air strength on the main convoy routes from

Canada to Great Britain has increased with the use of 'CAMS' (Catapult Aircraft Merchant Ships).

* * * * *

- Mediterranean -

There are now ten U-boats operating in the Mediterranean and more headed to that theatre.

The sinking of HMS *'Ark Royal'* by two U-boats, while celebrated wildly by the Germans, has proven to be a two-edged sword, in that the ship's aircraft are now based ashore and are consequently currently being used solely for antisubmarine work.

This means that operating a U-boat in these waters has become considerably more risky that it was before the sinking.

* * * * *

- Mediterranean and North Africa -

Seaborne supplies for the Axis forces in North Africa are suffering horrendous losses. More than sixty percent are going to the bottom. Less than half the seventy thousand tons that have been averaged over the past for months is achieved.

In that both Rommel and Auchinleck are in hopes of preparing an offensive, this does not bode well for the German forces.

* * * * *

- Resistance -

The strong resistance movements in some occupied areas are giving the German occupiers some real headaches and they launch a very active anti-partisan operation in Yugoslavia.

* * * * *

- November First -

- Eastern Front -

Marshall Shaposhnikov becomes Chief of Staff of the Russian forces.

The German Eleventh army takes an important Soviet communications center in the Crimea Simferopol.

* * * * *

- USA -

Roosevelt announces that the US Coast Guard will now come under the direction of the US Navy. This is a significant move, as this transition of authority is normally only undertaken darning a time of war.

* * * * *

- November Second -

- Yugoslavia -

Dissention in the resistance occurs as the Tito leftists argue with the conservative Serbs under Mihailovic's leadership.

* * * * *

- November Third -

- Eastern Front -

German attacks toward Leningrad with the aim of taking the important railroad center one hundred miles east at Tikhvin are underway in order to isolate Leningrad. The Soviets counterattack but rather than seeking the soft spots in the German lines, they take on the strongest forces aligned against them and are ineffective.

Kursk falls to the Germans.

* * * * *

- November Fourth -

- Eastern Front -

German forces of the 170th Division take Feodosia in the Crimea.

* * * * *

- November Fifth -

- Tokyo -

The Japanese make additional peace offerings to the US.

These contain no repudiation of the Tripartite Pact and include the Japanese maintaining some bases in China. They are rejected by the US. The Japanese go back to the table but have decided that if they do not get what they want from the US by the end of November, they will look to war.

US code breakers are intercepting the Japanese Diplomatic communications.

* * * * *

- November Sixth -

- Moscow -

On the anniversary of the nineteen-seventeen revolution, Stalin speaks for only the second time in his thirty years as leader.

He calls upon the peoples of the Soviet Union to increase their efforts to defend *'Holy Russia'*. He then goes on to play down the facts of the German invasion, claiming that only three hundred and fifty thousand Soviet troops have been lost versus four and a half million slaughtered Germans.

He tells his people that victory is near.

* * * * *

- USA -

President Roosevelt announces that a loan of one billion dollars will be extended to the Russians to help them purchase Lend-Lease supplies.

* * * * *

- Brazil -

A German blockade runner, the *'Odenwald'*, loaded with rubber from Japan, is captured, in the American Security Zone, off the Brazilian coast, by the cruiser USS *'Omaha'*

* * * * *

- November Seventh -

- Germany -
RAF Bomber Command makes heavy raids on Berlin, the Ruhr and Cologne and suffers serious losses.

* * * * *

- November Eighth -

- Mediterranean -

Malta based *'Force K'*, made up of two cruisers, HMS *'Penelope'* and *'Aurora'* and two destroyers, HMS *'Lively'* and *'Lance'* makes a night attack on an Italian convoy. They sink all seven merchant ships and a tanker and one Italian destroyer escort. The Italian covering force of heavy cruisers and destroyers does not intervene to engage the attackers.

* * * * *

- November Ninth -

- Eastern Front -

German forces heading for Leningrad successfully take Tikhvin, cutting the rail line into Leningrad. In the Crimea, Yalta falls to the German forces.

* * * * *

- November Tenth -

- London -

In a public speech Churchill states.
'Should the United States become involved in a war with Japan, a British declaration of war will follow within the hour'.

* * * * *

- November Eleventh -

- East Africa -

Allied regular forces, supported by local guerrillas, start the final battle to eliminate the Italians from Abyssinia. They begin by attacking Chilga to the west and Kulkaber to the southeast of the main Italian Gondar position.

These early attacks are initially rebuffed successfully.

* * * * *

- November Twelfth -

- Eastern Front -

German commander's meet at Orsha, where General Halder presents his plans for the continued attack against Moscow. The commanders accept the plans half-heartedly, which are to involve three Panzer Groups and three Infantry Divisions.

The temperatures around Moscow have dropped to minus twelve degrees centigrade. The Russians throw their first *'ski troops'* into the fight against the long-suffering German lines.

* * * * *

- Mediterranean -

The carriers, HMS *'Ark Royal'* and *'Argus'* deliver a full squadron of Hurricanes to Malta.

* * * * *

- November Thirteenth -

- Eastern Front -

As the muddy ground freezes solid, preparation for the renewed German offensive against Moscow begins.

* * * * *

- USA -

Congress passes changes to the Neutrality Laws, making it legal for armed US merchant ships to enter war zones. The vote for the changes passes with a very slim majority, clearly indicating that the powerful Congress is still not as committed to war as is the US President.

* * * * *

- Mediterranean -

On the return voyage to Gibraltar from Malta, HMS *'Ark Royal'* is attacked by U-81 and U-205. The U-boats manage a single successful torpedo hit which badly damages the aircraft carrier.

Attempts at damage control seem to be effective and the *'Ark Royal'* manages to struggle to within twenty-five miles of Gibraltar. Suddenly a serious fire breaks out and *'Ark Royal'* has to be abandoned and sinks.

* * * * *

- November Fifteenth -

- Eastern Front -

The recently ordered German attack against Moscow begins with converging attacks being directed toward the capital. These will come from both the north and south.

Guderian's Second Panzer Group moves forward from Tula to the south, while both the Third and Fourth Panzer

Groups advance toward the Moscow-Volga Canal.

The infantry armies on the flanks and the Fourth Army, occupying the front between the two armoured thrusts are ordered to make supporting holding attacks as the armour punch is commenced.

The Russians are planning to use what they believe will be a period of relatively stagnant winter battles, as a much needed opportunity to build up their reserves with troops from Siberia while holding any German attempts to move further on Moscow.

Consequently they are content to allow minor German successes for the next few days while the fresh troops are brought in to bolster the outer flanks.

The Germans are suffering from tired equipment that leaves them far under strength and the worst winter to hit the Soviet Union since records have been kept.

 Lubricating oil is freezing solid in the vehicles and metal parts, such as rifle bolts, are already becoming brittle and breaking. Panzer Divisions are no longer poroperly equipped numerically and now take to the field with numbers of machines more appropriate to the strength of mere Battalions.

* * * * *

- November Sixteenth -

- Eastern Front -
Kerch falls to one wing of the German attack in the Crimea while other forces move to besiege Sevastopol.

On the center front minor gains are made against Moscow.

* * * * *

- November Seventeenth -

- USA -

The US ambassador to Japan, Joseph Grew, cables the State Department that Japan has plans to launch an attack against Pearl Harbor, Hawaii. His warning is ignored.

* * * * *

- Berlin -

Head of the Luftwaffe's Production and Development Department, Ernst Udet, commits suicide over what he feels is his inability to perform his mission.

* * * * *

- Eastern Front -

The Nazi party's *'racial expert'* and ideologist, Alfred Rosenberg, is appointed to head the newly created *'Reich Ministry for Occupied Eastern Territories'*.

His mandate is to exploit these areas for German economic benefit and to rid them of the members of their population that are perceived as *'undesirable elements'*. The Baltic States and White Russia are to be included in his area of responsibility.

In the southern sector, First Panzer Group is making good progress near Rostov but the Soviets are beginning to organize counterattacks on their flank.

* * * * *

- November Eighteenth -

- North Africa -

British troops launch *'Operation Crusader'* crossing into Libya with the aim of relieving the siege of Tobruk.

Patrick Laughy

* * * * *

- Eastern Front -

Fresh Siberian troops counterattack near Venev, seriously damaging one of Guderian's infantry divisions. Several other short-lived assaults by these new Siberian fighters nip at Guderian's forces and are very effective at confining the German advance on this front.

* * * * *

- Pacific -

The Japanese send eleven submarines out from their home ports with orders to take up stations off Hawaii and carry out scouting missions in the area of the islands. Nine Japanese ships sail from Kwajalein toward the Hawaiian Islands.

* * * * *

- London -

It is announced that General Dill is to be replaced by General Brooke as Chief of the Imperial General Staff of the British Army. Dill will now be sent to Washington to lead the British military mission in the US. General Paget is chosen to take up Brooke's previous position as Commander in Chief, Home Forces.

* * * * *

- November Nineteenth -

- Australia -

The light cruiser HMAS *'Sydney'* clashes with the German auxiliary cruiser *'Komoran'* off the coast of Western Australia. The ships shoot it out and in the end sink each other.

* * * * *

- North Africa -

British and German forces lock horns, but each spreads its forces too thinly and little is accomplished. The British end with forty tanks out of service while the Germans lose only a few.

* * * * *

- November Twentieth -

- Vichy France -

Giving in to pressure from the Germans, General Weygand is relieved of his North African post.

* * * * *

- North Africa -

Both sides of the struggle are still suffering from spreading their armour too thinly. The British 4th Armoured Brigade faces yet another mauling from the Germans 15th Panzer.

The British 7th Armoured is active around Sidi Rezegh and 22nd Armoured is moving rapidly to support the 4th.

General Cunningham is confident enough to order the besieged forces in Tobruk to initiate break-out attempts but by the end of the day Rommel has begun to appreciate the British moves and orders his panzer divisions toward Sidi Rezegh.

Patrick Laughy

* * * * *

- Tokyo -

The Japanese continue to negotiate with the US.

Their suggestions for an interim proposal are found to be unacceptable after China's Chiang Kai-shek is successful in gaining both British and Dutch support for its rejection due to the concessions demanded in China.

In the interest of continuing the talks the Americans nevertheless make a negotiated reply.

* * * * *

- November Twenty-First -

- North Africa -

Rommel uses both his tank divisions to launch an attack on the British 7th armoured Brigade at Sidi Rezegh and within hours the British find themselves left with less than twenty tanks.

Cunningham's ordered break out attempts by the besieged forces in Tobruk is quickly thwarted by the Germans due to the inability of the expected relief to be provided by 7th armoured, who have problems of their own and are unable to offer support.

The British 4th and 22nd Armoured are moving as quickly as conditions allow toward Sidi Rezegh.

* * * * *

- East Africa -

Allied attacks on Kulkaber southeast of Gondor are reinforced after meeting strong Italian resistance and in short order the Italian defenders are forced to surrender.

This leaves the remaining Italian forces confined to the immediate area of Gondar.

* * * * *

- Mediterranean -

Axis convoy operations begin to expand in a desperate attempt to maintain the supply lines for their North African forces. Two escorting cruisers are badly hit, one by a British torpedo dropped from aircraft and the other by submarine attack.

A determined naval force from Malta attempts to find and sink the convoys but are unable to locate them.

* * * * *

- November Twenty-Second -

- West Africa -

While on patrol off the coast of West Africa, the cruiser HMS *'Devonshire'* runs across the German raider *'Atlantis'* while she is resupplying a U-boat and quickly sinks her. *'Atlantis'* has sunk twenty-two ships, totaling one hundred and forty-five thousand, seven hundred tons, during her war patrol.

Shortly thereafter and in the same area, a British cruiser sinks a second U-boat supply ship, the *'Python'*.

Both of these successful sinkings are brought about through British code-breaking accomplishments.

The sinking of these two supply ships causes Admiral Doenitz to cancel his plans to send off a force of U-boats to begin patrols off South Africa.

* * * * *

- Eastern Front -

The German forces on the southern section of the front take Rostov-on-Don, an important Russian transportation hub.

The British issue an ultimatum to Finland. They are to end the war with Russia or face war with the Allies.

* * * * *

- North Africa -

Rommel begins a strong counteroffensive. He retakes Sidi Rezegh just south of Tobruk, mauling and drastically reducing British armour strength. The Germans now have one hundred and seventy serviceable tanks while the British strength has been reduced to one hundred and fifty.

Rommel now holds the balance of power in the region.

* * * * *

- November Twenty-Third -

- Eastern Front -

In the center push toward Moscow the Germans continue to grind ahead slowly. Klin is captured and some German forces are less than thirty-five miles from the Russian capital.

* * * * *

- USA -

An agreement is reached with the Dutch exiled government for the US to occupy Suriname in Northern South America to protect the bauxite mines located there.

* * * * *

- North Africa -

The opposing forces meet in a violent struggle southeast of Sidi Rezegh. Both German panzer divisions and the *'Ariete Division'* charge headlong into the British armour and the two South African Brigades that have just joined in support of the British tanks.

By the time it is over the Germans are down to less than one hundred tanks and have suffered heavy infantry casualties. British losses are also high and Cunningham has concluded that the battle is lost.

Auchinleck, the ever confident British commander, then moves up to the front.

Rommel does not take a direct part in this battle, as he is leading his forces farther north around Gambut where the New Zealand infantry has captured the Afrika Corps Headquarters, along with much of Rommel's communication equipment.

* * * * *

- Mediterranean -

An Axis convoy carrying fuel from Greece to Benghazi is attacked by Malta based *'Force K'* and loses two freighters. The British Mediterranean Fleet puts out in support of this operation.

* * * * *

- November Twenty-Fourth -

- Eastern Front -

The Germans evacuate Rostov due to a threat to their rear from continuing Soviet counterattacks. This is done on the orders of Field Marshall von Rundstedt, despite the fact that such action has been specifically forbidden by Hitler.

* * * * *

- Atlantic -

The British cruiser HMS *'Dunedin'* is sunk by U-124.

* * * * *

- USA -

The Americans grant Lend- Lease to the Free French.

* * * * *

- North Africa -

Rommel, convinced that he has largely destroyed the British armour, decides to ignore the New Zealand infantry and he collects his armour together and begins advancing along the Trigh el Abd to the Egyptian frontier.
He meets little opposition.

* * * * *

- November Twenty-Fifth -

- Eastern Front -

German forces take Istra on the Moscow front.

* * * * *

- Mediterranean -

U-331 sinks the British battleship HMS *'Barham'* while she is on convoy duty.

* * * * *

- Pacific -

The US navy begins to establish compulsory convoying of merchant vessels.

* * * * *

- East Africa -

The British take Tadda Ridge, seven miles from Gondar, in Ethiopia.

* * * * *

- November Twenty-Sixth -

- North Africa -

Rommel's panzer divisions attack British positions around Capuzzo and Sidi Aziz and suffer appreciable losses.

The Field Marshall realizes that the British armour has been quietly regrouping in the Sidi Rezegh area and that the New Zealand infantry are still moving toward Tobruk. He orders his tanks to turn back in that direction, heading for Bardia for refuelling.

British General Cunningham is relieved of his command of the Eighth Army and Auchinleck replaces him with his Chief of Staff General Ritchie.

* * * * *

- Pacific -

A thirty-three strong Japanese attack fleet including six aircraft carriers, supported by auxiliary craft, sails from northern Japan for the Hawaiian Islands.

* * * * *

- Tokyo -

The so called *'Hull note'* ultimatum is delivered to Japan by the USA. This demands the complete withdrawal of all Japanese troops from French Indochina and China

* * * * *

- November Twenty-Seventh -

- Eastern Front -

The Soviet forces occupy Rostov and the German First Panzer Group retreats toward Taganrog. On the Moscow front Guderian's forces have been fighting around Kashira for three days and their commander makes the decision that they cannot continue their drive toward Moscow, unless they are sent reinforcements.

* * * * *

- North Africa -

The 4th and 6th New Zealand Brigades link up with the Tobruk garrison at El Duda and late in the day take up tank engagements in the Sidi Rezegh area.

The German Afrika Division is renamed the 90th Light Division and it joins the now infamous 15th Panzer and 21st Panzer to complete the *'Afrika Korps'*.

The 4th Reich

* * * * *

- East Africa -

The Allied attack on Gondar goes in and quickly makes progress despite the rugged terrain. General Nasi, commanding the Italian forces, decides to ask for terms.

* * * * *

- November Twenty-Eighth -

- East Africa -

The British come to terms with the Italians at Gondar and the twenty-two thousand Italian troops surrender.

Benito Mussolini's East African Roman Empire has ceased to exist.

* * * * *

- North Africa -

The battle between Rommel's forces and the British continues with the Germans trying to wipe out the link between the New Zealand infantry and the Tobruk garrison.

* * * * *

- November Twenty-Ninth -

- Eastern Front -

On the Moscow front, the forces commanded by General Reinhardt reach the Moscow-Volga Canal and mange to cross into the Dmitrov area. Fresh Siberian units are defending in this area and the German tanks quickly become bogged down against the fierce Soviet resistance.

* * * * *

- Mediterranean -

Two additional cruisers and two destroyers arrive in Malta to expand the fleet.

* * * * *

- Tokyo -

A Japanese government liaison conference reaches the decision that the final terms delivered by the US are unacceptable and that Japan must go to war.

* * * * *

- November Thirtieth -

- Eastern Front -

Field Marshal von Rundstedt is relieved of his command by a direct order from Hitler.

* * * * *

- Pacific -

British units based in Borneo report that Japanese naval forces are on the move. Several more repots of the same nature come in and this leads to an increase in tension in Malaysia and the East Indies.

No one however, links these with a possible threat against Hawaii.

The 4th Reich

* * * * *

- North Africa -

Rommel successfully forces one of the New Zealand Brigades out of the Battle near Tobruk.

* * * * *

- Hamburg -

The German raider *'Komet'* arrives back in home port after a patrol that has lasted five hundred and sixteen days. She has sunk three ships for a total tonnage of thirty-one thousand, as well as worked in conjunction with *'Orion'* to sink seven additional ships.

* * * * *

- Atlantic -

A British bomber equipped with *'Air to Surface Vessel radar'* (ASV), sinks U-206 in the Bay of Biscay, which is located on the west coast of France and Spain. This is the first success for this newly developed radar.

Patrick Laughy

CHAPTER TWENTY-THREE

- December -

- Hitler -

- Wolfsschanze -

An infantry reconnaissance formation reaches the outskirts of Moscow early in the month. It is quickly dispersed by several Russian tanks and an ad hoc emergency force made up of factory workers.

The German offensive is grinding to a halt.

Field Marshal von Bock is unwell, suffering from stomach cramps, as he speaks to Brauchitsch by phone and tells him frankly that the German lines no longer have any real depth and his troops are physically exhausted.

On the third von Bock calls Halder and repeats to him the situation as he sees it. He is depressed and the Chief of the General Staff attempts to bolster his spirits during the conversation.

Von Bock is pushing to go on the defensive but Halder has to report directly to Hitler and he doesn't want to hear any bad news. At the end of the call he tells von Bock: *'the best defense was to stick to the attack'.*

Those commanders at the front could clearly see that a continued offensive was impossible.

Those ensconced at *'Wolfsschanze'* were living in another world.

Guderian noted on the fourth that the temperature was down to thirty-one degrees below zero. In order to get their engines to turn over, his tankers had to build fires under them. The machines telescopic sights were frozen solid and would not function. His men still had no winter uniforms, no overcoats nor woollen stockings, they were suffering terribly from the severe cold.

Guderian didn't ask to stop the attack, he knew what the answer would be to that. He simply, on his own hook, selected a defensive line, dug in and pulled his foremost troops back behind it.

On the fifth the temperature at Moscow dipped another five degrees.

That night, the new Russian commander of the central front, General Zhukov, launched a massive counter attack against the German lines. He threw in one hundred divisions across a two hundred mile front.

It took the Germans completely by surprise and left the German Supreme Command in shock and filled with disbelief.

Von Brauchitsch, physical ill and discouraged, was ready to resign.

Even Hitler was taken aback and unsure of what he should do next.

He couldn't understand the ferocity of the attackers. The Russian troops he had fought against in the Great War had been poorly trained and ill-equipped soldiers. The hordes confronting the German lines at Moscow were proving to be anything but.

On the sixth of the month the Fuhrer admitted privately to Jodl, his Chief of the Operations Staff of the Armed Forces High Command, that *'victory could no longer be achieved'*.

To add to this confusing turn of events, Hitler's promise that if Japan should fight the United States, Germany would join her ally was about to bite him in the hind end.

On the twenty-eight of November, von Ribbentrop had summoned Japan's ambassador, General Oshima and urged Japan to declare war against both the Untitled States and Britain. The suggestion had come as a surprise to Oshima.

He replied: *'Is Your Excellency indicating that a state of actual war is to be established between Germany and the United States?'*

Without giving the question much thought, von

Ribbentrop responded with.

'Roosevelt is a fanatic, so it is impossible to tell what he would do. There is no possibility of Germany's entering into a separate peace with the United States under such

circumstances. The Fuhrer is determined on this point.'

Oshima reported this conversation to the Japanese High Command who, as they had already dispatched the carrier taskforce headed for Hawaii, were delighted with the news.

On November thirtieth they ordered Oshima to inform Hitler and Ribbentrop that the English and Americans were planning to move military forces into East Asia and such a move must be countered.

He was specifically told to tell them.

'say very secretly to them that there is extreme danger that war may suddenly break out between Japan and the Anglo-Saxon Nations through some clash of arms and add that the time of the breaking out of that war may come quicker than anyone dreams.'

This instruction was almost immediately followed by fervent orders to obtain specific pledges from the Germans in this regard.

Sensing his government's eagerness in this matter Oshima moved swiftly, arranging a further meeting with von Ribbentrop for the evening of the first of December.

When they met, Oshima was more than a little taken aback when von Ribbentrop was blatantly evasive over his request for firm expressions of the German position on the matter.

The German Foreign Minister promptly excused himself, saying that he would first have to discuss the matter with the Fuhrer, who was currently at *'Wolfsschanze'*.

Oshima was well aware of the fact that Hitler was fully occupied with the war on his Eastern Front and had little time for the intrigues that were going on in the Far East.

Although it did not overly disturb him that he had been rebuffed by von Ribbentrop, after all, as the head of state,

Hitler would be the one to make the final decision on any such agreement in writing; he nonetheless waited with some impatience for a response. It finally came on the fifth of December when he received a draft treaty to the effect that Germany promised Japan that it would join them in any war against the United States and would not conclude a separate peace with the US.

Late on the afternoon of December seventh, Otto Dietrich, Hitler's press officer, received by wire the news of the Japanese attack on Pearl Harbour. He called staff at the Hitler bunker and advised that he was bringing over a very important message.

For most of the day Hitler had been receiving negative reports from the Russian Front and he assumed that this would be more of the same. Obviously disheartened, he received Dietrich curtly when he arrived.

His press officer quickly read the message and Hitler was at first too stunned to respond.

Then the Fuhrer's dejected features suddenly brightened and, shaking slightly from excitement, he snapped out.

'Is this report correct?'

Dietrich replied that he had received confirmation from his office by telephone.

A giddy Hitler snatched the telegram from his hand and, not taking the time to put on his hat and coat, walked rapidly over to the military command bunker.

The unannounced visit took both Keitel and Jodl by surprise as Hitler burst inside waving the telegram. He shouted across to them.

'We cannot lose the war! Now we have a partner who has not been defeated in three thousand years'.

* * * * *

Receipt of the telegram had seemingly brought about a change in Hitler's outlook on life in general. The Fuhrer had undergone a remarkable transformation which was very obvious to those in his military inner circle.

In an about face, he had become confident again despite the reports streaming in from the Russian front. He brushed aside concerns over the situation and within twenty-four hours he had issued a new directive:

'The severe winter weather which has come surprisingly early in the East, and the consequent difficulties in bringing up supplies, compel us to abandon immediately all major offensive operation and to go over to the defensive'.

He then set out his concept and general principles of such a defensive line and instructed a relieved and delighted Halder to look after the nuts and bolts of issuing subsequent instructions to front line commanders.

This done, he promptly boarded his train and headed for Berlin to take personal charge of the situation now presented by the Japanese attack on Pearl harbour.

By the time he reached Berlin, Hitler's delight at the news of the Japanese attack had begun to dissipate as he realized what it meant to his current fight against the Russians.

The Japanese attack, while wonderful in the long term, was bound to bring about immediate problems for Germany.

Stalin would instantly recognize that the Japanese would now be far too involved in dealing with the Americans to give even the slightest consideration to mounting an attack against Russia. This meant that the Russians would now be free to transfer almost all of their forces currently guarding their Asian boarder and move them into their line of defense against Germany.

On the moring of the ninth, von Ribbentrop met with Hitler, bringing the unwelcome news that General Oshima was calling for an immediate German declaration of war against the Americans.

Aware of Hitler's changed outlook about the Pearl Harbour attack and it implications for Germany, von Ribbentrop informed the Fuhrer that in his opinion, Germany was not obligated to declare war against the US by their agreement with the Japanese. He based this conclusion on the fact that according to the Tripartite Pact, Germany was only bound to assist her ally in the case of a direct attack upon Japan, and this had not as yet occurred.

Hitler immediately dismissed such a response to the Japanese, telling his Foreign Minister.

'If we don't stand on the side of Japan, the pact is politically dead. But that is not the main reason. The chief reason is that the United States already is shooting at our ships. They have been a forceful factor in this war and through their actions have already created a situation of war.'

Despite von Ribbentrop's view and the strong advice against declaring war against the US by his own Foreign Office, Hitler sought his own council in the matter.

Hitler's resulting decision as to whether or not to declare war on America came quickly, but not without deep thought. The situation had come to a head at an inconvenient time where the war against Russian was concerned but that shortcoming had to be weighed against the overall value of the Tripartite Pact.

From a propaganda perspective, the public acquisition of a new and powerful ally would provide a powerful positive response internally in Germany and with her other allies. This would serve to soften the disappointing turn of events in Russian. Additionally the step towards a declaration of war with the American's was in line with his ideological world view.

Hitler firmly believed that he was intended by God to be the man to lead the suffering world in its fight against the two major enemies of human survival, that of international Marxism which resided in Russia and that of international finance capitalism which rested in the USA; both of whom he firmly judged, to be the creation of international Jewry.

* * * * *

On December eleventh Hitler convoked a sitting of the Reichstag to give himself a platform to publicly announce his decision. During his speech he said the following:

'Roosevelt is as mad as Woodrow Wilson. First he incites war, then falsifies the causes, then odiously wraps himself in a cloak of Christian hypocrisy and slowly but surely leads mankind to war, not without calling God to witness the honesty of his attack'.

He then offered his view that international Jewry was being fostered within both Bolshevik Russia and Roosevelt's America before continuing:

'I have therefore arranged for passports to be handed to the American ambassador today and the following....'

Thundering applause and shouts of support filled the huge room for some time and Hitler stood quietly, hands clasped, until it had died down. Then he picked up on his topic again:

'Germany is at war with the United States, as from today'.

Life had suddenly become much easier for the US President who had, up to this point in time, to deal with many prominent and powerful citizens who did not want to fight a foreign war.

The attack on Pearl Harbour and Germany's declaration of war had unified his country behind him like never before.

Jodl, the Chief of the OKW, left the Kroll Opera House, which had been used for the Reichstag meeting, filled more with concern rather than the enthusiasm which had been clearly demonstrated by the others who had been in attendance.

He called his deputy, General Warlimont, at *'Wolfsschanze'*.

"You have heard that the Fuhrer has just declared war on America?"

Warlimont confirmed that he had and went on to explain that he and other staff officers had been completely blindsided by the announcement and had just been discussing the situation.

Jodl responded.

"The staff must now examine where the United States is

most likely to employ the bulk of her forces initially, the Far East or Europe. We cannot take further decisions until that has been clarified."

A frustrated Warlimont replied.

"Agreed; this examination is obviously necessary, but so far we have never even considered a war against the United States and we have no data on which to base this examination; we can hardly undertake this job just like that."

Jodl sighed.

"See what you can do. When I get back tomorrow we will talk about this in more detail."

* * * * *

Privately, and with benefit of hindsight, Hitler later told Bormann.

'This war against America is a tragedy. It is illogical and devoid of any foundation of reality. It is one of those queer twists of history that just as I was assuming power in Germany, Roosevelt, the elect of the Jews, was taking command in the United States. Without the Jews and without this lackey of theirs, things could have been quite different. From every point of view Germany and the United States should have been able, if not to understand each other and sympathize with each other, then at least to support each other without undue strain on either of them'.

* * * * *

Within Hitler's military and domestic inner circles the anxiety of going to war with the US was quickly supplanted by the continued reversals on the Eastern Front. The situation there was extremely intense.

The Germans were being forced to retreat and the area west of Moscow was quickly turning into a frozen wasteland of abandoned German equipment.

Morale on each side in the clash was shifting, the

Germans becoming more desperate and the Soviets increasingly cheered. So much so, that the Russian's publicly announced that the Nazi's attempt to place Moscow in a situation of siege had failed dismally and two days later, to order the return of the entire government back to Moscow.

Hitler's response to this action, despite Brauchitsch's recommendation to continue the retreat to safer ground, was to immediately issue an order that would infuriate his field commanders.

'Stand fast, not one step back'.

Marshal von Bock, still suffering from a serious stomach disorder and long past a state of physical and mental exhaustion, promptly reported himself as unfit for duty. Hitler immediately replaced him with Field Marshall Gunther von Kluge.

On the nineteenth, Brauchitsch, who was just recovering from a heart attack, got up enough courage to face Hitler on the issue. They had a private meeting during which the two argued strenuously for a good two hours. After Brauchitsch left this meeting he went to see Keitel and told him: *'I am going home. He has fired me. I can't go on any longer'.*

Keitel responded with.

'What is going to happen now then?'

To which Brauchitsch replied.

'I don't know; ask him yourself'.

A few hours later Keitel was summoned to the Fuhrer's presence and Hitler read out an Order of the Day he had just composed. In brief terms it stated that Hitler was assuming personal command of the army, inextricably binding the fate of Germany with his own.

This was to be kept secret for the moment, although Keitel felt that Halder should be advised of the situation at once. Hitler agreed to this request.

Hitler then went on to belittle the consequences of the change in policy, saying.

This little affair of operational command is something

anybody can do. The commander-in-chief's job is to train the army in the National Socialist idea and I know of no General who could do that as I want it done. For that reason I have taken over command of the army myself.'

The German Army was now under the command of a man who's highest military rank ever achieved, was that of Corporal.

* * * * *

- Walther Hewel -

Born in Cologne on the second of January nineteen-four, Walther Hewel was one of the few persons that could really be considered as one of Adolf Hitler's personal friends.

Hewel was one of the earliest members of the Nazi party, joining when he was only a teenager.

He graduated in nineteen twenty-three and attended the Technical University of Munich. In that same year he took part in the failed Beer Hall Putsch. After Hitler's conviction for treason following the Putsch attempt, Hewel stayed in Landsberg prison with him for several months, acting as his valet.

Hewel then worked for several years as a coffee salesman and planner for a British firm in the Dutch East Indies were he organized the local branch of the Nazi Party drawing his membership from the German expatriates who lived there. By nineteen thirty-seven, Hewel's Nazi party had established branches in Batavia, Bandung, Semarang, Surabaya, Medan, Pandang and Makassar.

Hewel returned to Germany in the nineteen-thirties and entered the diplomatic service. He was then sent to Spain where he was almost certainly working as a German spy.

In nineteen thirty-eight, Hitler recalled Hewel back to Germany where Hewel served in a diplomatic post in the German Foreign Ministry and the two men resumed their friendship.

Hewel held the post of ambassador and was selected to serve as von Ribbentrop's liaison to Hitler. In fact the position was more honorary than functional and he held the title primarily due to his long ties to the party and his ongoing friendship with Hitler.

Hewel performed a general service for Hitler and could best be considered as his major-domo.

Hitler placed him in charge of co-ordinating his household, keeping peace between the military and civilians officials around Hitler and regulating contact between male and female members of Hitler's large entourage.

He was a pleasant, good natured man, not particularly brilliant but one who could usually deal with situations and events that Hitler could or did not, wish to deal with.

Hewel sincerely liked Hitler and enjoyed his company. He was one of the few men around Hitler who did not drift off during the Fuhrer's long monologues, honestly finding them both interesting and stimulating. He was as loyal to the Fuhrer as his faithful dog.

He was granted a great deal of freedom by Hitler and often played practical jokes on his boss, something that Hitler would not have tolerated from others.

A shy man when around women, Hitler often tried to play matchmaker for him. The Fuhrer often had longer private discussions with his friend, sharing with Hewel his most inner thoughts, especially those he had to guard from others, like the ones concerning his views on anti-Semitism, the problems caused by worldwide Jewry and the solution to these problems.

Over time, Hewel would reveal the content of many private conversations that he had shared with Adolf Hitler.

* * * * *

- Concentration Camps -

- Romania -

In excess of fifty thousand Jews had now been interned in Bogdanovka, a Romanian camp situated along the Bug River in Transnistria.

In December of nineteen forty-one Romanian troops, together with Ukrainian auxiliaries, moved in to empty the camp. The firing squads went on for more than a week and few internees survived.

Similar action was taken in the Domanevka and Akhmetchetka camps.

* * * * *

- Poland -

Six camps had now been built or were under construction in what had been Polish territory. Auschwitz and Majdanek were designed to function as concentration and forced-labour camps.

Chelmno, Belzec, Sobibor and Treblinka were all designed specifically as *'special handling'* camps.

Using *'gas vans'*, Chelmno began gassing operations in December of nineteen forty-one.

Belzec, Sobibor and Treblinka were built as part of *'Aktion Reinhard'* and used carbon monoxide gas produced by fixed stationary engines which were permanently attached to the gas chambers.

* * * * *

- Eric -

Hans, Eric, Heidi and the construction Superintendent, who was overseeing the building of the *'Operation Fatherland'* portion of the massive research and development complex and U-boat docking areas buried deep beneath the mining operation, were standing around a table in the control room of the U-boat holding area.

Being tucked within the enclosed space of this concrete structure, it was difficult for Eric to maintain his concentration as they discussed the designs for the U-boat facility, which were spread out on the table between them.

Construction was still going on in the area outside the room and the accompanying noise made it difficult for him to hear what was being said.

In addition, as one entire wall of the chamber in which they were standing was made up of floor to ceiling glass to provide those inside who would be working at the control panels with an overview of the entire massive water-filled cavern, whenever a U-boat entered or left: it was hard not to glance out, lose one's concentration and become absorbed in what was taking place as the workers hurried about the task of getting the large overhead cranes into place over the remaining three other, as yet incomplete, sub pens.

Other workers were spread out across the decks of his U-boat like a swarm of ants as they prepared cargo for the rapidly moving crane to lift and deposit onto the dock next to the gently floating craft.

Of course, his lack of concentration had nothing to do with the fact that Heidi stood across from him with her elbows resting on the table as she leaned forward to better view the plans and the complexities contained therein, that the Superintendent, also a distant cousin, was carefully explaining to them.

While this stance was probably all very innocent and had been helping her to gain a better perspective; it was also providing him with an excellent opportunity to take advantage of a clear view of the remarkable cleavage generated by the pressure her arms generated against the sides of the bodice of the low cut peasant blouse she was wearing.

* * * * *

- Gabriella -

On December second of nineteen forty-one, Gabriela gave birth to a healthy seven pound, six ounce baby boy.

Konrad was in the delivery room at the clinic when his son was born, although he had chosen not to personally bring his child into the world, allowing one of his subordinates to oversee the delivery.

Within hours of the birth, the young new family had received a congratulatory telegram from no other, than the SS-Reichsfuhrer himself, Heinrich Himmler.

That afternoon, a tired by delighted Konrad sent wires out to Berlin and Castle von Stauffer to share the good news.

* * * * *

- Karl von Stauffer -

The Count was at home, dining with his old friend and confidant, doctor, the Baron Heinrich von Kleist and Wilhelm when the telegram arrived from Konrad announcing the birth of a son and heir.

Congratulations exchanged, Karl found a bottle of champagne, opened it and they paused long enough in their ongoing discussions to finish it.

* * * * *

- The Countess -

Upon receipt of the telegram announcing the birth of her first grandchild, Erika made her first ever trip to the lower recesses of the castle with the intention of carrying the good news to Ursula and Friedrich.

An hour later she was on the phone with the Count urging him to make arrangements to have the family travel to Norway using their private rail cars as soon as the trip could be arranged.

* * * * *

- Eric -

As dinner on Friday evening was to begin, Eric sat on the right of the patriarch of the extended Brazilin wing of his family.

In celebration of yet another successfully completed voyage by Korvettenkapitan Eric von Stauffer and his massive U-boat, Klaus von Stauffer had invited over fifty members of his far-flung family to attend a weekend at his newly constructed mansion.

Eric had met a good thirty of these distant relations on his previous trips, as they were directly involved in either the family's mining operation and its resulting spinoffs, or supposedly so, while actually working as part of the secret *'Operation Fatherland',* research and development facility which was rapidly being completed within the caverns that rested just beneath the cover of the mining operation.

Eric had found himself hoping that he might be seated beside Heidi, however he was to be disappointed.

His beautiful distant cousin was seated far down the table from him. The table had obviously been set to put the older generations of the family, those who oversaw the various segments of the family and held positions of responsibility, close to him.

Conscious of his own important role and responsibility to represent his father's and immediate family's interest in what was transpiring in Brazil, Eric accepted this seating arrangement as the correct thing for Klaus to have arranged, but the truth be known, he would have welcomed an opportunity to spend more time with Heidi.

He had only been in Brazil for two days, but it seemed to him that the relationship with his bright and vivacious distant cousin that had seemed, to him at least, to be warming up since they had first meant, had taken a strange twist.

While she had certainly been welcoming of him upon

his arrival, something had changed.

As the serving began, he found himself wondering exactly what the change had been and he was only half listening to the conversations going on around him.

I wonder if she has met someone else and has a new and serious relationship.

She seems different now. More mature, definitely. And more confident and assured, yet somehow aloof and standoffish; unquestionably keeping her distance, yet still sending him signals that had been enough, on several occasions, to cause him to take mental steps to prevent a direct physical pronouncement of his interest in her physically.

It was bloody confusing.

He was having difficulty concentrating on anything but her and he would damn well soon speak to her about it.

* * * * *

- The Count -

The last of the champagne consumed, Karl and the Baron retired to his library and settled in, with brandy and cigars and returned to their earlier discussions.

Heinrich opened the topic.

"So, you have someone in place in Canada. Well, I think I can help with the US and perhaps Great Britain. I have an uncle in America and two cousins, much removed I'm afraid, in England. I would of course have to renew and expand contact with them to ensure they would be interested in meeting our needs, but the possibility is there."

The Count nodded.

"Yes I fully understand. I, myself, have had to tread gently when I recruited those from within the distant branches of my own family.

However keep in mind that we don't require loyalty from them in regard to *'Operation Fatherland'*. We don't need to apprise them of it in any way.

We only need to offer them a business proposal, one that will make them a great deal of money. We will only require of them to market our property in their own countries. We need them to act as intermediaries in selling the gold, precious stones and artwork we provide to them and they can fully expect a generous commission for doing so."

The Baron nodded.

"Yes, I understand that, but nonetheless, we will be putting into their hands articles of extreme value belonging to *'Operation Fatherland'* and we must therefore be certain that we trust them implicitly before we can afford to accept them into our financial dealings."

CHAPTER TWENTY-FOUR

- December -

- British air operations -

Raids by Bomber Command are smaller in scope. Brest, Cologne, Bremen and Aachen are hit and small sorties are made over northern France.

* * * * *

- Maritime Warfare -

Allied shipping losses rise to two hundred and eighty-five ships sunk, for a total of five hundred and eighty-three thousand, seven hundred tons. With Japan's entry into the war, losses by the Allies in the Pacific Theater make up the majority of these sinkings, more than four hundred and thirty thousand tons.

German U-boats have a poor month as they are primarily being sent on patrols to the less rewarding waters of the Mediterranean and off the coast of Gibraltar. Ten U-boats are sunk.

During nineteen forty-one, the allies have lost one thousand, two hundred and twenty-nine vessels, accounting for a total loss of four million, three hundred thousand tons.

The British have received just over thirty million tons of dry cargo for the year, far less than their normal peacetime average of approximately fifty million tons. Despite the strict rationing already in place, this has meant that more stringent restrictions must be faced by the English population as the war continues.

* * * * *

- December First -

- North Africa -

While Rommel's Africa Korps is able to force the New Zealanders to retreat at Sidi Rezegh, his units are exhausted and many of their senior officers have been captured or killed.

The British Eighth Army has taken a beating but unlike Rommel, they are getting excellent resupply and regular replacements for damaged or destroyed tanks.

* * * * *

- Eastern Front -

There is a short-lived Russian counter-offensive at Tula near Moscow.

* * * * *

- Malaya -

Acting on reports of Japanese preparations for an attack, the British declare a State of Emergency.

* * * * *

- December Second -

- Tokyo -

Japanese Prime Minister Tojo dismisses an American peace offer as unacceptable.

A special code order, *'Climb Mount Niitaka'*, is transmitted to the ships of the carrier force steaming across the pacific toward Hawaii. It confirms that negotiations have broken down and that the carriers are to execute the attack against Pearl Harbor on the morning of December seventh.

* * * * *

- Eastern Front -

German forces reach Khaki, located in the northern suburbs of Moscow and are less than twenty miles from the Kremlin. Hitler orders Kluge to move against the city from the west. Bock, commanding Army Group Center, is unwell.

* * * * *

- East Indies -

The British battleship HMS *'Prince of Wales'* and the battle cruiser HMS *'Repulse'* arrive at Singapore.

* * * * *

- North Africa -

Rommel has his hands full. He is trying to maintain the siege at Tobruk through fighting around El Duda, as well as moving against the British armor which is regrouping farther south near Bar el Gubi. At the same time he must send reinforcements to the Axis garrisons at Bardia, Sollum and Halfaya Pass, which are barely holding out against the 4th Indian Division.

In fact, based on his depleted supply and equipment situation, what he is attempting to do is impossible. He is being forced to spread what minimal resources he possesses far too thinly in each area and in so doing is bound to suffer serious losses to both men and armor.

* * * * *

- December Third -

- London -

Conscription is now expanded to include all men between eighteen and fifty. Women are now to serve in fire brigades and ancillary groups.

* * * * *

- December Fourth -

- Japan -

An Invasion force leaves Hainan bound for Malaya.

* * * * *

- Eastern Front -

The temperature falls to minus thirty-seven centigrade at Moscow and all German efforts founder.

* * * * *

- December Fifth -

- Eastern Front -

Hitler orders a halt to the German offensive.

* * * * *

- Mediterranean -

Hitler orders the transfer of the entire *'Fliegerkorps II'* from the Eastern front to the Mediterranean, with the intent of improving the movement of Axis supply convoys who are still having great difficulty in supplying Rommel.

* * * * *

- December Sixth -

- Eastern Front-

The Russians begin a massive counteroffensive along the full five hundred miles of the Moscow front.

* * * * *

- London -

The British declare war on Finland.

* * * * *

- Pacific -

Japanese forces leave Palau for an attack on the Philippines.

* * * * *

- December Seventh -

- Tokyo -

Japan launches an attack on Pearl Harbor, declares war on the United States and the United Kingdom and invades Thailand and British Malaya, while launching aerial attacks against Guam, Hong Kong, the Philippines, Shanghai,

Singapore and Wake Island.

* * * * *

- Ottawa -

Canada declares war on Japan.

* * * * *

- Berlin -

Hitler issues a directive titled *'Nacht und Nebel'* (Night and Fog).

This directive is aimed at removing from occupied lands all political activists and resistance helpers and anyone endangering German security.

Prior to this decree, the Nazis had been rounding up and imprisoning political prisoners from both Germany and occupied Europe. These consisted primarily of individuals whom the Germans felt in need of, 're-*education'* or resistance leaders in occupied Western Europe.

This activity had been accomplished according to national agreements and procedures such as the Geneva Convention, which other countries followed as well.

In issuing this decree however, Hitler has decided that Germany would no longer have to conform to what they considered, as *'unnecessary rules'*.

On the same date, Himmler issued the following instructions to the Gestapo:

'After lengthy consideration, it is the will of the Fuhrer that the measures taken against those who are guilty of offenses against the Reich or against the occupation forces in occupied areas should be altered. The Fuhrer is of the opinion that in such cases penal servitude or even a hard labour sentence for life will be regarded as a sign of weakness. An effective and lasting deterrent can be achieved only by the

death penalty or by taking measures which will leave the family and the population uncertain as to the fate of the offender. Deportation to Germany serves this purpose.'

* * * * *

- December Eighth -

- Declarations of War -

The United States, Great Britain, Australia, New Zealand, the Netherlands, the Free French, Yugoslavia and some South American countries declare war on Japan. China declares war on Germany, Italy and Japan.

* * * * *

- Pacific -

The Japanese take the Gilbert Islands. Clark Field in the Philippines is bombed and many US aircraft are destroyed on the ground. Japanese troops attack Thailand and begin the Battle of Prachuab Khirikhan.

Two days of Japanese air attacks hit Wake Island and an invasion force leaves Kwajalein escorted by a cruiser and six destroyers.

The Japanese 38th Division begins its attack on Hong Kong.

The city of Shanghai is taken by the Japanese and the small US garrison is captured.

* * * * *

- Eastern Front -

Soviet counterattacks are making headway against the desperate German defensive positions at Moscow.

Patrick Laughy

* * * * *

- North Africa -

Rommel, with dwindling forces available, decides to abandon the siege on Tobruk and begins an organized and well controlled retreat toward Gazala.

* * * * *

- December Ninth -

- Eastern Front -

The Soviet drive captures Elets in the centre front and at Leningrad the Russians take Tikhvin forcing the Germans into a short but pell-mell retreat.

Despite these achievements the Russians are still unable to sufficiently supply Leningrad and rations for the city are already well below the starvation level.

* * * * *

- Malaysia-

There are further Japanese landings at Kota Bharu, Singora and Pataini and in Thailand they take and occupy Bangkok.

* * * * *

- South China Sea -

Overnight HMS *'Prince of Wales'* and HMS 'Repulse' are sunk by Japanese aircraft, leaving the British without a single operational battleship available in the Pacific Theatre of war.

* * * * *

- December Tenth -

- Philippines -

There are Japanese landings and air attacks on Luzon. The naval base at Cavite is badly hit and weapon stocks are destroyed by air attacks. At Aparri, two thousand troops land, while in the northeast of the island at Vigan, a similar number achieve a beachhead.

* * * * *

- Marianas -

The Japanese take the island of Quam, capturing three hundred American troops.

* * * * *

- Hong Kong -

The Japanese have now advanced in force to the defensive line and have captured a crucial position at its west end.

* * * * *

- Malaysia -

British forces advancing into Thailand from Kroh reach *'The Ledge'* position where they have planned to meet and throw back the Japanese advance but find that the Japanese have arrived first and in much greater numbers.

The British forces are forced to retreat.

* * * * *

- December Eleventh -

- Declarations of War -

Germany and Italy declare war on the US. The United States declares war on Germany and Italy.

* * * * *

- Moscow -

The Soviets begin to announce successes in their counteroffensives surrounding Moscow. Guderian's forces have now been forced back from Stalinogorsk. Weakened, exhausted and suffering from poor resupply, many German units are unable to withstand the onslaught of the fresh Soviet forces being unleashed.

* * * * *

- Pacific -

The defending force of four hundred and fifty US marines on Wake Island successfully rebuffs an attempted Japanese landing. Two Japanese destroyers are sunk in the melee.

* * * * *

- Malaya -

The 11th Indian Division at Jitra is attacked by Japanese units advancing from Singora. The 11th has already lost heavily in some of their outpost actions and they are quickly pushed back from the Jitra position.

* * * * *

- Burma -

Japanese invasion forces begin their attacks.

* * * * *

- December Twelfth -

- Declarations of War -

The British and the US declare war on Romania and Bulgaria following those countries declaration of war on both. India declares war on Japan.

* * * * *

- Philippines -

Twenty-five hundred troops from the Japanese 16th Infantry land in south Luzon at Legaspi as Japanese aircraft launch additional air attacks against the remnants of the US aircraft on the island.

Japanese landings are also made on the southern Philippine Islands of Samar, Jolo and Mindanao.

* * * * *

- USA -

The Americans seize the French ocean liner *'Nomandie'*.

* * * * *

- December Thirteenth -

- Declarations of War -

Hungary declares war on the USA and Great Britain, who promptly reciprocate.

* * * * *

- Hong Kong -

Under Japanese attack, British troops withdraw from their defensive positions on the mainland to the island of Hong Kong.

* * * * *

- Burma -

British forces evacuate their airfield at Victoria Point in the extreme south of the country on the Kra Isthmus. Japanese troops quickly move in to occupy.

* * * * *

- North Africa -

Forward units of the British forces have moved up to the Gazala but almost immediately begin to lose heavily to German counterattacks. Despite these successes, Rommel quickly realizes that he cannot expect to hold these positions due to the strength of his forces.

The *'Africa Korps'* begins a slow retreat toward

Cyrenaica and beyond to what Rommel considers his next defensible position, at El Agheila.

* * * * *

- Mediterranean -

Two Italian cruisers carrying fuel to North Africa are sunk off Cape Bon by a force of three British and one Dutch destroyer.

Italy begins a major convoy with cover by their main fleet, which includes four battleships. Two of the transports in this convoy are sunk by a British submarine.

* * * * *

- December Fourteenth -

- Malaya -

The Japanese from Patani now push on beyond The Ledge, to Kroh.

* * * * *

- Mediterranean -

British cruiser HMS *'Galatea'* is sunk off Alexandria by U-557.

The Italian battleship *'Vittorio Veneto'* is torpedoed by a British sub and takes serious damage.

British convoy HG-76 sails from Gibraltar for the United Kingdom. This convoy consists of thirty-two ships and the escort includes the carrier *'Audacity'* and twelve other ships under the command of Commander Frederic John Walker.

* * * * *

- December Fifteenth -

- Eastern Front -

The Russian attacks northwest of Moscow reach Klin and Kalinin and these forces occupy both towns.

* * * * *

- Mediterranean -

Two British battleships, HMS *'Queen Elizabeth'* and HMS *'Valiant'* are sunk in the harbor of Alexandria by Italian *'human torpedoes'*.

The British begin an operation to bring supplies to Malta from Egypt. Six cruisers and sixteen destroyers take part as escorts.

The Italians abandon their convoy operation to bring supplies to Benghazi.

* * * * *

- Malaya -

The British forces have retreated to Gurun and are taking very heavy losses to the Japanese attack. They manage to hold the Japanese at Gurun.

* * * * *

- Hong Kong -

The Japanese endeavour to send a small force across the water from Kowloon to Hong Kong Island but are forced to retreat.

* * * * *

- December Sixteenth -

- Borneo -

At first light, with considerable naval support, the Japanese land at Miri, Seria and Lutong. The British and Dutch forces set their oil plants on fire before retreating under the onslaught.

* * * * *

- North Africa -

Rommel continues his organized retreat toward El Agheila where he plans to wait for reinforcements in the form of both men and armor.

* * * * *

- Mediterranean -

The Italians put together a second convoy for shipment to North Africa. This time they send a convoy escort consisting of four battleships, five cruisers and twenty-one destroyers.

* * * * *

- Malaya -

A second wave of Japanese landings begins. The British forces withdraw from Penang on the west coast.

* * * * *

- Eastern Front -

The Germans dig in, forming a battered and bedraggled defensive line on the Moscow front.

* * * * *

- December Seventeenth -

- Eastern Front -

The German forces in the Crimea begin their attack against the fortress city of Sevastopol.

* * * * *

- Mediterranean -

The British naval fleet of *'Force K'* from Malta joins up with Vian's *'Force B'* from Alexandria and as night falls, the covering forces of the two convoys, Italian and British, meet in an action that will be later classed as the *'First Battle of Sitre'*.

The engagement is indecisive due to each of the escorts turning their attention to the protection of their own convoys rather than attacking the enemies.

* * * * *

- Malaya -

The British pull back from their main defensive positions at Gurun, retreating south over the Perak River as they fight delaying actions to protect their rear.

* * * * *

- Washington -

Relieving Admiral Kimmel, Admiral Nimitz is appointed to the command of the US Pacific Fleet and leaves for Hawaii. Admiral Pye takes temporary command until Nimitz arrives.

This sudden change in command is unhelpful for the beleaguered island of Wake, in that no decisive leadership will be present on Hawaii until the newly assigned commander takes up his post.

* * * * *

- December Eighteenth -

- Eastern Front -

An ill Field Marshall von Bock is replaced by Field Marshall Kluge.

* * * * *

- Mediterranean -

The British convoy reaches Malta. *'Force B'* sails back to Egypt while *'Force K'* begins to search for the Italian convoy earlier spotted. Late that night 'K' runs into a minefield and loses one cruiser and one destroyer and both of its cruisers in the force are damaged.

* * * * *

- Hong Kong -

Overnight the Japanese manage to make landings on Hong Kong Island between North Point and the Lei U Mun Channel. The British counter attack but are unable to dislodge the Japanese forces.

Patrick Laughy

* * * * *

- December Nineteenth -

- Berlin -

Hitler formally removes Brauchitsch from his post as Commander in Chief of the German Army. He assumes the position himself.

* * * * *

- North Africa -

The *'Africa Korps'* continues its organized retreat through Cyrenaica.

* * * * *

- Philippines -

Overnight the Japanese land near Davao on Mindanao. The carrier *'Ryujo'* is in support of the force of five hundred men from the 56th Infantry Regiment.

* * * * *

- Eastern Front -

The German attack on Sevastopol continues.

* * * * *

- December Twentieth -

- Pacific -

Several Japanese ships are sunk or damaged as the battle for Wake Island continues.

* * * * *

- Eastern Front -

In the Battle for Moscow, the Soviet offensive continues to inflict considerable losses on the defending German positions. Northwest of Moscow, Volokolamsk is retaken by Russian forces.

* * * * *

- Washington -

Admiral King is appointed Commander in Chief of the US Fleet.

* * * * *

- Berlin -

Minister of Propaganda, Joseph Goebbels makes a public appeal for winter clothing for the troops serving on the Eastern Front.

* * * * *

- December Twenty-First -

- Philippines -

The Japanese make landings on Luzon at Lingayen Gulf. Tanks support a force made up from the 48th Division and they are provided with both air and naval support.

* * * * *

- Eastern Front -

A besieged Leningrad cannot be supplied sufficiently by the Russians and three thousand residents are now dying daily from starvation and disease.

The German forces at Sevastopol capture the outer ring of forts which surround the city. From the sea, the Russians are furiously reinforcing the city with supplies and manpower.

* * * * *

- Romania -

Some cases of typhus spread by lice and fleas break out in Bogdanovka concentration camp.

The German advisor to the Romanian administration, suggests that all the inmates of the institution should be given *'Special Treatment'* in order to eradicate the disease.

Forty thousand are promptly *'retired'*.

* * * * *

- December Twenty-Second -

- Wake Island -

The Japanese return to the island with renewed strength and determination. Planes from the carriers *'Hiryu'* and *'Soryu'* join the battle and two hundred Japanese troops manage to land.

* * * * *

- Washington -

Named the *'Acadia Conference',* the first official joint meeting between the British and American political and military leaders commences.

* * * * *

- December Twenty-Third -

- Wake Island -

Overwhelmed, the American forces on wake surrender to the Japanese.

* * * * *

- Philippines -

General MacArthur declares Manila to be an *'Open City'.*

* * * * *

- Burma -

Japanese air attacks begin on Rangoon.
There are only two allied fighter squadrons in Burma at this time, one from the RAF and one from *'Chennault's'* American Volunteer Group. They are able to offer only token resistance against the hordes of Japanese *'Zeros'* taking part in the operation against Rangoon.

* * * * *

- Borneo -

The Japanese make landings at Kuching, the capital of Sarawak. Two transports are sunk and an additional two are damaged by a Dutch submarine. A second sub sinks a Japanese destroyer but then, subsequently, the sub suffers the same fate.

The small British force billeted here puts up a fierce defense.

* * * * *

- North Africa -

Axis forces evacuate Benghazi as the Allied advance reaches Barce.

* * * * *

- December Twenty-Fourth -

- Philippines -

Seven thousand Japanese troops of the 16th Division land at Lamon Bay in southeast Luzon. To the north, American forces have moved to take up the first of five delaying positions planned to block the advance of the Japanese between the Lingayen Gulf and the Bataan Peninsula.

* * * * *

- Sulu Archipelago -

Japanese troops land at Jolo.

* * * * *

- December Twenty-Fifth -

- Borneo -

The small British force at Kuching withdraws under the pressure of the Japanese attack.

* * * * *

- Eastern Front -

At Moscow the Russian offensive continues.

The German forces there are now down to seventy-five percent of the numbers they had in June at the start of the battle. Guderian has fewer than forty tanks left and in Hoeppner's Panzer Group, only one of the four armoured divisions has more than fifteen tanks.

* * * * *

- North Africa -

Advancing Allied troops reach and take Benghazi and Agedabia as the German retreat continues.

* * * * *

- Hong Kong -

British forces in Hong Kong surrender.

* * * * *

- Philippines -

The US forces in north Luzon are attacked at their second line of defense at the Agno River.

* * * * *

- Crimea -

Amphibious forces from the Russian Army and Navy land and take up defensive positions at Kerch.

* * * * *

- December Twenty-Sixth -

- Eastern Front -

German attacks on Sevastopol continue, however the Russian landings in the eastern Crimea at Kerch now poise a threat to other German units of the Eleventh army.

* * * * *

- Norway -

Two hundred and sixty British and Norwegian commandos land on the Lofoten Islands at Moskenesoy to destroy the fish-oil factory.

* * * * *

- December Twenty-Seventh -

- Philippines -

The American forces now fall back to their third defensive line which runs east and west from Paniqui.

* * * * *

- London -

Air Marshal Brooke-Popham is replaced as Commander in Chief Far East, by General Pownall.

* * * * *

- Norway -

Six hundred British and Norwegian commandos land at Vaagso and Maaloy. They target fish-oil factories and radio stations. Merchant and patrol craft are sunk and two hundred and forty-three Norwegian volunteers are transported to Britain.

Hitler is furious. He directs Doenitz to station U-boats to guard against any further such endeavours and orders additional German forces to be sent to bolster German garrisons in Norway.

* * * * *

- December Twenty-Eighth -

- Eastern Front -

At Sevastopol the Germans make gains in the Fort Stalin area where the 22nd and 24th Divisions are leading the offensive.

* * * * *

- Philippines -

The Americans have now been forced back to the Tarlac-Cabanatuan defensive line and hare being attacked furiously.

* * * * *

- Malaya -

Patrick Laughy

British forces give up Ipoh to the Japanese. They move to defensive positions at Kampar and the River Slim.

* * * * *

- Burma -

General Hutton is appointed to command the British forces.

* * * * *

- Sumatra -

Japanese paratroopers land.

* * * * *

- North Africa -

Rommel surprises the British by ordering units from his well-planned and orderly retreat to turn on his pursuers in several sharp attacks. As a result, the British 22nd Armored Brigade takes severe losses.

Even in retreat the *'Desert Fox'* demonstrates that he will use his claws quickly and effectively if any opportunity presents itself.

* * * * *

- December Twenty-Ninth -

- Eastern Front -

Additional Russian forces consisting of the 51st and 44th Armies land at Feodosia in the eastern Crimea.

The German attack against Sevastopol is effectively halted as the Germans try to deal with these new forces and those landed earlier at Kerch.

* * * * *

- December Thirtieth -

- Philippines -

US troops fall back yet again, this time to their final prepared line before the Bataan Peninsula which is just north of Clark Field. They hope to hold this line against the Japanese long enough for the troops frantically retiring ahead of the invading Japanese in south Luzon to make it through Manila to Bataan.

* * * * *

- Eastern Front -

The Russian troops fighting near Moscow have advanced to, and recaptured Tula.

* * * * *

- Malaya -

The Japanese have now advance to a point close to Kampar in the west and Kuantan in the east.

* * * * *

- December Thirty-First -

- Australia -

General Brett takes command of the US forces in Australia.

** <u>Epilogue</u> **
By the end of nineteen forty-one, what had been mainly a European and Mediterranean war, had become the Second World War.

Other books by Patrick Laughy

Paperbacks

The Little Black Book

Alumni

The 4th Reich Books 1 and 2

E-books

The Little Black Book

Alumni

Atlantis-Ship of the Gods

The 4th Reich Book 1 Part 1

The 4th Reich Book 1 Part 2

The 4th Reich Book 2 Part 1

The 4th Reich Book 2 Part 2

The 4th Reich Book 3 Part 1

The 4th Reich Book 3 Part 2